BLACK CANARY ™

BREAKING SILENCE

− DC ICONS −

Wonder Woman: Warbringer
by Leigh Bardugo

Batman: Nightwalker
by Marie Lu

Catwoman: Soulstealer
by Sarah J. Maas

Superman: Dawnbreaker
by Matt de la Peña

Black Canary: Breaking Silence
by Alexandra Monir

BLACK CANARY ™

BREAKING SILENCE

– DC ICONS –

ALEXANDRA MONIR

Random House 🏠 New York

Copyright © 2020 DC Comics.
All DC characters and elements © & ™ DC Comics.
WB SHIELD: ™ & © WBEI. (s20)
Cover art by Jen Bartel

Excerpt of the song "Nature Boy" by eden ahbez used by permission of Geraldine Janowiak/GoldenWorld
Court of Owls nursery rhyme copyright © 2011 DC Comics (excerpted from *Batman* [Volume 2] #1, written by Scott Snyder and illustrated by Greg Capullo)

Visit us on the Web! GetUnderlined.com

Educators and librarians, for a variety of teaching tools, visit us at RHTeachersLibrarians.com

Library of Congress Cataloging-in-Publication Data
Name: Monir, Alexandra, author.
Title: Black Canary: breaking silence / Alexandra Monir.
Description: First edition. | New York: Random House, [2020] | Series: DC icons |
Summary: "In this thrilling origin story of Black Canary, the titular hero uses everything she has—including her voice—to fight against a world where women have no rights"—Provided by publisher.
Identifiers: LCCN 2020024616 (print) | LCCN 2020024617 (ebook) |
ISBN 978-0-593-17831-7 (hardcover) | ISBN 978-0-593-17832-4 (library binding) |
ISBN 978-0-593-17833-1 (ebook)
Classification: LCC PZ7.M7495 Bl 2020 (print) | LCC PZ7.M7495 (ebook) |
DDC [Fic]—dc23

Printed in the United States of America
10 9 8 7 6 5 4 3 2 1
First Edition

For the women who came before me
and gave me a voice:
my mother, ZaZa Saleh,
and my grandmother Monir Vakili.
Thank you.

Beware the Court of Owls,
that watches all the time,
ruling Gotham from a shadowed perch,
behind granite and lime.

They watch you at your hearth,
they watch you in your bed,
speak not a whispered word of them,
or they'll send the Talon for your head.

—OLD GOTHAM CITY NURSERY RHYME BY SS

CHAPTER ONE

The weeds climbed from soil to sky on all sides of Robinson Park, shrouding the abandoned grounds from the rest of Gotham City. Dinah Lance had grown up driving past this stretch, watching the once-flourishing park fade over the course of her childhood. The greenery had been the first to go, shriveling up and turning the color of mud. An army of vines came next, emerging from the ground and crawling up every bench, slide, and swing, until soon the whole space was too overgrown to see through. It used to be just another grim sight Dinah passed on her way to school, a reminder of all the ways the Court of Owls had failed their city. But today was different. Today she knew what was hidden inside.

"Please tell us you're not serious about this." Dinah's best friend, Mandy Harper, shuddered as she stared across the street. "That place looks like a hangout for serial killers."

"Yeah, it's clearly been shut down for a reason," Ty Carver, the third member of their trio, said with a grimace. "And traipsing around a sketchy old park was *not* what I had in mind for our second-to-last day of summer. Especially when we could be at Natasha Wycliffe's party right now."

"You guys can chicken out if you want, but I'm going in," Dinah said, striding ahead of them. "What we're about to uncover easily beats some party that—I hate to break it to you, Ty—we're not even invited to."

"Wait." Mandy gripped her arm. "What if someone sees us? Is your plan really worth the risk of—"

"Rotting in Arkham Asylum?" Ty finished her sentence. "Um, of course not. C'mon, let's go."

Dinah paused midstep. She couldn't exactly blame them for their reservations. Trespassing on closed government property was, technically, a crime against the Court—one that could warrant the Owls' favorite punishment. A prison sentence at Arkham used to be reserved for the most dangerous, deranged criminals in the city, but these days there was an entirely different group behind bars. The Court had "repurposed" Arkham, warping it into a torture chamber for anyone who dared to oppose them. It was a place where roles were reversed, with known criminals running the show and would-be heroes languishing in their cells. The kind of place you tried to avoid at all costs.

Still . . . Gotham City's rulers had far bigger fish to fry than high school students poking around a run-down park. Dinah hadn't heard of anyone their age winding up in Arkham—yet. Getting caught was a long shot. And for better or worse, her want was greater than her fear.

"It's totally deserted. No one's going to know we were ever there, much less throw us in Arkham over it," she said. "And if we did somehow get caught, I would be the one to take the blame anyway."

She looked back at the two of them as a beam of light from a streetlamp crossed their faces, highlighting Mandy's gold-flecked brown eyes, dark brown skin, and wary expression and Ty's pale skin and light blue eyes, jittery behind his glasses. Dinah felt a twinge of guilt for talking them into this.

"You don't have to come with me if you really hate the idea."

Mandy gave her a wry smile and pulled a tiny can of pepper spray from her skirt pocket.

"I mean, we're obviously not going to let you go in there alone."

"We're not?" Ty cracked. Dinah wouldn't have been surprised if he was only half kidding. As much as he cared about her, Ty also happened to be the furthest thing from a risk taker.

"This just better be worth it," Mandy added.

"It will be." Dinah grinned at her two oldest friends, looping an arm through each of theirs as they crossed to the darker side of the street.

The towering curtain of weeds rose up to meet them. It surrounded the park's perimeter, blocking every entrance.

"What are we supposed to do now?" Ty asked, raising an eyebrow.

"Just . . . follow me."

Dinah took a deep breath and slid sideways into the weeds, feeling them part just enough to let her through before swallowing her up in stems and leaves. They scratched at her skin as she elbowed her way forward, toward a half-buried entrance gate. A tangle of bare branches poked through the gate's iron bars, like spindly arms pushing her away. Still, Dinah moved closer.

The latch was rusted shut after so many years untouched. Dinah cringed—this wasn't going to be pretty, especially in her mandatory Gotham City girls' uniform. A starched white button-down and knee-length wool skirt weren't exactly made for fence jumping.

She tied her blond hair into a ponytail and backed up a few steps before breaking into a run, leaping up onto the gate. Her skirt snagged on the bars, and branches clawed at her bare legs, but she managed to hoist herself over to the other side, landing knee-deep in brittle, browned grass. And for the first time, Dinah was inside Robinson Park.

It looked wild, feral, in the twilight. Dead leaves and twigs littered the path ahead, ivy snaked around every surface, and even the trees drooped to the ground, as if hiding their heads in shame. Still, there were hints of the happier place this used to be. A pair of swings creaked as the breeze rattled their chains. A paint-chipped carousel swayed in the same wind, sending its porcelain horses on a slow turn they would never get to finish. Dinah stepped up to the horse nearest her, a gray Thoroughbred with a cracked white mane. Its mouth was open in an expression meant to be a smile, but time had reshaped it so that the horse now appeared to be baring its teeth. Dinah shivered, stepping back.

Just then Mandy came hurtling over the gate, landing with a flying leap. She actually managed to make it look graceful, even in her constricting uniform, and Dinah couldn't help but clap as her friend's feet hit the ground.

"Think of the gymnast I could have been," Mandy joked, dropping into a playful bow. It was a running gag between her and Dinah, albeit not a very funny one: remarking on all the different things they could have done or become if they had just been born a generation or two earlier—back when girls were allowed to be athletes.

Mandy's smile fell as she took in the scene around them. "Yikes. It's even more of a dump than I imagined."

A loud thump sounded behind them as Ty tumbled to the ground, glasses flying off his nose.

"Why is it that I always seem to wind up bruised whenever we follow one of your plans?" he complained, fumbling through the grass for his glasses.

"Sorry, T." Dinah reached out to help pull him back up to his feet. "But I promise—if what I overheard is even half true, you'll be thanking me for dragging you here."

"If you say so." Ty shook his head at her but then fell into step as Dinah led the way.

For a while, the only sound was of their shoes crunching leaves—until Mandy stopped abruptly and elbowed Dinah in the ribs. *"Look."*

Dinah glanced up and drew in a sharp breath. An old stone monument loomed ahead of them, like a temple plucked straight out of ancient Greece. Its front facade was bordered by twelve statues and, half buried among the leaves, twelve ornamented gravestones.

"The Forum of the Twelve Caesars," she murmured as they approached it. "That's what they used to call this—this mausoleum. I remember reading about it."

"Okay, well, you forgot to remind us there's a freaking *graveyard* in here," Mandy said with a gulp. "I vote we turn back now."

"I second that," Ty said quickly, but Dinah was already crouching to brush the leaves off the first headstone.

"Martha Wayne," she read, a pit forming in her stomach.

And she knew, without looking, who lay in the surrounding graves: Bruce and Thomas Wayne, James Gordon, Renee Montoya, and the rest of the heroes from Gotham City's past. These legends were the reason the Court of Owls had left Robinson Park to rot as soon as they took control of the city.

Suddenly, a sense of movement in her peripheral vision jolted Dinah from her thoughts. She could have sworn she had just seen a shadow flitting between the graves across from them. Dinah blinked, telling herself it was nothing, or that she'd imagined it—until she heard Ty jump.

"What was that? Did you see it?"

"Yeah, let's get out of here," Mandy urged her. "Now."

"You guys, chill," Dinah said, standing up and trying to ignore her own nerves. "We are in a wild park, after all, which means there's probably a dozen squirrels or other harmless creatures scurrying around. That's nothing to be afraid of. C'mon, we're so close."

She could hear Mandy and Ty muttering under their breath behind her as they advanced deeper into the park, passing a thicket of oak trees and a reservoir-turned-swamp along the way. Her eyes continued to scan the forest, alert for any signs of life that could threaten their presence. And then, finally, she found what she had come here in search of. It rose from the weeds like a decaying palace: the centuries-old Gotham City Opera House. A white marble outsider in a city of gray.

Fresh yellow police tape surrounded the building, its bold black letters shouting, NO TRESPASSING—GOV'T PROPERTY—DEMOLITION AHEAD. It was the only hint in this entire park that another human being had recently set foot in here.

Dinah ducked under the tape and gazed up at the structure in awe, as if she had just stumbled upon a holy relic. This opera house was built and run by a *woman*—back in the days when women still had the power to sing. When they had any power at all.

"Rumor has it there's a vault in there," Dinah called over her shoulder to Mandy and Ty, both of them lingering a few feet away from the police tape. "A Vault of Voices, where recordings of the old classical singers are hidden. *Female* singers." Her heartbeat sped up at the thought. What she would give to hear them . . .

"If that's true," Mandy said skeptically, "then wouldn't the Court have destroyed this place by now?"

"Apparently no one even knew about the vault until the police got an anonymous tip," Dinah replied, remembering the phone call she'd overheard between her dad and one of his fellow officers—the call that had led her here. She'd thought of little else since then.

Of all the things for her to dream of, to love most in the world, of course it had to be music—something she would never be allowed to pursue. Women were barred from singing or playing instruments, and yet there was nothing else in her entire life that had ever stirred her senses the way a song could. Playing one of her mom's old records was like slipping into a fantasy; the only thing missing was the female voice. To find those lost recordings, and get to hear what the women singers actually *sounded* like, would be the greatest historical discovery of her generation.

She just wished it didn't have to be.

"Well, that would explain the sudden demolition plans," Ty said darkly.

"And why we have to get in there before they do." Dinah quickened her pace. "Aren't you dying to hear it? A girl's voice, *singing* . . ."

Of course, it wouldn't technically be the first time Dinah heard the impossible, though she'd given up trying to convince anyone else that her childhood memory of hearing a girl sing was real. Her dad and her friends had all written it off as an eight-year-old's dream, which was no surprise. The idea of girls being able to sing, or do *anything* so powerful and free, was pure fantasy in the world they were living in. A world taken over by the Court of Owls, who ruled Gotham City as a patriarchal dictatorship while spreading their influence like a virus across the globe.

Dinah pressed her hands against the glass of a first-floor window and gasped as another world materialized inside: one with cobwebbed chandeliers, a sweeping staircase, and painted murals covering every inch of wall space. There was more color in this one room than she'd seen before in all of Gotham City.

Mandy and Ty joined her at the window, their interest finally piqued, while Dinah rifled through her crossbody bag for the lock-picking kit she'd "borrowed" from her dad. She hurried to the front entrance and got to work, angling the sharp pick into the keyhole. Just when she felt the pins in the lock start to budge, her eyes caught another flash of movement in the shadows. Goose bumps prickled a warning across her skin. And then—

A body leaped down from above, landing on the ground behind her with a nearly silent whisper of sound. A scream lodged in Dinah's throat as she recognized one of the unmistakable figures of Gotham City's nightmares. One that, until now, she had only ever seen in books and pictures—but never in the flesh.

The towering body was nearly seven feet tall, with muscles bulging beneath his black suit of armor. A chilling mask gave the twisted appearance of something half man, half avian, with a jagged beak where a nose should be and enormous, piercing yellow eyes. He lifted his hands to reveal the telltale steel-plated gloves, fingers ending in the sharp claws that gave this feared creature his name: *Talon*, faithful assassin of the Court of Owls.

And he was lunging straight toward her.

"Run!" Dinah shouted to Mandy and Ty before turning on her heel and breaking into a sprint behind them. Mandy tore off toward the maze of trees, gripping Ty's arm to keep him at her speed, but before Dinah could catch up to them, a gloved hand shot out and closed around her ankle. The Talon's claws dug deep into her skin, using the momentum to spin her roughly toward him. The breath left her lungs as Dinah looked up into those enlarged yellow eyes.

"Please, I didn't mean any harm," she managed to choke out. "I wasn't doing anything. Please just let me g—"

Instead of answering, the Talon gripped her neck with one steel glove and used the other to slide one of his claws from her chin down to her chest, drawing blood. Dinah opened her mouth to scream, but the Talon dug his fingers into her windpipe, and she couldn't make a sound. *He's going to kill me. He's going to kill me right here, right outside the place I've been dreaming of, and no one will hear me die.*

The pain from his roving claw seared through her till she could no longer think; all she had left was instinct. And it was instinct, coupled with years of Sandra Wu-San's training, that drove Dinah to reach up and seize the Talon's wrists in one lightning-quick move.

Her body acted on its own, ignoring her fear, ignoring the threat of retaliation, as she twisted his arms around her back in a standing arm bar. She wouldn't have stood a chance against him if not for the element of surprise. Girls weren't supposed to fight back—they weren't even supposed to know how. And so the Talon was caught off guard, roaring his fury as she yanked him toward the ground and then let go, sending his body falling backward.

Dinah shot forward, racing for the trees. But just when it seemed that she might actually make it, that she could have somehow succeeded against the odds—another monstrous figure pounced to the ground in front of her, and then one more. She was surrounded by Talons now, circling her with blades extended, eyes glittering with the promise of blood. Her amateur jujitsu skills were futile in the face of these three. Dinah squeezed her eyes shut, bracing for the end while silently praying for Mandy and Ty to make it out of there alive.

And then came the blare of a siren.

Dinah's head snapped up in surprise, just in time to see the police car come crashing through the gates. Even before the two officers jumped out, she knew her dad would be one of them. As Detective Larry Lance flew onto the scene, his gun aimed straight ahead, Dinah didn't know whether to feel relieved or even more afraid.

"Gentlemen—Talons—thank you for catching this intruder. The Gotham City PD will take it from here," Larry called out, feigning confidence. But Dinah could see the fear written across his face. Fear for her.

The Talons turned their attention to Detective Lance and his partner, blades curling in their direction now. Larry caught Dinah's eye and gave a slight nod toward the trees. But she couldn't run away, *couldn't* leave him alone with the Talons. Everyone knew they loathed the police and considered the GCPD far beneath them. It was the Court, not the GCPD, that had the authority to dump "offenders" in Arkham Asylum, the worst of Gotham City's prisons. Which meant one wrong move, and the Talons could make her dad their newest inmate—or their latest victim.

Now, Larry mouthed, eyes fierce. She forced herself to move, darting away from the Talons as her dad stepped closer, pulling their focus from Dinah. *If anything happens to him . . .* Dinah shook her head violently to rid herself of the thought. She had to find Mandy and Ty.

Dinah raced to the dark pocket of trees they had disappeared into, eyes scanning in every direction. Panic bubbled in her stomach as she combed through the weeds, growing more desperate the longer she looked, until—

"*Psst!* In here."

She whirled around. Her eyes welled up instantly at the sight of Mandy and Ty, huddled in the trunk of a split-open tree. They pulled Dinah in with them.

"I'm so sorry," she whispered.

She never should have dragged them into this; she knew that now. It was so easy to overlook the risks when she'd never encountered them in real life before, but now, at the thought of what could have happened, her chest was tight with guilt.

Mandy nodded. "It's okay. Let's just get out of here."

"My—my dad." Dinah swallowed hard. "I don't know

how they knew we were in trouble, but he and his partner are there right now, surrounded by Talons. I can't leave until—"

"They'll be okay," Ty said gently. "They have guns, remember?"

"But the Talons have something else. Something just as lethal."

Dinah shivered as the fabled word flew into her mind. *Electrum.* An elusive, highly conductive alloy that the Owls had controlled and hoarded for years, injecting it into their Talons to give them enhanced strength and instant healing capabilities. What chance did an ordinary pair of cops have against that?

Mandy wrapped an arm around her shoulders.

"Your dad just gave us an opportunity to escape, and the last thing he would want is for you to stay here and not take it. He knows what he's doing. Please—let's go."

Dinah forced herself to follow as Mandy and Ty climbed out of the tree trunk. The three of them crept back through the park with their hands clasped, holding their breath. The carefree energy that had propelled them over the gates just an hour earlier felt foreign now, as if it had been three entirely different people who entered Robinson Park. Dinah kept turning her head to listen in the direction of the opera house, but the quiet was even more chilling than the sound of Talons descending. If the unthinkable happened, she could be going home an orphan. And it would be her own fault.

Mandy cleared the gate first, followed by Ty, whose sweating palms kept causing him to slip off and into the dirt, until Dinah finally helped push him over. And then it was her turn. She could feel her muscles protesting, her adrenaline nearly spent, but she managed to give it one last hurdle over to the other side. When they finally emerged past the barrier of weeds and back onto the street, they were bruised and bloodied, their clothes torn by brambles and muddied by the forest. But they were alive.

"You were right about one thing, at least," Ty said to Dinah as they walked in a huddle toward the residential side of Gotham City, hidden in the shadows of the sidewalks and alleyways between buildings. He draped his jacket over her and Mandy to cover their frayed skirts, and they kept their heads down, trying their best to blend in.

"What's that?" Dinah asked numbly.

"The rumor must be true—about the Vault of Voices. Because whatever is in that opera house was obviously important enough to be guarded by Talons."

Dinah stopped in her tracks as another realization hit her.

"And it's something they haven't found yet. The Court must still be searching for the vault. Otherwise . . . why would the opera house still be standing?"

Mandy and Ty looked back at her with wide, uncertain eyes. And as they made their way home, the questions in her mind grew louder with every step.

CHAPTER TWO

She waited for hours, fear twisting her insides as twilight turned to pitch-black night. The apartment felt cold and empty in a way it never had before, making the worst-case scenarios playing in Dinah's mind seem all the more real. She curled up on the couch under a heavy blanket, one hand on her cell phone and the other on the police scanner, listening as intently as if she could will the sound of her dad's voice. But the time crawled by with no news, no word. Not even his fellow officers at the GCPD headquarters could tell her where Detective Lance was. All they knew was that he'd left the station in a rush after receiving a message on his private line.

Dinah threw off the blanket and rose to her feet, grabbing her jacket and keys from the hall closet. She had just decided to do the exact opposite of what her dad would have wanted—return to Robinson Park in search of him—when she heard the sound. *Footsteps.*

Dinah froze as a sea of wide yellow Talon eyes filled her thoughts. By now, they could easily know her name, where she lived. They could have come for her—to drag her away, to punish her for trespassing. And the only thing separating her from that torture was a flimsy wooden door.

The door swung open, and Dinah shrank back in terror, whipping her head wildly, desperate to find any method of concealment in these crucial next seconds. But when she saw who it was, she became dizzy with relief.

Dinah flew into his arms, and Larry scooped her up in a bear hug. *Dad's here—he's safe.* When he met her eyes, though, she saw that his smile was strained.

"Are you okay? What happened? Where were you this whole time?" Dinah's words tumbled out in a rush as he ushered her inside and locked the door behind them. "I'm sorry for putting you through that—*really* sorry."

Larry sank down onto the couch, and Dinah noticed how pale he looked.

"Dad? What happened?"

He gave her another smile that didn't quite reach his eyes.

"I'm okay. More important, you are." He paused. "I . . . made a deal with them."

"You what?" Dinah frowned. "What kind of deal?"

"Nothing that concerns you," he said vaguely. "It's police business."

Dinah studied him, unsure what to believe. But then he shifted in his seat, his face creasing into the Frustrated Father look she knew too well.

"Why did you do it, Dinah? I *told* you to never go near that place. How could you betray my trust like that, putting not just yourself but your friends at risk? Do you even realize what could have happened?"

Dinah lowered her eyes, regret knotting her stomach. Her dad was right, of course. She had known the risks and ignored them—because in the moment, nothing had seemed as important as getting inside the opera house and rescuing those stolen voices.

"You think you know better, but you don't." Larry's voice hardened, and Dinah winced. "I shouldn't have to remind you what precarious times we're living in. If you want to stay safe and out of harm's way, then you need to follow not just the Court's rules but your father's rules, too."

"I know," Dinah mumbled. "I will. I'm sorry, Dad."

She hoped the conversation would end there, but Larry gave her a scrutinizing glance and said, "You still haven't told me what you were doing in that park."

Dinah looked away. She really didn't feel like diving into a touchy subject, but there was no other excuse she could think of that he would believe.

"I just wanted to hear it. The sound of a girl singing," she said quietly. "Like the voice I overheard when I was little. After what you found out about the opera house, I thought if I could just make it inside . . . maybe I'd find it again."

Larry's face clouded over at her words. He let out a long exhale.

"But we talked about this back then, a dozen times. What you think you remembered just isn't possible. It was a figment of your imagination—a natural coping mechanism, after what we'd been through."

Dinah shook her head.

"I know what I heard."

It was the kind of memory that left a mark, tilting her identity to one side and twisting the path in front of her.

And while the memory was blurred around the edges, some of the details lost to time, there was no forgetting the moment when eight-year-old Dinah Lance leaned against the window and heard a girl's voice echo through it.

If she closed her eyes and concentrated hard enough, she could still relive that day. The smell of takeout leftovers wafted in from down the hall, where her dad ate alone in front of the TV while Dinah stayed in her room with no appetite. There was the peculiar way the wind rippled into her bedroom, causing her to get up from the floor to shut the window—and then the shock of the *voice*, breaking through the silence. High and clear, with a sweetness behind it so beautiful that tears sprang to Dinah's eyes. She'd never known a sound like that before, never known it could exist. It was undeniably the sound of a *girl*.

As the voice grew in strength, soaring into a rich melody, it was like a tightly wound knot unraveling, a wave crashing. It was freedom. Dinah was afraid to move, terrified that the spell might break, as she drank in every bend and swing of the notes, every lilt of the voice. The song was one she had never heard before, with words she didn't understand, but even at eight years old, she knew the emotion she was hearing in the unseen girl's voice. *Longing. Nostalgia. Love.* The same things Dinah was feeling herself as she clung to memories of her mom.

It was the first time she had recognized the magic of music—how it could connect you so deeply, through feeling, to people you'd never seen before, people you would never meet in your life. But this mystery singer outside her window, hidden from view, was one person Dinah was desperate to meet. She needed to know how it was possible, and how

Dinah could be an exception just like her: a female voice in a chorus of men.

"You know how I feel," Larry said gruffly. "I don't want to hear any more about phantom voices, and I don't want to see you waste another second chasing after them. Do you understand me?"

Dinah nodded, but his conviction couldn't shake hers. The "phantom voice" was as real to Dinah as her mother's smile, or the sickly-sweet scent of the white lilies that filled their apartment those first months after she was gone. And a large part of Dinah believed that if she could just manage to find the voice again . . . then maybe it could fix everything else that was broken.

By the time morning rolled around, the events of the previous day felt more like a disturbing dream than anything resembling reality. As Dinah and her dad bustled through the kitchen going about their morning routine, with Larry brewing coffee and Dinah scrambling eggs, it seemed impossible that just yesterday they were facing off against the Talons. Until she stepped out the front door.

Something was lying on their doorstep, bloody and mangled. Dinah covered her mouth in horror at the sight of the grayish-white clump, matted through with dark red blood. *Is it . . . alive?* She inched forward, and after a few heartstopping seconds, Dinah recognized the plumage and porcelain, the gaping round hollows for eyes. It was an owl mask. And her hands began to shake.

Everyone in Gotham City knew what this grisly symbol meant, and everyone feared finding one at their door.

It was a clear message from the Court of Owls. She'd been caught in an act of resistance, and this was her first—and likely *only*—warning. The mask would have to hang in their front window for a full week now, a law of the Court, to show the Owls their warning had been heard and to admit to their neighbors that someone in this house had committed an offense. A second infraction, if one dared, would mean a prison sentence at Arkham or death by Talons—and there was never the luxury of a judge or jury. This was life in an autocratic society.

Larry appeared over her shoulder, swearing under his breath at the sight.

"Get back inside," he ordered her, rolling up his sleeves and wincing as he picked up the mask. Blood dripped a path from their door to the kitchen as Larry carried it to the sink, and Dinah watched, frozen.

She should have known this was coming. No one got away with breaking the rules in Gotham City, and she'd been so stupidly confident to think they could escape the park unscathed. But there was something else simmering beneath her remorse—fury that this was happening at all. Anger that she even *had* to stoop to trespassing, just to see inside an opera house that used to belong to all of them. And the unavoidable fear of what would come next.

"This wasn't supposed to happen," Larry said, dropping the mask under running water and turning to face her. "We had an understanding. The Court wasn't supposed to find out we ever went near the opera house."

"'The Court of Owls, that watches all the time.'" Dinah's voice wavered as she quoted the dark nursery rhyme. "I didn't realize just how true that was."

Dinah stood silent for a moment, the cogs in her mind

turning. Something was bothering her about the Talons' presence at the opera house. The first Talon had attacked soon after she approached the front doors, almost like he was *waiting* for someone to attempt to break in. But she was just a teenager, virtually harmless. Were they waiting for someone more dangerous?

"There's something I don't understand," Dinah said, staring at the mask. "Why would the Court show their hand and make it so obvious they're guarding something valuable in there? Because without a Vault of Voices or something equally big hidden inside, why would they even care about a high school student trying to get into a deserted opera house?"

"It's their property, and it's a symbol of Before—a symbol of everything they're against. You trying to break in is an act of resistance, however unspoken," Larry reminded her. "They don't need any other reason than that."

He moved toward the window and Dinah followed, guilt tugging at her chest as she watched her dad, forced to hang up this emblem of shame. Her spirits sank even further at the thought of how many people would walk past their building and see it, just this morning alone. Of all the weeks to draw negative attention to herself, this particular timing might sting the sharpest: Tomorrow was the start of senior year.

CHAPTER THREE

The first day of school at Gotham City High always played out like a popularity pageant. Students lingered on the quad and outside the front doors in tight clusters, pretending to be deep in conversation when they were really only half listening to one another. Their eyes kept flitting to the stairs with each new arrival, silently scoring who drew the biggest crowds of friends and admirers, and whose presence caused barely a ripple. The results would become clear enough when invitations went out for the most exclusive parties, the ones thrown by the likes of Natasha Wycliffe. Maybe it was because Gotham City was ruled by the old-money, elitist Court, but it seemed the one thing the high school had an abundance of these days was snobbery.

Dinah was used to flying under the radar as one of the less-popular, less-wealthy students, living on the outskirts of the school's social hierarchy with Mandy and Ty. But now, with the bloodied mask in her window for all to see, suddenly it was Dinah who everyone was looking at. Her skin burned under their collective stares as she walked up the steps, whispers and snickers trailing her inside. She kept her head down until she got to her locker, where Mandy was already waiting.

"Don't worry," Mandy said, linking her arm with Dinah's. "They'll find a new scandal and move on from you soon enough. Someone else is bound to piss off the Court before long."

"Yeah. I'm just grateful they spared you and Ty the bloody-mask treatment," Dinah said. "Can you imagine having to explain that to your parents? You wouldn't be allowed to hang out with me anymore."

Mandy grimaced. "I'd like to think they would be cooler than that, but . . . you're probably right. Anyway, I don't think the Court or the Talons spare anyone if they can help it. They must not have seen me and Ty in the park."

"Ty has you to thank for that," Dinah said soberly. She didn't even want to think about how they would have fared without Mandy's speed in that moment.

Dinah stopped in front of her first class and gave Mandy a quick hug before stepping inside. "See you at lunch."

Twelfth-grade history was taught by one of the few women teachers, Mrs. Pritchard, who was notoriously pro-Owls. A quick glance around the room made it clear that Dinah didn't have any friends in this class, so she slipped into a desk toward the back.

"Welcome, seniors!" Mrs. Pritchard greeted them, bright-eyed and over-caffeinated. "I hope that you all had a wonderful summer and you're ready for an even better school year. This fall is already shaping up to be a *very* special one, and I'm sure most of you know why." She paused for effect. "This year marks the twentieth anniversary of the Silencing—the event that dramatically reshaped Gotham City."

Dinah gaped at the teacher in disbelief. She wasn't serious—*couldn't* be serious—about celebrating one of the darkest times in women's history. Or was she?

"The Court of Owls is honoring the anniversary and celebrating a record fifth term for Mayor Cobblepot with a Patriarch's Ball at Cobblepot Manor next Saturday," Mrs. Pritchard continued. "The mayor is planning to make a big announcement that night, and luckily for us, Gotham City High students and faculty are all invited."

A buzz rippled through the class at that, but Dinah made a face behind her textbook. She'd heard rumblings of a gala being planned to kick off the mayor's new term, but never guessed that she would have to attend. The thought of having to spend an evening "celebrating" the most loathsome people on the planet was a punishment—one she would rather spend the night in a sewer than endure.

"We'll begin our first semester with a deep dive on the Court's Coup. Turn your textbooks to page three."

The famous illustration of seven men in gray cloaks and owl masks, standing before a burning fireplace, filled the page. A video screen unfurled across the teacher's whiteboard with the same image magnified. There was no looking away from it.

"Midway through the twenty-first century, a cabal of powerful, wealthy men from Gotham City's founding families banded together to seize back control of their city," Mrs. Pritchard began to recite. "Long operating behind the scenes as the Court of Owls, the group was angered by the modernization of Gotham City and the prominence of caped vigilantes who had toppled the balance of power and changed the face of the city. These so-called superheroes pushed what they called an 'egalitarian' agenda." Mrs. Pritchard pursed her lips, as if she'd just uttered a dirty word. "This meant that anyone, even those born to the lowest ranks, could pursue the highest levels of education and stature. Of course, we all know what ended up happening."

No. We don't all know. Most of us only know the lies you've been force-feeding. Dinah dug her nails into her palms, barely able to stomach this propaganda.

"Gotham City in this 'kumbaya' age of superheroes failed dramatically on the world's economic stage. Incomes plummeted, and local businesses barely held on. Meanwhile, women's rights movements led to looser morals and declining numbers of marriages and births."

Excuse me? There was something physically wounding about being forced to sit there in her seat, mouth clamped shut, in the face of all these lies masquerading as education. None of it was even *close* to true. Gotham City had been thriving in the age of superheroes, of women's rights. But Dinah was one of only a few her age who knew the truth, because her parents hadn't been afraid to tell her. They told her about the women-run businesses that exploded onto *Gotham Gazette*'s "Most Profitable" lists, about all the formerly struggling denizens of the East End who were employed and rising above everything that was once expected of them. Until all that progress came to a grinding halt.

"Vowing to restore the Court's once-mighty influence and return Gotham City to its roots," Mrs. Pritchard continued, "the Court of Owls built up an army of indomitable fighters, known as the Talons, to wage their war against the 'superheroes.'" She smiled thinly. "It was a war easily won—especially without the interference of a certain Batman, who had finally died of old age the year prior. After unseating the existing government, the Court of Owls began ruling Gotham City as a dazzlingly successful autocracy."

Is this a joke? Dinah glowered down at her textbook, trembling with rage. The only people who could consider the Court's rule a "dazzling success" were the Owls themselves. Gotham City's entire middle and lower classes had seen their prospects fall, to say nothing of what had happened to its female population. But Mrs. Pritchard's grossest omission was the way she just glossed over *how* the Owls had won the war. They used the most cowardly tactic of all: sending their Talons on a sneak-attack murder spree during the Night of Terror. They had moved under the cover of darkness, breaking into the homes of superheroes while they slept, stabbing them to death before they woke. Only the few whose identities were unknown were spared, but they soon disappeared, too. *And just like that,* Larry had told her through gritted teeth, *Gotham City's superheroes were gone.*

Dinah glanced around the room at her classmates, but most of them looked more zoned out than outraged. Then again, none of them had Detective Lance for a father, to tell the truth about those nightmarish years. They had all been born and grown up after the Silencing. This was all they knew.

"It was the women of Gotham City who raised their voices the loudest against this new regime, who used protest music to start a revolution." A new image filled the screen, a crowd of faceless women storming City Hall. Painted to look like the enemy. "A resistance they paid dearly for."

It didn't matter how many times Dinah heard the story,

or that she already knew what was coming—it still made her skin crawl. She had to bite her tongue to hold back her fury as the teacher continued.

"The Court tapped Chester Cobblepot, of the renowned Cobblepot dynasty, to serve as mayor of their reconstructed Gotham City. A gifted chemist, Mayor Cobblepot had developed a gas that, once unleashed, would cause a very specific and permanent effect on females—to teach them an important lesson." Mrs. Pritchard paused, relishing the grand finale of her vile tale. "And so the women and girls of Gotham City woke up the next morning to find . . . they *could no longer sing.* They had been silenced, just as the next generation of women would be, and the ones after them. The message was clear: stay quiet and loyal to the Court, or risk losing even more. And as the gas spread across our city, the last of the female singers faded into silence."

How can she do it? Dinah stared at Mrs. Pritchard, wondering how it was possible for this woman to recite those words without screaming, without feeling the same fire of rage burning in Dinah's chest over what had been taken from them.

But then the classroom door swung open, halting the teacher mid-drone. And someone new walked in.

He had the greenest eyes Dinah had ever seen. Eyes so striking, they blurred everything else in the room. There was an expression behind them, one she couldn't quite place, which drew her in all the more. Somehow, Dinah could tell these were the eyes of someone who had seen more than most.

He had sun-streaked brown hair and an athlete's build, tall and muscular, highlighted by the deep blue V-neck sweater he wore over his khakis. The sweater instantly marked him as different—the only person in the room wearing a hint of color.

As he sauntered up to the teacher, full of the easy confidence that comes from having never spent a day in an awkward stage, a hush came over the class. Glancing around her, Dinah could see that she was far from the only one intrigued by the stranger, and she felt a self-conscious twinge. This wasn't her. She wasn't the type to follow the masses in lusting after a handsome face, and she wasn't about to start now.

"Ah, there he is!" Mrs. Pritchard trilled. "Everyone, meet your new classmate: Oliver Queen."

The new guy sized up the class with one lofty glance and then looked away, probably bored by them already. Dinah knew the type: big man on campus at his last school. Too handsome for his own good. They would likely exchange no more than two sentences all year.

Mrs. Pritchard directed Oliver to the empty desk behind Dinah and told the class, "Oliver joins us from Star City, California."

Dinah felt a wave of sympathy for him at that. Who would ever want to trade the seaside and sunshine of Star City for cutthroat, gloomy Gotham City? His parents must be gluttons for punishment.

Mrs. Pritchard launched back into her lecture, but Dinah couldn't concentrate even if she wanted to. She was too aware of the guy behind her—his chair squeaking as he leaned back in his seat, the sound of him scrawling something into his notebook when there was nothing for them to take notes on, the feel of those green eyes on her back.

Dinah wasn't sure if she wanted to slide her desk away from or closer to this Oliver Queen from California.

He took his time gathering his things when the bell rang, as if purposely avoiding the rush of students. Dinah swallowed her nerves and blurted out the question foremost on her mind.

"Hey. So . . . why did you leave Star City?" *Well, that didn't come out so smooth.* She cleared her throat awkwardly. "I just meant, I can't imagine anyone choosing Gotham City over California."

"I didn't choose this," Oliver said flatly. "My parents died in an accident, and I got shipped here to my uncle's."

Dinah stopped short, the color draining from her face. Oliver gave her a wry look. "Saddest story you ever heard, right?"

She surprised herself then, taking a step closer and placing a hand on his arm.

"I know how you feel. My mom died when I was seven. There's nothing worse."

This time he actually looked at her. The edge in his voice seemed to soften as he said, "Yeah. The worst." They held eye contact for a moment, and that was when Dinah realized what it was about his green eyes that had struck something in her when he first walked in. There was a sadness behind them—a sadness she recognized too well.

"So, I guess I'll see you around. . . ." He glanced at her questioningly. "What's your name?"

"Dinah. Dinah Lance."

"See you later, Dinah Lance."

Dinah watched him go, a strange sensation bubbling in her stomach. She hadn't expected it . . . that moment of connection. He was the first person she had ever talked to at school who actually understood what it was like to lose a parent. How it irrevocably changed you, giving you a darkness that others got to blissfully skate past. As close as she was to Mandy and Ty, they could never relate to her in this way.

But Oliver Queen could.

Dinah had just slid into her seat at the cafeteria table she shared with Mandy, Ty, and two of Ty's gamer friends, who only spoke in mumble-grunt, when the singing started. The school's all-male a cappella group sauntered into the cafeteria, their voices ringing out proudly as they inaugurated the school year with Gotham City's new anthem.

". . . And we vanquished invaders,
drove out caped crusaders.
Now Gotham is ours, ours alone.
The Court of Owls took back our home."

"Ugh, not this song," Ty grumbled. He took a vigorous bite of his BLT. "Like, who wants to celebrate getting rid of *superheroes* and replacing them with a bunch of creepy dudes wearing owl masks? Where was our vote in that?"

"We were born at the wrong time," Mandy said gloomily.

"But at least Ty gets to sing," Dinah said, still staring at the a cappella group. Sometimes, her longing to join them was too much to stand. In those moments, it felt like the harmonizing notes were reaching straight through her, burrowing into her chest, and if she just opened her mouth, surely the music would come pouring out. But, of course, it never did.

"You know I won't," he said, draping one arm across her shoulders and the other across Mandy's. "Not as long as you can't."

Dinah managed a smile for her oldest friend. "It's stupid that I care so much, I know. . . ." She trailed off, distracted by the sight of someone new joining the most exclusive— and loathsome—table in the cafeteria. The one populated by Zed Cobblepot, Thom Elliot, Natasha Wycliffe, and the other sons and daughters of the Court of Owls. It was Oliver Queen.

"I guess the new guy isn't so different after all," Dinah remarked, the disappointment catching her by surprise.

"Well, yeah. He *is* the heir to Queen Industries," Mandy pointed out. "It would only make sense for his family to be in cahoots with the Court of Owls."

"Queen Industries—of course." Dinah shook her head. "I should have known."

A newspaper headline flashed in her mind, about an orphaned teenage heir to the Queen manufacturing fortune. It hadn't meant anything to her at the time, just another kid with massive inherited wealth. But after seeing the sadness in his eyes today, she felt a pang of remorse that she'd been so flippant before.

Just then, Zed caught Dinah staring. The look that crossed his face sent a chill through her body.

"Saw your window decor today, Lance," he called, raising his voice so that no one in the cafeteria could miss his words. "What were you and your old man trying to do? Follow your mom to an early grave?"

Dinah was up from the table before she knew what hit her, forgetting the promises she'd made to keep her martial arts training a secret. She lunged toward Zed with a fury that could have sent his body reeling to the floor—and likely would have, if not for the stupid new guy, Oliver Queen, jumping between them and blocking Dinah with his muscled forearms.

"Not worth it," he muttered in her ear while Zed laughed at her attempted strike. Dinah shook off Oliver's arm, shooting him a glare before trudging back to her table.

Senior year was off to a seriously crappy start.

After what felt like a never-ending school day, the final bell rang at last, and Dinah shot out of her seat. She was desperate to be alone, away from all the curious, gossipy eyes—but first she had to walk through the heavily guarded Downtown Gotham City on her way home. She could only hope the eyes wouldn't continue trailing her there.

Downtown was the beating heart of the Court, where the Owls' influence could be felt in every brick and stone. They had taken over Gotham City's landmark buildings twenty years ago, and it was only thanks to her parents that Dinah knew the real origins behind the architecture. She could gaze up at the tallest building in the city, with its domed spire and gargoyle statues, and see not just the Court's current seat of government, but its former identity as the Old Wayne Tower, home of the once-flourishing Wayne Industries. She could walk past the Gotham City Courthouse and recognize the place where lawyers and judges once worked together in search of justice, even though it was now little more than a glorified holding pen for whomever the Owls wanted to dump in Arkham Asylum. And when she passed the grand Powers Hotel, she didn't just see the notorious spot where Mayor Cobblepot, Marcus Powers, and the other Owl Masters carried out their bribes and schemes—she saw the restaurant where, years before, her father had proposed to her mother.

But that old Gotham City her parents had known couldn't have been farther from the reality Dinah was looking at today. She thought of her godmothers, Anissa and Grace, who used to walk hand in hand through the city, laughing and kissing without garnering a second glance, but who were now forced to live in hiding. If she hadn't known better, it would have been easy to think her parents had fabricated the old way of life—that it was just a bedtime story written in wishful thinking.

Crossing into Downtown's main thoroughfare, Dinah found every corner crawling with uniformed Owl Guards on active patrol. There was a hush in the streets, as if the locals were all holding their breath. Businessmen were dressed to the nines in suits and hats, while women over eighteen covered up in ankle-length skirts and three-quarter-sleeve tops, forced to abide by the public dress code. Dinah's uniform was only a slight improvement. She had never cared much about clothes, but Mandy was particularly irked by the monotonous dress code, and was always searching for subtle ways to subvert it—like coming to school with her grandmother's vintage leopard-print hair scrunchie worn like a bracelet around her wrist, or leaving her shirt half untucked. She and Dinah had to get their kicks from these tiny morsels of rebellion.

Dinah passed Wall Street, where the professionals on the steps and darting in and out of office buildings were all men. Women were only spotted on the residential blocks, pushing baby carriages or hauling groceries. As soon as she graduated, that would be expected of her, too. Dinah felt a stab of panic at the thought.

Even the opportunity to go to school now, seen as a "gift" for girls, was really just the Court's way of indoctrinating them into their system of beliefs. But at least it was something—the chance to go where the boys went, to take (most of) the same classes. They could all at least pretend there was a somewhat level playing field—well, not when it came to sports, of course. They weren't allowed to play sports, either.

Dinah was just about to make the turn onto her street when she changed her mind at the last minute and kept going, toward a boarded-up building. She reached up to touch the windowsill, where her own initials had been carved a lifetime ago.

This used to be her mother's shop, D. Drake Florals. With women only allowed to work in one of a few "appropriate" fields designated by the Court, Dinah Drake had considered herself lucky: florists were on the "feminine-safe" list. She could keep her job—but the infuriating catch was that she had to lose ownership of her business; her husband would own it now. Still, Larry made a point of keeping the name of the shop the same, after Dinah's maiden name. It was still *hers* . . . even if they were the only two who really knew it.

The younger Dinah still had fuzzy memories of her mom bringing her to work on Saturdays, where she would always let Dinah design her own makeshift flower arrangements. Those were her favorite days.

Dinah swallowed the lump in her throat and turned away. She shouldn't have come back here—it hurt too much. But then her eye caught the familiar awning of Rags 'n' Tatters, the old antiques shop farther down the street that Dinah and her mom used to pop into after their Saturdays at the flower shop. It was always a treat to see the owner's collection of wares from the early twenty-first and twentieth centuries, and though everything on display had to be approved by the Court's team of Culture Enforcers, so far they hadn't found a reason to remove the owner's upright piano. Maybe, if she was lucky, she would get to hear him play this afternoon. She was almost at the shop door when the silence in the streets was suddenly shattered.

A flock of bodies came running in a flash of blue and black—blue jeans and black shirts with the yellow outline of a bat sketched across the front, an homage to the superhero who protected them and kept the Court in their place for as long as he lived. This was the unmistakable uniform of the Resistance. It was a group of twenty, made up of mostly women who flouted the dress code while holding up signs and screaming a chant. *"Bring back our voice! Bring back our rights!"*

Dinah couldn't look away, something kindling in her chest at the sight. And then she caught a flash of a vaguely familiar face from within the crowd. She darted forward, scanning the group of protesters for the face—when the tear gas hit. Bodies scattered in a cloud of smoke, some falling to the ground while others went running, as the Court's guards swooped in with their ammunition. Dinah tried to move toward the bodies on the ground, but her nose, mouth, and eyes all felt like they were on fire; it was too hard to see, to breathe.

A pair of hands clamped down on her shoulders. Dinah jumped, a scream lodging in her throat, as the hands yanked her backward.

CHAPTER FOUR

Through the blur of smoke, Dinah struggled to see who was connected to the hands gripping her shoulders. It looked like the kind of face only found in a horror film. Mismatched scraps of leather covered every inch of the stranger's skin, plastering his mouth shut, hiding all but his flashing blue-gray eyes. He towered over her in a hooded brown cloak, and Dinah shrank back, trying to yank out of the monster's grasp. And then she heard a faint voice in her ear.

"Dinah. It's only me."

She blinked rapidly, and the smoke in her eyes began to clear. The figure that seemed so intimidating through the smoke was . . . barely two inches taller than her, and as he lowered the scarf covering half his face, the weathered features of an older man came to light. The sole similarity between him and the monster she thought she'd seen was the hooded patchwork coat, which looked like it had been pieced together from a variety of clashing fabrics. Relief flooded her chest as she recognized the crescent-shaped scar under his eye and the quirky fashion that marked Rory

Regan, owner of Rags 'n' Tatters. It must have been close to a year since Dinah saw him last.

She let him pull her away from the crowd and chaos toward his shop door, which opened with a familiar bell chime. Rory ushered her into one of the stiff antique chairs inside and then disappeared to the back of the store, returning moments later with a glass of water and a wet cloth for her soot-covered face.

"Thank you," Dinah mumbled, gratefully taking both. After gulping down the water, she looked into Rory's kind eyes and said, "It's been forever since I've come to visit. I'm sorry."

"No apologies necessary," he said lightly. He'd been close to her parents once, when Dinah Drake was alive and had her own business two doors down. It occurred to her now that all three of them had basically abandoned him, and she felt a pang of regret.

Dinah turned back to the window, and her stomach lurched at the sight of the protesters. Their bodies were still crumpled on the ground.

"Are they . . . they . . ."

"They'll be all right," Rory finished her sentence. "Hurt and dazed, yes, but they will live."

"How do you know?"

"Because it happens a few times a year, especially around the anniversary of the Silencing. Someone usually gets a brave and noble idea in their head, ropes in others who share their hopes, and then they march together until they fall. The gas is usually enough to stop them, but not kill. The Court knows that if they murder everyone who opposes them, they'll have no one left to rule."

"I just stood there," Dinah muttered. "I don't want to be the kind of person who just stands there."

Rory placed a gentle hand on her shoulder. And then Dinah saw something through the window that froze her insides cold.

Officers from the Gotham City PD were storming onto the scene, crouching down to slap handcuffs on the battered protesters, forcing them to their feet. And right there, working alongside them, was Dinah's father, his expression blank as he cuffed and dragged a pair of protesters to a waiting cop car.

"I'm going to be sick," Dinah blurted out, before bolting through the cluttered shop to a tiny corner bathroom. She retched into the bowl twice, the image of her dad's betrayal searing across her brain, even as a voice tried reminding her that he had no choice. This was his job. And with a target on her back now, his position was that much trickier. He couldn't afford to put a foot out of line.

But it still killed her to see it.

When Dinah came wobbling out of the bathroom, Rory was there waiting for her, his face creased with concern.

"Dad wasn't supposed to . . . to be like them," Dinah said numbly. "He was always my strongest ally against the Court."

"He still is, I'm sure," Rory said. "Sometimes, in this new world we're living in, the only way to survive is to wear a different face for the public—for the Owls."

"That doesn't make what I just saw okay," she muttered. She braved another glance out the window, but the protesters and police were gone now. All that was left was a soot-filled street with bloodstains on the ground from those who tried fighting back.

"Why don't you pick out something from the store, for old times' sake?" Rory offered, clearly trying to distract her. "My treat."

"It's okay. You don't have to," she said, her eyes still on the window. "I'm not a little kid anymore."

"True. But what's the fun of owning a shop like this if I can't pass on treasures to friends now and again?"

Dinah hesitated, and then turned from the window to face him.

"You—you don't happen to have anything from the old opera house, do you?"

"No." Rory gave her an appraising look. "But something came in just last week that you might like."

Dinah followed him across the room, her heartbeat picking up speed as he stopped in front of a safe and unlocked it with his ring of keys, revealing a thick folder labeled *Sheet Music: 20th Century*. He handed her four pages from the top of the pile, yellowed with age—even though music was illegal for her to possess. Rory was risking his neck to give her this gift. She would be risking her own by accepting it, if anyone found out.

But it was a risk she would have to take. There was no way she could say no to something she wanted this much.

Dinah glanced down at the first lined page, with the words *ELEANOR RIGBY—Lennon/McCartney* inscribed at the top. Dancing across the lines were curled black symbols that Dinah recognized as musical notes, with the lyrics in tiny font underneath. She felt a jolt of excitement.

"I actually *know* this song." She beamed at Rory. "Thank you."

And as she gazed down at the notes and lyrics, she

couldn't help drifting into a fantasy. One where she could sing the melody, the words, herself—just like any man.

Dinah could feel the eyes again, tracking her from the shadows as she walked home from Rory's shop. She tightened her grip on her book bag, where the sheet music was hidden inside like some kind of weapon. If any of the Court's guards on patrol decided to pull her aside for a stop-and-search . . . Dinah's stomach lurched at the thought of being caught with something so illicit. *My second offense.* She could get sent to Arkham.

She shook her head, trying to rid herself of the thought. It would be okay; she would just have to act normal, be on her best behavior for the rest of this short walk. Give them no reason to look at her twice.

Rory had offered to walk Dinah home, but she'd waved him off, assuring him there was no need—especially since Dinah was pretty confident that she was a lot better equipped to fend off trouble than the soft-spoken, fragile-looking shop owner anyway. But she was regretting her decision with every snap of a twig and rustle of movement that echoed uncomfortably close behind her. She kept turning to look over her shoulder, but the passersby were all farther away than the sounds would indicate. Dinah spotted two middle-aged businessmen mid-argument, a girl pushing a double stroller who looked far too young to be a mother, and a red-haired woman in a wheelchair who briefly met Dinah's eyes. None of them appeared all that interested in her, but she still couldn't shake the feeling of being watched.

Finally, Dinah reached the front door of the walk-up brownstone apartment she and her father called home. She glanced behind her one last time before turning the key in the lock, breathing a sigh of relief once she was inside.

The sheet music was practically burning a hole in her backpack, and Dinah's eyes flew to the clock above the fridge. She'd have the place to herself for another forty-five minutes at least. . . .

Dinah turned and dashed across the apartment to her room. At first glance, the bedroom was nothing special: stark white walls, a tidy twin bed and matching desk, and a dresser showcasing just two framed photos. One was of Dinah and her parents, the other of Dinah, Mandy, and Ty at her sixth birthday party, when they were a newly formed trio. Both pictures were from a time when she still had a mom.

The photos were the only personal touches in the room until you reached the walk-in closet. That was where Dinah's true personality was hidden, and she stepped inside now, grabbing the sheet music from her backpack on the way.

The closet walls were a joyful mess of a collage, covered in cutouts from books and magazines she and Mandy had found hidden in the Harpers' attic. They were both stunned that Mandy's parents had managed to hold on to this contraband: magazines with names like *Rolling Stone* and *Vogue* that showed women—actual flesh-and-blood *females*—singing on-stage, speaking at podiums in front of world audiences, wearing lab coats at hospitals, even in astronaut uniforms. Most astonishing of all was the magazine with a woman president on its cover. Dinah had never seen anything like it—certainly not in the world they existed in now. The pictures of these forgotten women covered every square inch of wall space in her closet, reminding her of all the careers and opportunities and freedoms women were once allowed, all the lives they once got to live.

She could pass hours just staring at them, heroes of all different shades and sizes. But she especially loved her section of cutouts featuring musicians, *singers:* a twentysomething blonde in a midriff shirt giving the camera a piercing gaze; an elderly African woman onstage under a marquee that read THE VOICE AND SOUL OF CAPE VERDE; and a dark-haired, dark-eyed Iranian opera singer in elaborate costume. All that was missing from her collection was the sound of them. The Court of Owls might have overlooked a few magazines in their burning of history, but they succeeded in destroying every shred of audio and video evidence of female singers. Except for—*maybe*—whatever lay in the Vault of Voices.

Dinah reached under the rack of identical school uniforms and pulled out a small trunk that used to be her mother's. Sitting inside was her mom's old record player, with a stack of vinyl albums underneath.

Before her mom died, there was always a record playing in the house. Her dad even had a corny catchphrase about it: *I'm getting tired of coming home to the sound of other men serenading my wife!*

After she died, he'd wanted all of it gone—the record player and her carefully chosen vinyl collection—until young Dinah stepped in and refused to let them go. But even now, he wanted nothing to do with music, and Dinah sometimes wondered if there was more to it than grief. Either way, Dinah was careful to keep them hidden in her closet. Her father was allowed to own records and music, but she certainly wasn't.

Dinah rifled through the pile until she found the black-and-white album cover she was looking for. *Revolver.* Sure enough, there it was, listed on the back: "Eleanor Rigby," track two. She glanced from the record to the sheet music in awe, and then on a whim she reached for the ballpoint pen sticking out from one of her journals on the closet floor. This was the first item of music Dinah had ever owned herself—she had to mark its importance by writing her name and today's date in the corner. And then she slid the record from its sleeve and placed it on the turntable, lowering the needle onto the second groove to cue up track two.

A smile lit Dinah's face, and she held the sheet music to her chest. *"Ah, look at all the lonely people,"* a young man sang a century ago, his plaintive emotions frozen in time.

Dinah replayed the track over and over again. It was after the tenth listen that she took a deep breath and decided to try.

"Ah, look at all the lonely—"

In her head, she could do it. She could sing along with McCartney in perfect harmony, floating across the notes with him. But while her mouth formed the words, nothing happened. Her throat closed up instead, a visceral reminder of Mayor Cobblepot's dark science, weaponized against her gender.

Dinah tossed the sheet music to the floor and slammed the record player shut, the song skidding to a stop with a loud scratch. *Stupid.* What did she expect, that Rory Regan had given her magical sheet music? She'd never be able to sing.

"Dinah? What's all that noise in there?"

She stood up a little too quickly, banging her head on one of the closet shelves, and bit her tongue to keep from letting out a string of expletives. Larry was waiting in the doorway when Dinah stepped out of the closet, her head still throbbing.

"What were you doing in there?" Larry eyed her suspiciously. "Was that . . . the Beatles I heard?"

"So what if it was? Are they illegal now, too?" Dinah asked evenly.

Larry looked taken aback by her tone.

"Um. No. But in light of the symbol hanging in our window, it would be wiser to not draw any more attention—"

"Is that why you were out arresting innocent protesters today?" she said, cutting him off. Her voice was harsh enough to make him wince. "To get in good with the enemy?"

"You don't know what you're talking about," Larry snapped, the softness gone. "There are things I've had to do to keep you—us—alive, and for you to stand there and judge when you know *nothing* of—"

"So tell me!" Dinah pleaded. "If I've got it all wrong, then just tell me why."

Larry stopped short, the energy draining from his face like air from a pricked balloon.

"The less you know, the better," he finally said. "It's for your own safety."

As soon as he walked away, Dinah slammed the door shut, throwing her pillow at it in frustration. How was it that the person closest to her could also be a complete, infuriating mystery?

Dinah was just climbing into bed for the night when her phone pinged with a text. When she grabbed it from the bedside table, a message from Mandy was waiting on-screen.

And so the fawning begins . . .

Her message linked to a blog post in the gossip section of the *Gotham Gazette*. Dinah leaned back against propped-up pillows as she clicked the link.

THE BILLIONAIRE BOY NEXT DOOR

The streets of Gotham City are abuzz over our newest arrival, the fabulously wealthy, gorgeous, yet desperately tragic Oliver Queen. Sources say the popular "Ollie" left a string of broken hearts behind in Star City, none more than his own after the shocking death of his parents just six months ago. Heir to a fortune rumored to be in the $1 billion range and set to take the reins of Queen Industries from his uncle upon graduating from college, Oliver is the closest thing we have to a prince on this side of the Atlantic. So now the pressing question is: Will one of our Gotham girls be able to charm this orphan out of his sadness . . . and become his chosen *Queen*?

Dinah cringed.
Okay, ew, she texted Mandy. Can certain gossip columnists PLEASE be barred from making bad puns?

It feels like they're trying to turn him into the sexy version of a Charles Dickens character or something, right? Mandy wrote back. I mean, fine, he's obviously hunky, but only if you're into that type. Personally, I don't want a dude with dreamier eyes than me. Anyway, if you read more of the article, it kinda sounds like he needs a therapist a lot more than a girlfriend.

A part of Dinah felt like she was snooping as she scrolled down to continue reading, but it took a few more paragraphs before she finally put the phone down.

> **Rumors of family drama have long dogged the illustrious Queens, but none of the familial discord lessened the sting of losing his parents. When Oliver did appear in public after the tragedy, Star City sources say, he could be found drinking and partying even though he was underage, a key factor in his uncle's stepping in as his guardian and moving him across the country.**
>
> **Luckily, Gotham City is just the right place for Oliver Queen. Insiders report that the Court of Owls is keen to welcome this high-profile arrival to their inner ranks.**

"Yeah, that's *exactly* what a troubled guy needs," Dinah muttered. "To get swept up in a creepy cult."

But it wasn't her problem. She might have felt a kinship with Oliver when they first met, but it seemed that all they had in common was a sad backstory. He was one of *them*.

There was just one thing that didn't fit this narrative— the look of concern on Oliver's face earlier today as he held her back from lunging at Zed Cobblepot. Why had he even cared? The others at his table would have loved nothing more than to watch Dinah make a fool of herself attempting to fight the king of Gotham City High, but for some reason . . . not Oliver. Maybe he wasn't soulless like the rest of them after all.

CHAPTER FIVE

Dinah walked up the front steps to school the next morning in a fog, groggy from a night of insomnia. The events of the previous day had kept her mind wide awake as she replayed the wrenching sight of protesters covered in tear gas, of her father standing over them. But when she stepped through the double doors into the main hall and glanced up at the overhead clock, Dinah realized she'd somehow made it ten minutes early . . . which meant she could catch the final minutes of a cappella practice. She'd made a habit of it last year, arriving with enough time to listen in outside the music room door. It was pretty embarrassing, fangirling over a school a cappella group like that, and it probably only heightened her bitterness at not being able to sing herself. But their harmonies were just too beautiful. She couldn't stay away.

As she drew closer to the lush blend of voices carrying toward her, Dinah spotted someone else lingering by the closed door. Her eyebrows shot up. Was that . . . Oliver Queen?

He turned quickly, as if sensing her presence, and flashed a brief smile.

"Hey. Dinah, right?"

"Yeah." *He remembered.* Although—duh, of course he remembered. After the whole altercation with Zed Cobblepot at his lunch table, it would have been hard for him to forget the name *Dinah Lance.*

"What are you . . . doing?" she blurted out, gesturing to the closed door.

"Someone told me you don't have much of a music scene in Gotham City, so I figured this was the closest I could get," he joked.

"Well, sadly, that might be true," Dinah said with a wry smile.

"I was just walking by and noticed how good they sound." He leaned in closer to the door and Dinah followed suit, feeling her skin prickle with self-consciousness, as if the close proximity could give away that she spent last night reading up on him. "This song is a lot better than that weird one from yesterday," he added.

So he's not a fan of the new Gotham City anthem, either. That was a point in his favor.

They fell silent, listening to the blend of voices inside coming to a crescendo on the chorus.

"California dreamin' on such a winter's day . . ."

"Does that make you homesick?" she asked, glancing up at him out of the corner of her eye.

He paused, an inscrutable expression crossing his face.

"It's not really the words in the song, but just . . . music in general that makes me homesick."

Dinah's breath caught in her throat.

"I know what you mean." She was about to say more when she caught sight of Zed Cobblepot sauntering down the hall—toward Oliver. There was no way she was going to hang around long enough to hear his amusement and scorn that *she* was talking to his buddy. "I should go. I'll see you in class."

"Wait—"

Dinah darted away from him, turning in the opposite direction and heading toward her locker. But their short exchange kept replaying in her mind . . . until she saw something that yanked her right out of her thoughts. It seemed she wasn't the only one making conversation with somebody unexpected.

Natasha Wycliffe was leaning against her locker and smiling up at *Ty*, of all people. His face was so flushed, it practically matched the red shade of his hair. Dinah felt a twinge of worry as he chatted her up. It had to have been Natasha who initiated the conversation; Ty wouldn't have made the first move. So what was she after?

Dinah hung back, peeking around the corner and waiting for Ty to finish his awkward flirt-fest. Finally the bell rang and Natasha pulled her books out of her locker, then stopped to give Ty a . . . *hug?* She sauntered off and Ty watched her go, a lopsided grin on his face. Dinah hightailed it over to him.

"Excuse me. What was that?"

Ty glanced at her, taken aback by her sudden appearance.

"Oh—that. I helped her with her calculus homework yesterday. We're seated next to each other this year." He grinned. "Talk about good luck, right?"

"Ty-*ler*," Dinah chided. "You know who she is. I thought

we promised each other we'd never cozy up to the spawn of the Court!"

"Just because her parents are in the Court doesn't mean she is," he said defensively. "She's nothing like them."

"And you know that how?" Dinah retorted.

Ty gave her a disgruntled look and started walking.

"Can't you just let me have this one good moment, Dinah? Not everyone connected to the Court of Owls is all bad."

Dinah stopped short.

"You wouldn't be able to say that if you were me."

And it hit her then—that as much as he could sympathize and rail against the regime along with Dinah and Mandy, he would never fully understand what their experience, every day, was actually like. Not when he still had his voice and all the other privileges of Before. He could have whatever career he wanted, he could play instruments, he could sing out loud, he could wear *pants*. He had no idea how lucky he was.

"I don't want to fight with you, Dinah," Ty said wearily. "Let's just drop it. I'll see you at lunch."

He walked away, leaving her with a pit forming in her stomach.

The sound of marching footsteps outside the classroom door brought first period to an abrupt halt. Mrs. Pritchard practically flew out of her chair to open the door, where two men in unmistakable uniforms advanced through the halls, their eyes straight ahead, looking at no one. They wore the Court of Owls' livery colors, deep burgundy tunics under gray hooded coats, with a long, sharp dagger glinting from the bandolier strapped across each of their chests. Dinah's throat turned dry. What were the mayor's cronies doing here at *school*?

"All right, students!" Mrs. Pritchard clapped her hands together, a slightly manic look in her eyes. "The mayor's office notified us that they'd be calling a school-wide assembly, and it looks like that's happening . . . right now. Please line up and follow me to the auditorium."

The air turned thick with tension as the students slid out of their desks and made their way to the door. Oliver Queen fell into step with Dinah.

"Any idea what this is about?" he asked quietly.

Dinah shook her head.

"Zed didn't tell you anything?" She kept her tone light, but the subtext was clear: *Aren't you on the inside?*

"No," Oliver replied, meeting her eyes. "I'm as clueless as everyone else."

They walked the rest of the way in silence, Dinah's heart thudding louder the closer they got to the auditorium. Any surprises involving Mayor Cobblepot were always the worst kind, a punch to the gut. Like, for example, his biggest surprise of all: stealing the voices of an entire population.

The class shuffled into their row of seats, joining the monotonous sea of white button-downs, beige khakis, and gray wool skirts. Dinah sat sandwiched between Oliver and another back-row student, sleepy-eyed Logan Rogers. As Oliver's arm brushed against hers, Dinah felt goose bumps rise. She inched away from him. Whatever that involuntary reaction was—it wasn't going to happen again.

"Attention, Gotham City High!" The Court-appointed,

mustachioed, and middle-aged Principal Samuels addressed them from the foot of the stage. "We are *honored* to be in the presence of our mayor's deputy secretary and Culture Enforcer, Mr. Ruben and Mr. Dwight, respectively, who are here to make a special announcement."

Dinah swallowed hard, bracing herself. Bringing out the Culture Enforcer never meant anything good.

The uniformed men strode up to the stage, sweeping the principal aside as they took the podium.

"The upcoming Patriarch's Ball will honor both the anniversary of the Silencing and Mayor Cobblepot's illustrious tenure, as well as the Court of Owls' formidable history," the dour-faced Mr. Dwight began. "As such, we will be paying tribute to the Court's origins by featuring elements from the early Patriarch's Balls, of several hundred years ago."

Dinah's shoulders relaxed. For once, the news was something trivial instead of horrifying. She could feel a wave of relief rippling through the student body as everyone came to the same realization.

"This will be an opportunity to educate you further about the history of your rulers," the Culture Enforcer continued, always ready to prick the fun out of anything. "For example, we'll be bringing back the tradition of the quadrille, an aristocratic formal dance of the eighteenth and nineteenth centuries that began in the court of Louis XIV and was introduced to America by the Court of Owls' founding families."

Dinah rolled her eyes. This sounded insufferable already.

"The quadrille was the highlight of all formal occasions, as it featured the four most important, top-tier couples present at any function. These eight individuals were chosen to open the ball with a quadrille d'honneur, where they would perform the intricate, five-part dance while moving through the room in the shape of a square."

"That doesn't sound weird or anything," Oliver said under his breath, echoing Dinah's thoughts.

"Yeah, and what's a 'top-tier couple'?" she snorted.

On the other side of her, Logan Rogers flashed Dinah a disapproving look. Someone, apparently, was taking this seriously.

"The dance was frequently performed to opera melodies of the day, and you might recognize some of the steps from our modern iterations of the waltz and ballet," Dwight said.

Dinah's ears perked up at the mention of opera. She wondered if any of the women whose voices lay in the opera house vault had participated in this upper-crust tradition.

"Now, to symbolize the merging of the old generation with the new, your mayor and the Court of Owls have selected four esteemed students to serve as guests of honor and lead the first quadrille of our own Patriarch's Ball, accompanied by the respective girls of their choosing."

Their choosing. Dinah stiffened at the phrase. Naturally, the poor girls wouldn't have a choice in whether or not to suffer through the night with one of the blowhards handpicked by the Court.

The deputy secretary, Mr. Ruben, leaned in to the mic. "The first guest of honor is . . . also known as our first son, Mr. Zed Cobblepot!"

"Duh," Dinah whispered to Oliver. "He really needed to consult his note cards for that one?"

Oliver laughed, and it was a surprised sound—like he almost wasn't used to laughing.

After pausing for a round of applause, Mr. Ruben continued, "Next up, we have Desmond Clark."

The cheers that followed his name were even louder than Zed's. Desmond was the star of pretty much everything he did—a cappella, sports, school—and his father was rumored to be the current Grandmaster of the Court of Owls. It was a role shrouded in secrecy, but one that clearly put him at the top of the chain.

"Thom Elliot."

Ty wouldn't like that one. Everyone knew Thom was on-and-off with Natasha Wycliffe, and she was the obvious choice for his date.

"And our last honored guest is . . ."

Dinah yawned. So far the announcements had been utterly predictable, names she could have guessed in her sleep. The final name would probably be—

"Oliver Queen."

Dinah's mouth fell open. Oliver shot up in his seat, looking just as stunned as she felt. For a society that was all about the old, *why* would they pick the new guy over one of the four remaining sons of Owls?

There was a beat of surprised silence, followed by applause, with even a few whistles of approval. As the words from the gossip column floated back to her mind, Dinah realized it wasn't that much of a shocker after all. Oliver might have been new to their school, but he wasn't new to the Court. His family must have been a part of the Owls' inner sanctum since long before he moved to Gotham City. And here she'd been joking around with him just moments ago, like she could be honest with him about how she felt about the regime—like he was *safe*. Oliver Queen was clearly anything but. She'd have to remind herself to be more careful around him moving forward. Maybe by avoiding him entirely.

"Now we'd like to invite our four honored guests up to the stage, where they may formally select their dates," Dwight said, and Principal Samuels clasped his hands together in glee. Dinah cringed in her seat. So they were going to put the girls on the spot *now*? The insults didn't end.

Oliver's face was flushed as he slid out of their row and followed Zed, Thom, and Desmond to the stage. The other three sauntered up full of back-slapping self-congratulations, but Oliver at least had the decency to look embarrassed by the whole thing. He kept his eyes trained on the uniformed deputies, ignoring the stares coming his way from the audience.

"First up, young Master Cobblepot." Dwight bowed his head in deference. "Which lucky lady would you like to call up to the stage?"

Zed's sometime-girlfriend, Maya Powers, took that dubious honor, while Desmond chose his hookup du jour, Camila Orchard, from one of the fancy families. Thom invited Natasha, as predicted, leaving Oliver Queen the question mark. He'd barely been at their school long enough to *know* anyone, much less ask someone out, and Dinah couldn't help her curiosity as she watched him survey the room. If he was going off looks and Owl-approved pedigree, then it would probably be Rochelle Rose, or maybe—

"Dinah."

Okay, now she was imagining things. She'd heard wrong; there was no way—

"Dinah Lance."

CHAPTER SIX

The whole room seemed to gasp at once. Zed's cruel laugh reverberated through the auditorium, saying what the rest of them were thinking. Oliver had an entire school to choose from, and of all people he picked . . . *her?*

Dinah sank lower in her seat. Maybe her name was just the only one he could remember, and if she stayed put he would come up with another—

"Get up," Logan Rogers hissed next to her. Everyone was turning in their seats to stare, and she had no choice but to stumble to her feet, making the painfully awkward trek to the stage. She kept her eyes on the floor to block out her gawking classmates but glanced up when she felt a hand reach out for hers. It was Mandy, sitting in an aisle seat and flashing her a mile-wide grin, as if this were the thrill of a lifetime. But on the other side of Mandy was Ty, eyeing Dinah in disbelief. *And you had the nerve to give* me *a hard time about liking Natasha,* she could practically hear him saying. Dinah hoped he could read the truth in her expression, that she had nothing to do with this.

When she climbed the steps to the stage and took her place next to Oliver, he gave her a sheepish smile.

"Hope you don't mind me putting you on the spot like that," he said in her ear.

"Why . . . why me?" she whispered back. "Don't you know who I am?"

"What do you mean? Are you famous or something?" he teased.

"I *mean*, I'm the one with the bloodied owl mask hanging in my window right now. I'm the last person the Court would want you to bring." The thought of being so exposed to them, practically handed to the Owls on a gleaming ballroom floor, sent a stab of panic through her. She gestured to their classmates in the audience. "You have a few hundred way more suitable options right in front of you."

"I don't want suitable," he said simply.

Ah, so that was it. This wasn't some kind of twisted Cinderella moment, but Oliver's softball attempt at rebelling. Being the "wrong" girl made her the right date. She couldn't really argue with that, but she bristled at the idea of being used. And, on a deeper, more secretive level . . . she sort of wished that Oliver had chosen her for a reason other than trying to shake things up.

"Now that we've introduced our four pairs who will lead the quadrille d'honneur," Mr. Dwight said, overpronouncing every syllable of French, "it's time to learn the steps. I understand one of your teachers has been given special authorization to learn this historical dance, for the purpose of instructing you?"

He held out a hand toward Mrs. Pritchard, who looked like she might faint from excitement. She teetered up to the stage and joined Dwight for a demonstration, the two of them wearing dead-serious expressions as they circled and chasséd across the stage. When the stuffy pair demonstrated a particular move called "pigeon-winging," jumping in the air and striking their legs together, Oliver met Dinah's eyes and they both nearly lost it, covering their mouths to hold back their laughter.

Mr. Dwight turned back to the audience, oblivious to the comedic effect he was having.

"Now it's your turn. Everyone, form into pairs and follow along with the couples onstage as we teach them the steps."

If the Court wanted Dinah Lance to die of embarrassment, they were off to a good start. Having the whole *school* watch her attempt a decidedly unflattering, old-fashioned dance for the first time was nothing short of mortifying.

The auditorium filled with the sounds of chairs scraping back and students rising to their feet, as Mrs. Pritchard cued up the PA system. A jaunty melody of strings and piano floated from the speakers, and Dinah tried to pretend she was somewhere else—some*time* else. Away from this stage and the hundreds of judgmental eyes, and back in the ballroom of the old opera house, where maybe the singer whose photo hung on Dinah's closet wall once performed this same strange dance, too.

Oliver held out his hand, grinning at Dinah like he was in on her secret, and something swooped in her chest at his touch. *Get it together, Dinah Laurel Lance.*

The moment of spark soon gave way to chaos, as Dinah and Oliver were swept up in a blur of choreography. The four couples bumbled their way through the steps, all of them nearly colliding at one point, while Mr. Dwight yelled out foreign terms such as *jeté* and *assemblé*. The dance called for the eight of them to switch partners as they moved through the routine, and when Dinah found herself in front of Zed, she froze.

His gray eyes glittered, enjoying her discomfort. And just as she moved forward, reluctantly following the steps, he slid his foot out right in front of her—sending her faceplanting to the front of the stage. The music screeched to a stop.

"Ouch. You okay?" Oliver reached out to help her up, but Dinah pushed his hand away. Her face burned with humiliation as she peeled herself off the floor to the sound of her classmates' laughter.

"*Someone* is going to need more practice!" a voice shouted gleefully from the audience, followed by another wave of laughs.

Dinah stared daggers at Zed, imagining what she could do to him right now—a front kick/side kick combination to knock him to the ground, a guillotine choke hold to finish him. Her limbs were pulsing, itching to fight back, but she kept her fists clenched at her sides. She would have to hold it all in and keep the anger buried until after school, when she would finally get to see Sandra.

"Quiet!" Dwight snapped, and the smiles slipped off the students' faces. They'd all seen what could happen when Mayor Cobblepot got angry. If his staff was anything like him—

"Contrary to what you might think, we're not doing this for fun. The Patriarch's Ball is a serious occasion." The Culture Enforcer's voice dripped with disdain, especially as his beady eyes lingered on Dinah. "Yes, it's a dance, but more important, it's a showcase of our civic and military powers. The mayor and the Owls won't be the only figures celebrated, but the Talons as well." A ghost of a smile played across his face. "One Talon in particular will be in attendance—an especially lethal new member of our forces, one who bridges the gap between past and present. You'll want to be at your best for him. For all of them."

Dinah felt her stomach drop to the floor. *Talons and civilians . . . in the same room?* That never happened. Not unless massive blood was being shed. The Talons lived and operated in the darkness, only venturing into the light if there was someone to kill—or something to defend. Why—*how*—were they supposed to stand under the same ceiling, share the same walls? She'd be dancing straight to her death. This was clearly a sign from the Court, a show of public power to remind everyone of the control they held. But why were they choosing now to do that? Did something happen that might have threatened their rule, prompting a defense?

I'm not going, Dinah decided. She'd gotten lucky once, escaping them with her heart still beating. She wasn't about to chance it again.

But then she heard Oliver let out an exhale, and reality hit her with a jolt of panic. Dinah wasn't getting out of anything. Oliver Queen had made sure of that when he asked her, in front of everyone, to be his date.

Dinah huddled up in her window seat on the bus ride east, watching the scenery transform outside. Sleek skyscrapers and steel bridges gave way to pothole-filled roads and ramshackle tenement buildings as they crossed from Downtown

Gotham City into the East End, a place most people tried to avoid. But for Dinah, this neglected neighborhood—and one tenement in particular—represented the closest thing to freedom she'd ever known.

"Miss! Declare your destination."

Dinah glanced up at the bus driver's sharp tone, but it wasn't her he was addressing. There was another girl under his gaze, and, based on her uniform, Dinah could tell they were around the same age. Her stomach clenched as she watched the driver give the girl a once-over, his eyes narrowing in on the spare inches between her knees and skirt hem. But his expression wasn't leering; it was . . . worried. Which was creepy in a whole other way.

"The Court's guards will ticket you for that clothing infraction," he warned, pointing a stubby finger at the sliver of exposed thigh. "You'd best cover up. Now, where are you headed?"

The girl's face moved from embarrassment to fury while her voice remained calm, emotionless. "I had a growth spurt. It changed the way my clothes fit. And I'm going to Ellis Convalescent Home, to see my grandmother. Anything else?"

The driver marked her answer on his dashboard tablet and then waved the girl off, clearly missing the sarcasm in her voice. She slumped into a seat a row ahead of Dinah, and Dinah leaned forward to place a gentle hand on her shoulder. The girl turned around and the two of them exchanged a look that said it all—their shared frustrations and indignities, communicated in a single glance. *No singing, no driving, no showing skin.* They were sliding farther backward with each passing day.

By the time the bus arrived at her stop, Dinah's muscles

were already heating up, raring to fight. She quickly signed her name on the bus driver's tablet and scribbled *W. S. Tutoring Center* beside it, only a slight fudging of her destination. Location tracking was another one of the Court's methods of exerting control, and it was for that reason that Dinah tried to avoid public transportation whenever she could help it.

She hurried the four blocks from the station to Sandra's tenement, not pausing for so much as a breath, until she heard something unexpected. It was a soft voice singing, with a sweetness that couldn't be more out of place in this gritty environment.

Dinah turned to find a little boy standing on the sidewalk, dressed in dingy clothes and holding a cup of change. *"It's a new dawn, it's a new day, it's a new life for me . . . ,"* he sang with a solemn, quivery vibrato, and Dinah felt her hardened heart start to thaw. She reached into the zipper of her backpack where she kept her lunch money and handed the wad of small bills to the boy.

"You have a beautiful voice," she told him. "It could take you far. Far from here."

The little boy stared at the money in awe and then beamed back at her. His song followed Dinah the rest of the way to Sandra's street. *A new day, a new life for me . . .* It sounded like a dream.

Once she arrived at the faded brick building, she buzzed W. S. TUTORING on the intercom, and the front door creaked open. Dinah ran up the four flights of stairs, her regular training warm-up, until she reached Sandra's apartment—and a figure flew toward her.

She was all limbs, long and lean, her raven braid whipping

across her face as she launched at Dinah with a jumping knee. Dinah leaped back, guarding her lower body and blocking the incoming knee—but that's when Sandra reversed strategy in midair, extending her leg in a sky-high front kick that landed clean against the side of Dinah's exposed face. She tumbled to the floor, face throbbing.

"You tricked me," Dinah griped, wobbling back up to her feet with her cheeks and jaw stinging from the pain.

"No, I taught you my bait and switch," Sandra replied, looking unruffled as usual by Dinah's bruises. "It's highly effective, as you just saw. Body language can be as powerful as the sharpest blade. If you can use your body language to manipulate your opponent, making them anticipate and react to the wrong moves, then the fight can be yours. Now, let's see you do the same front kick."

Dinah nodded and assumed fight stance in the middle of Sandra's living room, repurposed as a makeshift training ring. The room was mostly bare, the few pieces of existing furniture pushed back against the wall, while a punching bag dangled from the ceiling. Instead of plates and silverware, her dining table was covered with martial arts weaponry: throwing knives, brass knuckles, and a pair of Sandra's signature kusarigama, heavy weighted chains with blunt ends that could capture, immobilize, and strike an opponent all at once. But Dinah wasn't allowed to touch any of these yet. Their training was solely in hand-to-hand combat—and Sandra was determined to make her pupil one of the best.

Dinah bounced lightly on her toes, gathering speed, before swinging her right leg up in the air for the front kick. But Sandra was shaking her head before Dinah's leg even left the ground.

"That foot shuffle you're doing is a dead giveaway of what you're planning. You need stronger setup and positioning if you want to catch your opponent by surprise. Like this."

Sandra stalked toward Dinah, using slow, controlled movements, her fists front and center. Suddenly her body went rigid, like a dancer who'd forgotten the next step. And then her leg flew up out of nowhere in a powerhouse kick, her foot turning and driving into the side of Dinah's face. If she'd used her full strength, Dinah would have been knocked unconscious in about two seconds. She watched her instructor in awe, too impressed to care about the blood that was starting to trickle down her cheek.

"How did you *do* that? I always thought a kick like that needed speed behind it."

"It requires an extreme level of skill and focus." Sandra gave Dinah a pointed look. "Two things our training is meant to instill in you. Let's go."

The rest of the afternoon sped by in an adrenaline rush as the sensei led her protégé through ninety minutes of combined kickboxing, judo, and jujitsu, practicing everything from punches and elbow jabs to takedowns and grappling techniques. By the time they reached the end, Dinah was a sweaty, red-faced mess—and loving every second of it. She kept picturing Zed Cobblepot as her opponent and relishing the imagined look on his face if he could see her now; what they would *all* say if they were watching her and Sandra spar. The sight of the "gentler sex" raging and sweating and throwing down in a drafty tenement room would likely be enough to send all members of the Court into cardiac arrest.

After training, Dinah took a quick shower in Sandra's closet-sized bathroom and changed into the freshly pressed spare uniform she always kept in her backpack. If she hadn't known well enough already, the incident on the bus made it all too clear: looking anything less than immaculate in public, or failing to follow the dress code to a T, only invited scrutiny. She couldn't afford to give the driver or fellow passengers any reason to question her whereabouts.

When she returned to Sandra's living room, she found it back in decoy mode already. The punching bag was gone and the sparse furniture had moved up to center stage, including a desk with a textbook open across it, to help sell the "tutoring center" this was supposed to be if anyone came checking up on Sandra. As she watched the trainer she idolized set the false scene, Dinah blurted out, "How do you stand it? I mean . . . aren't you just *dying* to unleash what you can do on those psychotic Owls? I know I am, and I'm a fraction of the fighter you are. How do you keep it all held in?"

Sandra paused, and when she spoke again, her voice was razor-sharp.

"What I'm teaching you is only to be used in self-defense. You know that, Dinah. Even if I were the best martial artist on this side of the globe—and chances are, I am—MMA skills alone can't compete with the electrum the Owls and Talons possess. I've seen too many accomplished fighters die at the hands of Talons to consider myself invincible. So, it's as I always say: We don't go looking for a fight. The best we can do is be prepared if, and only if, one comes our way."

"I know. And . . . I was." Dinah couldn't help smiling a

little. She'd been waiting for the perfect moment to bust out this humblebrag. "Believe it or not, I managed to fend off one of the Talons and live to tell the tale—thanks to your standing arm bar technique."

Sandra whipped her head up so fast, her braid nearly hit her in the face.

"You *what?*"

As Dinah filled her in on the Robinson Park debacle, Sandra's face grew more and more severe. Dinah gave her a sideways look. This wasn't quite the reaction she was expecting.

"Okay, obviously it wasn't great that I got caught, but of all people, I thought you would at least be a *little* proud," she said, throwing her hands up in bewilderment. "I mean, I used what you taught me, and I actually escaped from a Talon's clutches! For a minute, anyway."

Sandra looked away, her expression inscrutable.

"Better to never enter the ring than to leave your opponent unfinished. Whatever protection your father was trying to surround you with when he approached me to train you . . . well, you've gone and pricked the bubble. Your biggest advantage was the element of surprise, and that's gone now. They know you can fight, and they'll be watching you."

Dinah flinched.

"But I'm still standing here, aren't I? If the Talons wanted me dead, they would have done it by now."

"Yes," Sandra agreed. "Unless there's something else they want from you."

Dinah felt a cold wave of trepidation run through her.

"What could that be?"

"I don't know," Sandra said after a moment's pause. "All I

know is that you need to stay under the radar. At least until the Owls turn their attention to someone else."

"Well, that's not going to be possible." Dinah covered her face with her palms and groaned. "Of all the times to get asked out by a guy, it had to be for a date I can't get out of— one that'll probably get me killed."

CHAPTER SEVEN

Dinah had just turned onto her street when she saw them on the front stoop: her father, his face tight with tension, opposite an unfamiliar woman. Dinah was too far down the block to hear what they were saying, but she could see her dad talking and gesticulating rapidly, his eyes flashing the way they always did whenever he was upset. He wasn't even supposed to be home for another hour—so what was he doing there now, mid-argument with a stranger?

When she got close enough to their brownstone to see who was on the receiving end of her father's anger, Dinah stopped short with a shock of recognition. *Dark red hair. Bright blue eyes. Beautiful, maybe around Dad's age. Wheelchair.* It was the same woman Dinah had seen on her walk home from Rory Regan's shop—when she was so certain she was being watched.

Dinah ducked around the side of the apartment building, peeking her head out just enough to get a partial view. Whatever was going on between her dad and this not-quite-stranger, clearly they weren't about to pause their arguing to fill her in. The only way to get any answers would be through old-fashioned eavesdropping.

"If you won't let me talk to her, then please, just tell her yourself," she heard the woman saying insistently. "You know it's what her mother would want."

Dinah's stomach flipped. *She knew Mom?*

She could hear her dad reply through gritted teeth, his anger barely controlled, as he said, "How dare you speak for my wife?"

"I knew her long before you did, Larry. And we both know I'm right. The tide is starting to turn. We might finally have a chance—"

"There's no way I'm letting you jeopardize my daughter's future. So just leave us alone," he snapped, before turning his back on her and disappearing inside, slamming the door behind him.

Dinah could barely breathe. *The tide is starting to turn.* What did that mean—and what could it possibly have to do with her?

She waited, all senses heightened, as the woman let out a frustrated sigh and then turned around, wheeling in her direction. On instinct, Dinah stepped out of her hiding spot, in full view of the mysterious redhead. They locked eyes. And as the woman passed, without saying a word, she reached out her hand and pressed a small card into Dinah's palm.

Dinah watched her go, transfixed, and then turned the card over.

BARBARA GORDON
Gotham City Public Library

She frowned at the words, even more perplexed now. What in the world could a librarian have to say that her dad would be so anxious to keep her from hearing?

"Who was that lady I saw you talking to?" Dinah asked as soon as she walked through the door. "And why are you home early?"

"Nice to see you, too," her father said drily. "How was school?"

"Long story. But I asked my questions first."

"That was Jim Gordon's daughter," Larry muttered.

The name stopped Dinah in her tracks. The late Commissioner Gordon was Larry's mentor and idol, the whole reason he got into chasing criminals in the first place—and the reason he and Dinah were stuck in this godforsaken city. Larry had made Jim a promise before he died: that he would finish what the commissioner started and clean up Gotham City, especially its corrupt police force, for good. So far, things hadn't exactly turned out the way either of them had hoped.

"It didn't look like a very pleasant visit," Dinah remarked. "I would have thought you'd be a whole lot nicer to Commissioner Gordon's daughter."

Larry shot her a look.

"Who says I wasn't nice to her? How long were you standing out there?"

"Just . . . long enough to see you slam the door on her," Dinah fibbed. "She looked familiar, too. Where do I know her from?"

"She was your mother's friend," Larry said evenly. "Whenever the two of them were together, trouble seemed to follow. And that's all I'm going to say about that."

Dinah stuck her hand into her pocket, fingers tracing the

edges of Barbara Gordon's card. They used to tell each other everything . . . or so she'd thought. But if her dad wanted to keep more secrets, so be it. She would get the truth straight from Barbara herself.

She swept past Larry into the kitchen to start dinner, and he followed.

"So what was the long story about school? Something happen today?"

"Nice segue, Dad." Dinah raised an eyebrow at him. "But yeah. I might as well tell you now. You know that upcoming Patriarch's Ball?"

Larry's face tightened.

"What about it?"

"Well, they chose four 'notable sons' to open the ball as guests of honor, and one of them—the new guy, Oliver Queen—asked me."

Larry looked at her blankly.

"Asked you what, exactly?"

"Um. To be his date." At the astounded look on her dad's face, Dinah added, "Okay, is it really *that* hard to believe?"

"That boy—he's Robert Queen's son." Larry gripped the back of a chair, his knuckles turning white. "You know I'm not one to speak ill of the dead, but Robert was a power-hungry, greedy bastard who could make Scrooge look like a humanitarian. And that's not even his worst offense." Larry paused his rant to take a breath, and Dinah's stomach clenched as she waited for him to continue.

"Robert Queen was a key ally for the Court of Owls in their war on democracy. He helped them rise to power, and for that reason, the Queens are forever linked to the Court. So it should go without saying—I don't want Robert's son anywhere near you."

Dinah sank into the nearest chair, trying to digest this news. She already had her own preconceptions about Oliver, ever since she first saw him sitting cozy at lunch with the sons and daughters of the Court . . . but still, it was difficult to imagine the guy she'd laughed with during today's disastrous dance rehearsal being the threat her dad was describing. Ty's words from this morning echoed through her mind, and she wondered if she might have been too quick to dismiss them. *Not everyone connected to the Court of Owls is all bad. . . .*

"Do I have a choice?" she wondered. "I mean, Oliver asked me in front of the mayor's staff, in front of the whole school. How would I get out of it?"

Larry raked a hand through his hair in frustration.

"I'm not sure you can," he admitted grudgingly. "It would make too big of a statement to say no to him now. But listen to me, Dinah." He sat opposite her, his eyes wide with worry. "Whatever Oliver Queen does or says, just know you can't trust him. There's something about the timing of all this. . . . Him showing an interest in you so soon after you came to the attention of the Court, right after he moves to Gotham City, seems suspect to me."

"I understand," Dinah said, her appetite suddenly gone. "I won't trust him."

The sound of static and muffled voices broke through the room, and Dinah jumped in her seat before realizing what it was. The police radio.

"Detective Lance, do you copy?" came the harried voice Dinah recognized as Officer Stevens. "We need backup at—"

"Copy that," Larry interrupted with a punch of a button. He pulled his phone out of his pocket as it vibrated with an alert. "The address just came through. I'm on my way."

He turned to leave the room but then hesitated, looking back at Dinah. "You'll be okay?"

"I always am," she said wryly. Her dad dipping out on dinner for work was becoming a near-weekly occurrence at this point. "Go do your thing."

She waited till he drove off, siren blaring, before grabbing her keys and typing a quick text.

I'm coming over.

"Dinah. I didn't realize you were joining us for dinner." Ty's mom gave her a tight smile as she opened the door to their apartment, just three blocks down from the Lances'.

"Oh—no, that's okay. I just wanted to talk to Ty for a sec. It's . . . homework related."

"He's in his room," she said, stepping aside to let Dinah in. "But we'll be expecting him at the table in twenty minutes, so please make it quick."

There was something chilly in her demeanor tonight. Dinah was about to ask what was wrong, when she remembered. *The mask.* For a parent as rigid as Mrs. Carver, obsessed with rule-following and staying on the "good" side of society, the Court's symbolic strike against Dinah would seem like the ultimate scandal. It was no wonder she was in such a rush to close the door, before anyone saw Dinah Lance enter her house.

It was hard to believe their moms had been so close, with Dinah Drake the carefree, hippie florist and Meg Carver the polar opposite. But their friendship went all the way back to elementary school, and that kind of history proved hard to break. Just like her and Ty.

Dinah made her way through the Carvers' apartment, as familiar as her own, till she reached his room. She was about to knock on the door when it swung open.

"Well, if it isn't Oliver Queen's new flame," Ty said, an edge to his voice. "What was that lecture you gave me this morning again? You know, about staying away from anyone who's close to the Court?"

"Come on, Ty. Obviously I had no clue he was planning to ask me. That's why I'm here." Dinah stepped into the room, taking a seat at the foot of the bed. "I knew you would think I was being a hypocrite, but I really had nothing to do with . . . today. Trust me, I wasn't going out of my way to charm or tempt the guy."

"You mean—he just noticed you on his own?"

Ty's wide-eyed amazement was too much.

"Okay, I'm getting a little tired of everyone's shock here," Dinah said drily. "Shouldn't the people closest to me be the *least* surprised by someone else finding me appealing?"

"It's not that." Ty grinned at her, the ice between them starting to thaw. "You're a solid eight, at least."

Dinah lobbed a pillow across the room at him as he said, "It's more about the fact that . . . well, those people just never notice *us*."

"Until now, apparently." Dinah fell silent. "I don't trust any of this, and my dad is even more suspicious, but I have no choice. I guess we're about to find out if I was right or wrong to give you a hard time over Natasha. I'm sorry for bursting your bubble either way."

"It's okay," he relented. "I have to admit, I'm kind of

jealous. I wish I were the one getting asked out on an epic date . . . with her."

"That would involve her having a choice," Dinah reminded him. "Something we just don't get to have."

"*Ty-y!*" Mrs. Carver's voice carried across the apartment. "Dinner!"

Ty rolled his eyes. "Coming, Mom!"

"She told me we had twenty minutes," Dinah said with a frown. "I think she just wants me gone."

"You know my mom," Ty said. "Born with a timer in one hand and a schedule in the other."

They walked out of his room laughing together, the tension broken. But when they got to the kitchen, they found it empty. Ty's parents and fourteen-year-old brother, Gabriel, were frozen in front of the radio in the den instead.

"What's going on?" Ty asked.

"Police chase," Gabriel said breathlessly. "A group of armed Resistance fighters just broke into Robinson Park, and now the GCPD is after them. The police actually interrupted the classical music station with a news alert, telling everyone to stay away from the streets around the park since gunshots were fired. Isn't that wild?"

Dinah's head snapped up. She and Ty stared at each other. *Robinson Park?* It couldn't be a coincidence . . . could it?

And then she thought of the way her dad had gone rushing out the door, cutting off the police radio before letting Dinah hear the address. What were the odds that the Resistance was after the same thing she was—the opera house, and the Vault of Voices?

CHAPTER EIGHT

Larry left the apartment at the crack of dawn the next morning, before Dinah had a chance to grill him about the night before. Her only indication that he was even safe was a text message blinking on her phone screen from the middle of the night.

> All OK. I have to leave for the office early in the morning, so will see you at dinner. Love you—have a great day at school.

Dinah stared at the text in frustration. That was it? That message could have been written by an accountant on a humdrum week, not a cop who likely spent last night in a standoff between the Resistance and the Talons—if, as she suspected, the opera house was where they'd been heading.

She grabbed her phone and refreshed the *Gotham Gazette*'s daily news feed. But barely anything had been written about last night's police chase, save for one simple line: **ARMED "RESISTANCE" CRIMINALS APPREHENDED**

BY GCPD OUTSIDE ROBINSON PARK. In their censored news media, where anyone aligned with the Resistance was automatically labeled a criminal, the real news came out in dribs and drabs, more from the whispers of those in the know than the Court-supervised reporters. And suddenly, Dinah was in a rush to get to school.

She showered and dressed quickly, gulping down coffee and two bites of toast before heading out the door. Right away, she noticed something new on her street—an uptick in the number of armed guards. As if they were anticipating something. Their eyes narrowed on Dinah as she moved forward, scanning her school uniform for any breach of propriety, her face for signs of rebellion. And then came a light of recognition that made her heart sink.

"Dinah Lance! This way."

Her throat turned dry; her face burned hot. For a split second, she contemplated running, but that would only make it worse. She forced her feet into motion, following the Owl Guard, who gripped her arm and dragged her to the end of the sidewalk. And there, in front of gawking passersby, the guard patted her down roughly, his gloves slapping against her skirt and blouse, as if there was anything she could possibly manage to hide in there. Dinah stood frozen even as her muscles begged to move, to send that boorish guard tumbling backward with a sharp knee to the chest. But she couldn't afford a single act of rebellion. She knew it was because of the mask in her window that she was subject to this extra "attention"—and the only option available to her now was playing the part of a dutiful, obedient Court subject. No matter how unbearable a role it was.

The guard's hands pulled at Dinah's backpack next, digging through her textbooks and binders before finally accepting that there was nothing to see. He sent Dinah on her way with a scowl, his scrutiny moving on to the next girl, as she tried to calm her fraying nerves and press forward.

The swarm didn't end on her block. The entire walk to school was filled with them, men in burgundy-and-gray Court uniforms with the shadow of an owl on their chests— watching. It wasn't until she was through the school doors and safely inside that she could breathe.

"What's wrong?" Mandy asked the second she saw Dinah in the locker hall.

"I got searched on the way here. I'm fine, but . . . it was worse than I expected," Dinah said. She swallowed hard, meeting her friend's eyes. "Have you heard anything? Like, what's all this extra security about?"

Mandy shook her head, looking at Dinah in concern.

"I have no idea. All I know is that something serious must have gone down last night for the Court to be on this much of an alert."

The tide is starting to turn. We might finally have a chance. Dinah drew in a sharp breath as the words she overheard from Barbara Gordon to her father echoed in her mind.

"What just happened?" Mandy peered closer at her. "You went pale on me."

"There's someone I have to go see today," Dinah realized. "Barbara Gordon."

She filled Mandy in as they walked to class, her friend's eyes growing huge as the story unfolded.

"Whoa," she breathed. "That's some serious intrigue. And I've definitely seen that name before."

Dinah stopped in her tracks.

"Really? Where?"

"We get a card in the mail from a Barbara Gordon every year on my mom's birthday," Mandy revealed. "Your dad was telling the truth about one thing, at least. They were all friends. But how weird that she lives here and hasn't once come over."

"All of it is weird," Dinah said slowly.

They stopped in front of Mr. Garcia's math classroom, where Mandy had first-period trigonometry. Before heading inside, she whispered to Dinah, "I'm coming with you today. We'll go right after school."

The faces on the wall were the first thing Dinah noticed as she walked into her political science class. Sharp eyes, lofty expressions, and noble clothing filled each canvas, lining the room in a series of seven vivid oil paintings. Dinah would recognize these faces anywhere: the current governing members of the Court of Owls surrounding the largest portrait of all, their chosen figurehead and mouthpiece, Mayor Cobblepot.

"This semester, we'll be comparing and analyzing the different sovereign governments around the world, starting with the most powerful," the teacher, Mr. Bauer, began. "Our own Court of Owls, of course. As your parents will remember well, the initial reaction to the Silencing and the rise of the Owls among some camps was one of dismay, with many attempting to flee the city—unsuccessfully, I might add. But what the dissenters failed to realize was that the Owls had galvanized followers around the city and seized on a moment: a reckoning of roles, a return to tradition. They soon realized how futile it was to fight, and settled into a vastly improved Gotham City."

Dinah bristled at yet another teacher glossing over a despicable truth. Naturally, Mr. Bauer would fail to mention the armed militia and Talons posted at train stations and city borders, the *real* reason everyone stayed. Under the Court of Owls, Gotham City was a place you could enter—but never leave.

Mr. Bauer cleared his throat, surveying the class. "So what would you say was the key to their success, the reason they were so victorious?"

A half-dozen hands rose in the air, and the teacher called on Logan Rogers.

"It was because the Court had this unbeatable combination of chemical and military weapons," he answered confidently. "Between their electrum-infused Talon army and a gas that could control or silence voices, who would even bother going up against them?" He paused. "That's why those Resistance people are all out of their minds. Either that, or they have a serious death wish."

Dinah flinched as the teacher nodded approvingly.

"Quite right, Logan. But what I'm talking about is something else—a skill the Court used to powerful effect in its earliest days and then deployed again centuries later, when it came time to overthrow the democratic government and its so-called superheroes. A talent that gained them countless loyal followers of their own. Does anyone know what I'm getting at?"

Mr. Bauer looked out at a sea of blank faces. And then Dinah spoke up without raising her hand.

"Rhetoric," she said. "The Owl Masters had a way of speaking that lit people on fire. They ended an entire way of life, and it all started with words."

"Exactly!" Mr. Bauer nodded triumphantly, missing the disgust in Dinah's tone. He looked away from her and at a group of boys in the front row. "As we discuss political and military strategy in class this year, you will learn that the single most dangerous weapon, before any ammunition, is your voice—and how you choose to use it."

Dinah's hands balled into fists under the desk. Her teacher's words were a slap across the face, a reminder of the power that more than half the students in this room would never fully possess. The Owls could have used their weapons in a myriad of ways—and they'd known just what they were doing when they attacked the female voice.

"After that comes having the right argument," Mr. Bauer continued, writing *argument* in block letters across the whiteboard underneath *voice*. "In the case of the Owls, there was plenty for them to point to when arguing that a democratic, women-dominated government was failing our country, while traditional autocratic regimes across the world were prospering. Add in skyrocketing divorce rates and plummeting birth rates, and you had a clear crisis to work with."

"How true was all that?" Dinah couldn't resist blurting out. Of course, she knew the real answer, which should have been the third item on the teacher's list: *propaganda*.

"True enough," he said, brushing past her question. "The next step for the Owls was *strategy*, which included finding the right figurehead to lead under their control. Enter the legend of Oswald Cobblepot, also known as the Penguin."

Mr. Bauer lifted the painting of Mayor Cobblepot, revealing another framed canvas underneath: the portrait of an ancestor. A man under the shadow of an umbrella's hood, a face marked by wild eyes and a pronounced, pointed nose. Of all the portraits on the wall, Oswald was the only one smiling in his. But the smile twisted his features, making his expression that much more unnerving.

"As one of the founding families of Gotham City, the Cobblepots always had a presence in the Court of Owls. Before our current mayor, his great-uncle Oswald was the most notable example. He enjoyed something of a double life in his time, an aristocratic property owner and chemist by day and lord of the underworld by night with his Penguin alter ego." Mr. Bauer looked fondly upon the portrait, as though the Penguin were some kind of revered figure instead of a sniveling monster disguised in gentlemen's clothes.

"While the Court *certainly* opposes crime"—Mr. Bauer paused, making sure to hit that point hard—"when it came to the Penguin's issues with the troublesome superheroes, he and the Court were in full agreement. In terms of strategy, Oswald's mind was an unquestionable asset. It was the Penguin himself who first dreamed up the idea of a voice-stealing gas, leaving the plans to his nephew to finish after he died. So with the Court installing Chester Cobblepot as mayor in exchange for him working under their direction, they achieved something much bigger than simply the right public-facing figurehead. They were able to tap into the mind of the Penguin and use his ideas for their benefit."

A slow smile spread across the teacher's face. And in that moment, Dinah could have sworn she saw a flash of movement in the portrait behind him—the slightest turn of the Penguin's head, a curl of his lip.

She was imagining it, of course. She had to be. But that didn't stop the cold trickle of fear seeping through her, or the shivers on her skin.

Sixth period was a stark contrast from the rest of the school day, the hour when students were divided for gender-specific classes. While the girls had year-round home economics, the boys alternated between leadership in the fall and gym in the spring. Both of those alternatives sounded like paradise to Dinah, especially now, as she sat down in front of her relentlessly dull cross-stitching assignment. But before she could prick her finger on yet another sewing needle, the teacher tapped her on the shoulder.

"Dinah, you and Natasha are needed in the music room today. Mrs. Pritchard called a dance rehearsal for the four couples opening the Patriarch's Ball."

"Really?" It was a stroke of luck. Dinah tossed her mess of a cross-stitch aside and headed for the door. Envious murmurs and grumblings followed her and Natasha out of the classroom, and this time Dinah could understand the fuss. Getting out of home ec was a serious perk.

"Um. Do you know where we're going?"

Dinah looked up in surprise as Natasha gave her a tentative smile. She hadn't said two words to Dinah before this.

"They must have forgotten that girls aren't usually allowed in the music room," Natasha said wryly.

Because of people like your dad, Dinah came close to blurting out. But instead, she told Natasha, "I can lead the way. I've never been inside, obviously, but I know which door is the one that often has music playing behind it."

"Oh—cool. Thanks."

"Sure." Dinah eyed Natasha, still caught off guard by the fact that she seemed sort of . . . nice. Had Ty been right, that she wasn't just another follower of the Court?

They continued down the hall in silence at first, until Natasha glanced at her and said, "So, how do you know Ollie?"

Those two are on nickname terms? Dinah felt a strange twinge in her stomach as she answered, "I don't, really. I mean, he sits behind me in history class and we've talked a little, but that's it."

Natasha raised an eyebrow.

"Well. Sounds like you made quite the first impression."

Was that a shade of *envy* in Natasha's voice? Dinah wondered if maybe she had hoped to be asked by "Ollie," but instead got scooped up by Thom Elliot first. And poor Ty wasn't even an afterthought.

They arrived at the music room to find the other two couples already inside, lounging on the raised platform seating, while Mrs. Pritchard flitted around the room in preparation. Zed Cobblepot let out a snort when Dinah walked in, but she ignored him. She was too entranced by the sights in front of her to care.

A gleaming piano stood in the corner of the room, surrounded by a five-piece drum kit, guitar, and upright bass, while the wall shelves above them held golden trumpets, trombones, and saxophones, all more tempting than any priceless jewels. On the other side of the room were the music stands and microphones, arranged in a perfect line for the boys' a cappella group rehearsals. Dinah felt the familiar pull in her chest at being so close, yet so removed, from her dream.

While the others chatted among themselves, Dinah stood apart, her eyes on the piano. The keys were like a lure, drawing her in . . . but she would never be able to slip behind the bench and rest her hands on the ivory. She would never make the keys sing with sound. And just as she was starting to feel dangerously close to tears, a hand touched her shoulder.

Dinah looked up into the vivid green eyes of Oliver Queen, peering at her with concern.

"Hey. You okay?"

"Yeah. Of course." She forced a smile. "Why?"

"You just looked so . . . sad for a minute there."

Dinah was too taken aback to respond at first. Aside from Ty, who was practically a brother to Dinah, none of the guys at this school had ever asked how she was doing, or so much as noticed when she was down.

Oliver Queen really was different.

"You might be right," she said quietly, her eyes returning to the piano.

"I can't imagine how it must feel," he said, following her gaze. "Seeing all these instruments right in front of you and knowing you're not allowed to play them."

Dinah felt something tighten in her chest. She nodded, not quite trusting herself to speak.

"Maybe one day that'll change," he added under his breath. Dinah's eyebrows shot up.

"What? You think so?"

He shrugged. "Anything can happen. It would be cool,

though, wouldn't it?" He cracked a smile. "I'm getting seri-ously sick of hearing the same voices all the time."

Dinah grinned back.

"My thoughts exactly."

With a flash, she remembered the one other time they had spoken about music: the morning when they'd both found themselves listening in on the a cappella rehearsal outside this same door. It felt like ages ago. "So, you're a music fan, then?"

"Yeah. Well, my mom was, so there was often music in the background growing up."

Dinah drew in her breath. *Just like our house, when Mom was alive.*

"Same," she said. "Who . . . who were her favorites?"

"She was always playing these old jazz records." Oliver looked away from her now, and she felt a pang of recog-nition at his expression. *That feeling of wanting so much to talk about Mom, to remember her—and the fear that if you do, you'll lose control and start to cry.*

"There was one record she used to play a lot. I don't know if it was her favorite . . . but I had this connection to it." He kept his tone light, but Dinah sensed something deeper.

"What was it?" she asked.

"You know the song 'Nature Boy'?" Dinah shook her head, and Oliver said, "Oh, it's a good one. So many of the greats from the past have recorded it."

"Really? How does it go?"

Dinah couldn't remember the last time she'd talked about music like this with someone, and she was riveted as Oliver began to sing softly, loud enough for only her to hear.

"There was a boy,
a very strange, enchanted boy.
They say he wandered very far, very far,
over land and sea. . . ."

His voice was warm, husky, and for once Dinah was grateful for her school uniform—so he wouldn't catch the goose bumps rising on her arms at the sound of it.

"That's really nice," she said softly. *And haunting, and beautiful.* She wasn't about to go overboard and say all that out loud, though. "So what was the connection? Between you and that song, I mean?"

He paused, as if weighing what to say. But then Mrs. Pritchard's voice broke through their bubble.

"All right, you two! We're about to get started." She beckoned Dinah and Oliver to join the others in the center of the room.

"Remind me to tell you later," Oliver said quickly in her ear. "Maybe on our way to the ball."

It felt like a promise of something. She nodded, her heart beating faster.

They followed Mrs. Pritchard to the makeshift dance floor, where the teacher had already managed to lose everyone's attention. Zed and Maya Powers were reading and cackling over something on Zed's phone, while the other four crowded around them to look. Mrs. Pritchard clapped her hands loudly.

"Opening the Patriarch's Ball is a *big* responsibility," she said, possibly overstating the matter, "and we only have about a week to prepare. So, without further ado, assume your opening quadrille positions."

Still snickering, Zed stuffed his phone back in his pocket, but not before smirking at Dinah. And it wasn't just him. Thom, Desmond, Maya, and Camila were all making a show of glancing at her and then quickly looking away, pretending to muffle their laughter. Only Natasha stayed quiet. Dinah felt her cheeks begin to flame.

"What's so funny?" she called out, meeting their eyes dead-on. "Something on your phone you wanted me to see, Zed?"

"That's enough, *please*." Mrs. Pritchard swept between Dinah and Zed before he could answer. "I don't want to hear another word unless it has to do with your dance steps."

Dinah continued glowering at Zed as Mrs. Pritchard moved the four pairs into position for the start of the dance, with each couple making up one side of a square. While their teacher demonstrated the first chunk of choreography, Dinah stood on her tiptoes to hiss in Oliver's ear, "Why did you ask me to this, knowing how your *friends* would react?"

At least Oliver had the decency to look chagrined.

"Zed's just being . . . Zed. I've known him since we were kids, and he makes fun of everyone, really."

"What a great personality trait," Dinah deadpanned. "I totally understand the friendship now."

Oliver laughed, the pleasantly surprised sound that she'd been starting to like.

"Sometimes you inherit friends," he murmured in her ear. "Haven't you experienced that?"

"Of course. But I only keep the good ones around."

Dinah got to have the last word there. The sound of strings filled the room as the quadrille music began to play through the speakers, and Oliver offered her his arm. The two of them were soon clumsily following along with the teacher as she led the couples through the routine. But even as her mind scrambled to keep track of the steps, she was all too aware of one thing—that Oliver still hadn't fully answered her question. *Why*, in spite of everything, did he ask her to be his date?

CHAPTER NINE

Dinah could feel her stomach somersaulting as she stepped off the bus in Old Gotham, a preserved section of the city virtually unchanged since the mid-twentieth century. Mandy and Ty followed right behind her, chattering under their breath and formulating theories about Barbara Gordon as they walked to the Gotham City Public Library, but Dinah was too nervous to join in. If her dad thought she'd gone against him by sneaking into Robinson Park, then this would be considered a true betrayal. Every few steps, she considered turning back—but her need for the truth kept her going.

"The big surprise here is that your dad apparently has so many people he doesn't like," Ty was saying now. "First he's yelling at your mom's old friend, then he bashes Oliver Queen's family. I've always thought of him as the warm and fuzzy type." He paused. "Well, maybe that's just in comparison to my straitlaced parents."

"Dad definitely seems a little more . . . stressed these days," Dinah said slowly.

"Hey! What if your mom left you some secret inheritance or something that only this Barbara person knows about?" Mandy said suddenly, her eyes lighting up.

"Oh, come on. You really think Larry would angrily turn away free money?" Ty gave Mandy a dubious look. "No, it has to be something else. What was it you heard your dad saying again? Something about jeopardizing your future?"

But Dinah didn't answer. She was gazing up at the hulking structure of the historic library, looming ahead on Fifth Street and taking up an entire city block. The marble columned building reminded her of the opera house, both structures like jewels in an austere crown. They must have been built at the same time—a time when music and letters were celebrated.

Dinah started up the grand stairway, passing the pair of stone gargoyle statues. And then, as the front doors drew closer, she stopped in her tracks.

"This is stupid," she blurted out to Mandy and Ty. "I mean, we don't even know if she's working here today."

She didn't say what she was really thinking: *What if Barbara tells me something about Mom that I don't want to hear?* But Mandy gave her a gentle push forward.

"We'll find out soon enough, won't we? C'mon, you're dying to meet her. And so are we."

They stepped through the vaulted-ceiling stone lobby and into the first reading room, a carpeted space with stacks upon stacks of Court-approved books lining the shelves. When Dinah was little, she loved holing up in a beanbag chair in the children's reading room with a pile of books at her side. But it hadn't taken long for her to realize that the stories were all the same—books from two-hundred-plus years ago about the "heroic" boys who got to go on all the adventures, and the "proper" young ladies who tended to the home. The characters always looked the same and acted the same, with a giant gaping hole where the more diverse, recent literature should have been. She had abandoned the library soon after that. And at the realization that *this* was what Barbara Gordon represented—this false, censored knowledge—her unease began to grow. *Maybe Dad was right not to trust her.* . . .

But Ty was nudging her in the ribs, pointing to the information desk. "Go on."

She hesitated, one voice telling her to bolt, the other to stay. But with her friends looking at her expectantly, Dinah took a deep breath and stepped forward.

"Excuse me? Is . . . is Barbara Gordon here today?"

She secretly hoped the man behind the desk would tell her no, to try back tomorrow. But instead, he nodded and pointed her toward a sign that read CHILDREN'S LITERATURE. Following his gaze, Dinah spotted a flash of red hair—and another wave of nerves hit.

"I . . . I think I should do this alone," she said, swallowing hard. "Is it okay if I fill you in after?"

"Really?" Ty looked deflated, but Mandy elbowed him. "We understand. Should we wait outside, or—?"

"No, that's okay. I don't know how long I'll be, so . . . I'll call you after."

Mandy reached over to give her a squeeze.

"Okay. Good luck!"

Dinah watched them go and then ventured forward into the Children's Literature room, a cozy space decorated with kid-sized reading tables and chairs, with framed illustrations of classic book covers lining the walls. From afar, it might have seemed like an idyllic haven for kids, but when you looked closer, the Court's not-so-subliminal messaging was everywhere—starting with the reading tables. Each one held a propped-up copy of *An Illustrated History of the Court of Owls*, the ridiculously fabricated retelling designed to be more "palatable" for children than the murderous truth. Dinah felt sick to her stomach at the sight. *What kind of person would peddle this crap?*

She was just about to turn on her heel and run out the door, when she saw Barbara's wheelchair pause before a half-finished display. Barbara held a book close to her chest before lifting it to place it on the display, and Dinah peered closer, curious to know which antiquated title would be chosen. And as soon as she saw which book it was, Dinah knew without a doubt—Barbara Gordon wasn't one of them. She couldn't be.

She had chosen *Matilda*. The only book starring a powerful female heroine in this entire section of the library. In fact, Dinah would have bet money that the Owls didn't even know *Matilda* was in here. There's no way they would have allowed that one—but Barbara was sneaking it in, behind all the Court-approved books.

Dinah stepped forward, heart hammering in her chest as she approached the woman.

"Barbara?"

Barbara Gordon looked up from the book display and her face froze. She gazed at Dinah, silent for a long moment, taking her in. And then her eyes welled with tears.

"You . . . you look just like her." Barbara blinked rapidly, took a shaky breath. "Forgive me, I—I was best friends with your mother."

Dinah's heart jumped. *Best* friends. She would know everything, then. Everything Dinah always wanted to learn but never wanted to pain her dad by asking, Barbara would have the answers to. But then . . .

"Why don't I know you?" she asked. "I—I'm not trying to be rude, but I'd never even heard of you before yesterday, and my mom's other close friends are all people I know well."

"You mean the people you were allowed to know." Barbara gave Dinah a sad smile. "I tried to be in your life, countless times, but there was no getting past your father. If you need proof, though . . ."

Barbara pulled down the edge of her sweater at her neck to reveal her shoulder, and Dinah let out a gasp. Two small birds in flight were etched just beneath her shoulder— the same image, and in the same spot, as her mother's tattoo.

Tears swam in Dinah's eyes; her knees turned weak. Barbara reached out a hand to steady her, and Dinah took it.

"How—why would my dad turn you away?"

Barbara's gaze dropped to the floor.

"Larry has his reasons for being overprotective. I think he blames me for what happened to your mom, and—"

"What happened to my mom?" Dinah stared at her, perplexed. "She was in a car accident. What did you have to do with it?"

Barbara's mouth snapped shut just as it hit Dinah: *Dad lied. Again.*

Something else must have happened to her mom,

something so bad he couldn't tell her. She took a gulp of air, feeling suddenly woozy.

"I'm not trying to come between the two of you," Barbara said. "And Larry should be the one to tell you more about . . . who she was. But there's something Dinah always intended to give you when you were old enough. I've held on to it all these years since she died, and I can't shake this feeling that now is the time. Come with me."

Dinah didn't move at first, her thoughts waging their own debate about who to trust, what to do. But then her eyes returned to Barbara's shoulder, where the birds lived on in secret. And she went with her gut, following Barbara through the winding stacks of children's books toward a locked back office.

Whatever she'd expected a librarian's office to look like, this wasn't it. Her long desk, overlooking a window to the reading room, was covered with not one or two but *three* different computers, a tablet, and a cell phone, giving the office a curious tech-company feel.

Barbara reached for her purse, nearly buried among the gadgets on the corner of the desk, and retrieved a large brown envelope.

"Open this when you're alone," she instructed. "And please—come find me again."

Barbara handed her the envelope, and Dinah reached for it with trembling hands.

Dinah sat across the dinner table from her dad, her palms growing sweaty under the pressure of trying to act normal and hide her secret. She wondered if he could read it in her face or hear her sped-up heartbeat from his chair. The image of the envelope from Barbara kept swimming in her mind, and it took every ounce of self-control to carry on with dinner and some semblance of conversation instead of tearing straight into her room to open it. But she did have something to ask her dad, and she shifted her focus to the question.

"What happened last night? I heard you were called back to Robinson Park."

Larry glanced up, his expression guarded.

"Yes. There was another demonstration attempt by the Resistance, close to the park entrance. It's a shame that—"

"Wait, where in the park?" Dinah interrupted him. "Were they heading for somewhere in particular?"

He gave her a knowing look.

"If they were, they didn't make it far. I wasn't about to risk another appearance from the Talons. It took a team of officers, but we managed to get the protesters under control and haul them out of there just in time."

"What do you mean, 'under control'?" Dinah asked suspiciously. "You didn't arrest them all, did you?"

"After what you saw with your own eyes a few days ago, Dinah, you of all people should know they're better off toughing it out in jail than being torn apart by Talons," he said, exasperated. "I'm just doing my job. Protect and serve, remember?"

"Who are you serving, though? And . . . doesn't it feel like the wrong side?"

Her words came out in a rush, and Larry's eyes narrowed. He leaned forward in his seat, about to say something, when they heard the three sharp raps at the door.

They both froze. There was only one source for that particular knock. *Owl Guards*. Defenders of the Court, who stalked the streets looking for offenders to deliver to their Talon army—to *Arkham*.

Larry swore under his breath and pushed back from the table.

"Let me do all the talking. Got it?"

She nodded shakily, fear holding her in a tight grip as Larry paced toward the door, his face grim.

Two burly men in uniform stood on the front stoop, one in front of the other, distinguishing the first-in-command from the second. They towered over Larry in their burgundy-and-black suits, another spin on the Talons' warrior uniform, featuring only a slightly less extreme version of the Talons' spiked gloves. Dinah's insides turned to ice at the sight of them.

"Evening, guards. How can I help you?" Larry asked, feigning calm as he opened the door a sliver. But the guards pushed past him, forcing the door's release and sweeping into their home uninvited.

"The Owls have taken an associate of yours into custody," the first-in-command said brusquely. "This man has been charged with supplying prohibited goods to his customers, and security footage identified *her* as one of his last visitors."

As the guard pointed his long, gloved finger at Dinah, she could have sworn her heart momentarily stopped. She shrank back in her chair, her knuckles white as she clung to the edge of the seat—until it hit her who the guard was referring to. She jumped up in alarm, forgetting her promise to stay quiet.

"Are—are you talking about *Rory*? What happened to him?"

Larry locked eyes with Dinah and gave the slightest shake of his head, his message clear: *Say no more. Don't react, don't give them anything.*

"Leave the questions to us." The second guard stalked toward her, leaning in close enough for Dinah to smell the onions on his breath. "What did you buy from that man?"

"N-nothing!" she insisted. "I can't think of—"

"We need to search your apartment." Guard One flashed his Owl badge at Larry and kept moving, as a sputtered protest escaped Dinah's lips. "In light of your daughter's recent transgression against the Court, we must determine whether or not she is aligned with Rory Regan in any Resistance or rebellion efforts whatsoever."

Dinah stared at them in shock while Larry said coolly, "No daughter of mine would ever be a part of the Resistance. I can assure you, the incident in the park that you're referring to was just . . . immature teenage antics. Nothing more."

But the guards ignored him and moved forward, surveying the apartment with eagle eyes. She could feel the blood roaring in her ears as the terrifying reality set in: they were only steps away from finding her secret closet. And if they did . . . it was over for her. Dinah would be thrown in Arkham Asylum, the rest of her life reduced to a prison cell, with Talons and equally vicious wardens as her only company, providing daily torture to remind her of what she'd done—

No. She couldn't let that happen. As soon as the guards' backs were turned, Dinah grabbed her dad's arm.

"Come on, do something," she whispered urgently. "You're a *cop*—you can stop this!"

But to her astonishment, Larry shook his head.

"We must never act like we have something to hide," he said out of the corner of his mouth. "I'll step in if I have to, but not yet."

"But—but—" Dinah opened her mouth to warn him about what she was hiding in her closet, but the second guard whipped his head toward her, narrowing his eyes at the sound of her whispers. She clamped her mouth shut, following her dad in agony as the Owl Guards threw open doors and rummaged through cabinets on the way to their true target: Dinah's bedroom. The only silver lining there was that her backpack, with the envelope from Barbara Gordon, was still buried under her coat in the den.

The guards pushed open her bedroom door and Dinah watched in horror as they barged inside, rifling carelessly through her belongings and sending the framed photo of Dinah and her parents tumbling to the floor. Tears of fury burned her eyes—and that's when the first Owl Guard made a move for her closet.

Dinah gasped, accidentally giving herself away. If there was any chance of them ignoring the closet, her involuntary reaction just killed that possibility altogether.

The nightmare unfolded in slow motion. Dinah had just enough time to look over her shoulder at her dad and whisper "I'm sorry" before the closet door creaked open and the light flickered on. And then, a sight none of the men in this room had seen for decades appeared on the walls: women onstage, in front of microphones, dressed in as much or as little clothing as they wanted—*free*.

Larry jumped in front of her, shielding her with his body, as the guards turned their enraged faces on Dinah. But the first guard shoved him aside, tossing Larry against the wall with brute strength, before seizing Dinah's wrists. His spiked gloves dug into her skin and she cried out in pain, while Larry peeled himself off the floor and raced to her side, trying in vain to pry the bladed gloves off her arm. Meanwhile, the second-in-command spat at the photograph of the sultry blond singer on the wall, before tearing the picture in half.

"Where did you find this filth?" he barked. "Rory Regan sold it to you?"

"N-no! I just—I found these old news magazines in a public trash can a long time ago, I can't remember where, and I was curious. . . ." Her voice broke as the guards' sights seized on her mom's beloved record player, with her carefully curated stack of records underneath.

"Those are mine!" Larry shot forward, inserting himself between the guards and the stack of records. "I must have left them in here. My mistake—"

But now the first officer was holding up her gift from Rory, the "Eleanor Rigby" sheet music that she'd left on top of the *Revolver* album. And Dinah's spirits sank even lower as she remembered how she had scribbled her name and the date in the bottom right-hand corner, so foolishly confident that this historical sheet music was hers to keep forever. Now the guard was staring at it like it was something incendiary—like the contraband that it technically was.

"What use could a female have for this?" he hissed, his other gloved hand still clinching her wrist in a sharp grip.

"It was only—just a souvenir—"

"And yet you know women are barred from owning any form of music." His voice dripped with cruelty, and as he fixed her with a cold stare, Dinah could see the threat in his eyes. *He's going to take me away. These are my last moments before Arkham—*

She felt Larry's protective hands grip her shoulders, pulling her away from the guards ever-so-subtly, as he addressed them.

"My daughter lives according to the law, just as I, her *police officer* father, taught her. Any curiosity she's shown about these . . . these characters from the past has no bearing on the person she is or the blameless life she leads. You can be sure that Dinah will be fully disciplined, both by me and by the police department."

The guards paid no attention to his words. It didn't matter what he said—Dinah had already shown the Owl Guards that she couldn't be trusted. By carrying her secret torch for the old way of life, she'd proven herself to be on the opposing side.

The first officer lunged forward, slapping a pair of handcuffs around Dinah's wrists in the span of a breath. She heard Larry yell something indecipherable as she was pushed to the floor, and then came the unmistakable sound of paper ripping. Dinah's head snapped up to see the guard using his sharp-tipped glove to shred the sheet music to pieces. Something cut deep within her at the sight.

The second officer flipped crudely through her mother's record collection, declaring with disgust, "This is the precise kind of music that tarnished the character of the past generations." He exchanged a sinister glance with his superior—and then, together, the guards went wild.

Priceless records snapped in half with sickening cracks. Pictures were clawed down from the walls, heads dismembered from their bodies, leaving nothing but shreds of paper where the prized photos used to be. The guards ripped, smashed, and tore apart everything Dinah cared about in this room, until all that was left of her treasures was a pile of scraps. Handcuffed and helpless, she could only watch in horror, as every part of her body started to burn.

She squeezed her eyes shut, half believing that when she opened them, everything would be all right. The despicable men in front of her would be gone and her room intact, proving that it was all just a nightmare. But of course—it wasn't.

"You're coming with us, little girl," growled the first guard. "The Talons are waiting for you at Arkham."

Dinah recoiled in terror. She whipped her head around, looking for her dad. But—he'd *disappeared* from the room. Dinah started shaking, from rage as much as fear. How could he leave her alone with these two monsters?

And then she had her answer, as Detective Lance came sprinting back into the room, this time holding his gun. He aimed it straight at the guards, who quickly seized their own weapons.

"You're not taking her anywhere," he said, his voice a steely threat. "You've done enough. The GCPD will handle it from here."

"You're tragically out of your league, Lance." The first guard laughed, a mirthless sound. "Everyone knows the

GCPD falls far below the authority of the Owl Guards and the Court."

"Luckily for me," Larry said calmly, "I'm working for both."

Dinah's mouth fell open. What was he *doing*? There was no way the Owl Guards would fall for that bold of a lie.

But then, just as one of the guards lunged at Larry and she was certain her dad had blown it, that they'd both be carted off to Arkham together now, he raised an arm and caught the guard's wrist in his palm. And before the guards could retaliate, Larry leaned in and murmured something that made them both pause . . . a foreign phrase Dinah had never heard before. They dropped their guns to their sides, staring at Larry with an odd look on their faces—a mix of respect and loathing.

"Don't think we won't still be reporting this to the Court," the guard finally said, his sharp gaze flickering from Dinah to Larry and back again. He uncuffed her roughly, his lip curled in a snarl. "Get your daughter in line, Lance. We'll be watching."

Dinah stayed frozen in place as her dad marched the guards out of her room, leaving it a wreckage of smashed vinyl, ripped photos, and upturned dressers and cabinets. It didn't feel like her room anymore; it had been soiled by their presence. And as she looked around at all she'd lost, her most precious possessions destroyed, Dinah found she couldn't fight the tears any longer.

Larry returned minutes later, his face looking like he'd aged ten years in a day. He knelt down beside her, wrapping an arm around her shoulders, but she pulled away.

"Why didn't you stop them sooner? How could you just let them come in here and—and do this to me?"

"You never told me what you were hiding in here." Larry looked at the tornado of debris surrounding them. "I had no way of knowing there was something they shouldn't see. And how do you think it would have looked if I'd tried refusing the guards their search? That's basically an admission of guilt."

Dinah stewed silently. He might have been right, but that didn't make it any easier to swallow.

"It wasn't true what you said, was it?" she asked. "You can't really be working for the *Owls*, too . . . right?"

Larry hesitated, and she stared at him in shock.

"You wouldn't."

"Remember when I said I'd worked out a deal with the Talons after the events in the park?"

"Yes . . ."

"Well. That was part of it."

"But—but—we're on their Undesirables list! Who else that's working for the Owls has a bloody mask hanging in their front window?" Dinah sputtered.

"That mask was meant for you," Larry said quietly. "And now I'm playing the part of a devout Court follower, using my position in the police department to be of service to them—while reforming my wayward daughter." He gave her a sidelong glance, and Dinah could see it in his eyes, how much it hurt him to play this false game. She thought of his blank expression while rounding up protesters that day outside Rory Regan's shop, and her heart twisted.

"Let's get away from here," she said. "I know that it would

take some serious strategizing to figure out an escape, but it would all be worth it. At least then we wouldn't be right under the Court's nose."

Larry smiled sadly.

"After what you saw today . . . you really think they would ever let us leave?"

CHAPTER TEN

Hours after Dinah had cleaned up the mess the guards left, her room still felt like a stranger's. She sat on the floor hugging her knees to her chest, her spirit almost as crushed as the broken records surrounding her, the ones she couldn't bear to throw away. She could hear her phone pinging with text messages, no doubt Mandy and Ty clamoring for the scoop on her meeting with Barbara Gordon, but Dinah was too drained to even pick up her phone. The conversation with Barbara felt like something from the distant past now anyway, considering what had come after.

And then Dinah sat up suddenly, a swoop in her chest as she remembered—*the envelope*. The one thing the guards failed to find.

She raced out of her room and into the den, unearthing her backpack from the messy coat pile on one of the armchairs. Throwing it over her shoulder, she hurried back to her room, passing her dad's closed door with the TV blaring from inside.

Once sequestered in her room, Dinah reached into the

backpack, where the envelope lay hidden between two textbooks. Whatever was inside—would it change what she always thought she knew about her mom?

Dinah pulled a sheaf of papers out of the envelope and her heartbeat sped up, imagining what she might find on the other side. *Letters? A diary?*

But instead, what she found was . . . lined staff paper, covered in musical notes. Just like the Beatles sheet music from Rory Regan's shop that the Owl Guards had torn up in front of her.

She could feel herself deflating like a balloon. All that anticipation for something personal, and *this* was the long-lost message from her mom? What was Dinah Drake trying to tell her—that she was a Bach fan or something?

Her eyes skimmed the first page. And Dinah's mouth fell open.

The Black Canary Sings
Music & Lyrics by Dinah Drake

Her mom was a *songwriter?* Since when? It was—it was impossible. Dinah Drake was a florist who had never once hinted at having a speck of musical talent. So how . . . ?

She grabbed the rest of the pages, poring over the sheet music and searching for answers among the notes. But something else happened. Something extraordinary.

As she stared at the lines and symbols on the page, without having ever heard the song, something started playing in her mind. A beautiful melody, winding upward in a minor key, full of rich notes and stirring chords. And Dinah realized that for the first time, she was *reading music*—all on her own.

She could see tiny words scribbled underneath the notes, in her mother's handwriting, and the melody and lyrics joined together in her mind as she read.

No more staying quiet when our world's gone wrong.
There's no time for silence when they steal our song.
So, ladies, let's stand up and find our own way.
Our time to be heard begins today.

It was as though her mom was seeing into Dinah's heart and mind when she wrote these words. Even just hearing it in her head, the melody was both infectious and achingly beautiful. It was the kind of melody that demanded to be sung.

Dinah whispered the words of the chorus, imagining her voice rising and falling along with the notes.

"Hey, ladies, we're taking back our dreams.
There's no limit to what we can achieve,
no more barriers to what we're fighting for.
Make that move up to the highest floor.

"Hey, ladies, coming out the other side,
now we know just what it takes to survive.
One day soon our winning bells are going to ring.
Play them loud when the Black Canary sings."

A wave of astonishment flooded through her as Dinah realized what this was: a song of resistance. Her quiet, unassuming mother hadn't just been composing music in secret—she'd been rebelling against the Court.

Dinah read on, hungry for more. But when she reached the second verse, there was only blank space where lyrics should be. Her mom never got to finish it. And suddenly, on wild impulse, Dinah grabbed a pencil from her desk.

In all conversations, they stripped out our voice.
They made our decisions, relinquished our choice.
But time's moving fast and the tide's got to change.
Our words and our song light the city's flames.

Dinah dropped the pencil, stunned. She'd never done that before, yet it felt as natural as . . . breathing.

And she could feel a new world beginning to open.

The next morning brought a second bloodied owl mask to her door, this one more mangled than the first. It was repulsive, but Dinah would take that over a prison sentence at Arkham any day. The mask didn't come on its own, though. There was something else with it: a letter written in black script on thick parchment, under the burgundy-and-gold seal of the Court of Owls. Dinah quickly began to read.

Attn: Dinah Laurel Lance
It has come to our attention that you were to attend the Patriarch's Ball with one of our four honored guests, Mr. Oliver Queen. However, in light of your second transgression and subversive behavior, we are withdrawing your invitation to the ball. You would be wise to learn from this unfortunate situation and

dedicate yourself to honoring the rules of the Court from this day forward, if you wish to remain in society.

Signed,

The Press Secretary of the Court of Owls

Dinah read the letter a second time and then began to laugh out loud. For the press secretary of the entire Court to be addressing a letter this threatening to a teenager . . . they must have *really* been looking for some way to pass the time. And if the Court only knew how little she cared about the ball, they would have realized they were doing her a favor. No more needing to shop for an overpriced, hideous ball gown; no more practicing antiquated dance steps for hundreds of people to see her inevitably butcher.

But then an involuntary image flashed through her mind: Oliver Queen holding another girl's hand on the dance floor, smiling at her instead.

Well, good, Dinah thought grumpily. *I didn't want to be that girl anyway.*

For the first time in their decade-long friendship, Dinah held back from confiding the whole truth to Mandy and Ty. The discovery of her mom's song felt too precious, too new, to share with anyone just yet—and a part of her wondered if they were better off not knowing anyway. In the Court's eyes, possessing knowledge of Resistance activities without reporting them was almost as big a crime as being an active participant.

It took her best amateur acting skills to convince them

that the Barbara Gordon meeting was nothing newsworthy, just an old friend of her mom's from their younger, wilder years who wanted to be part of Dinah's life. And for better or worse, her latest clash with the Owls was enough to overshadow the Barbara update completely.

"I never should have given you those magazines," Mandy said guiltily as the three of them huddled under an oak tree on the quad before school. "I should have known no good would come from us finding them."

"Are you kidding me? Those gave me *life*. I never would have known what women were capable of if I hadn't seen those pictures with my own eyes," Dinah told her.

"What they *used* to be capable of," Ty reminded her. "Wasn't it a depressing reminder of how much has changed?"

"Weirdly, no," Dinah said. "Having those images on my walls, and imprinted on my brain, gave me . . . hope."

"Well, that hope just got you axed from the biggest date of your life," Ty said grimly. "When are you going to tell him?"

"Now might be a good time," Mandy said, pointing at the front steps. Oliver was climbing up them now.

Dinah felt an unexpected wave of nerves as she crossed the quad to meet him, especially when he caught her eye and grinned, revealing the dimple in his left cheek.

"Hey," he greeted her.

"Hi." She pulled the letter out of her backpack, figuring she might as well get straight to the point. "So, um. This showed up today."

Oliver took it from her, his eyebrows shooting up as he read. A look of disappointment flashed across his face, and Dinah felt a strange warmth in her chest. So he really had wanted to go with her. Maybe the truth wasn't an ulterior motive.

"You couldn't have saved your rebellion for after the party, huh?" he asked wryly. "What did you do, anyway?"

The bell rang, pausing Dinah's answer. As they fell into step together on the way to first-period history, Dinah filled him in, giving only the bare facts and leaving out the emotions behind them. But there was no hiding the catch in her voice when she described the Owls smashing her mom's record player, tearing up the sheet music and the photos on the wall. Oliver stopped midstride, his eyes flashing.

"Are you serious?"

She nodded. And suddenly Oliver was taking her arm, leading her away from the hallway traffic and back toward the row of lockers.

"I'm sorry," he said when it was just the two of them. "That's just—that's beyond unfair. To be punished like that, for something as natural as listening to music?" He shook his head in disbelief.

She blinked up at him, taken aback by his surprise. And besides, when was the last time someone of his status had empathized with her?

"Was it so different in Star City?" she asked.

"I mean . . . no, not really," Oliver admitted. "I was probably just more blinded to it. No one was going to come after my mom for owning records, because of—well, who she was. Who she was married to."

"Yeah. That makes sense." She forced a laugh. "No such privileges over here, though."

"I'm really sorry," he said again, his lips twisting in disappointment. *Why am I looking at his lips?* Dinah forced herself to change the subject.

"Well, I guess this means I . . . I won't get to hear the rest of your story," she said.

"What story?" Oliver's eyebrows knit together.

"The one you were going to tell me on the way to the ball. About your favorite song. 'Nature Boy.'"

"Oh. That." Oliver chuckled.

"Tell me now?" she asked, wanting to draw out the moment a little longer. After this, there wouldn't be much for them to talk about . . . not when he would soon be taking another date to the ball.

Oliver fixed his gaze at a point on the wall as he spoke.

"So . . . a few years ago, my dad got it in his head that he needed to make a man out of me. He thought I was too pampered and 'soft,' not ready to face the big, bad world. And his solution for that was to force me to spend a summer on a survivalist island—by myself."

"Um. *What?*" Dinah looked at Oliver sideways. "You're kidding, right?"

"No." He laughed, but there was a bitter edge to it. "I shouldn't complain, though. I gained a lot on that island, let me tell you. But in the early days, when I was just barely getting through, I found the most random thing that made it a little better. I started to sing that one song—and pretend it was about me." A ghost of a smile played on his face. "That I was the 'strange, enchanted boy' the song was talking about, built for land and sea. I pretended, until I *was* him."

Dinah couldn't look away, moved by his words. He really had lived through more than most—just as her instincts had told her when she first glanced into those green eyes.

"How did the song go again?" she asked, inching closer to him.

Oliver glanced down at her, and then, so quiet only she could hear, he sang the opening bars. Dinah's heart twisted at the melody, at Oliver's surprisingly tender voice—and at all the ways he'd been tested at such a young age.

". . . And while we spoke of many things, fools and
kings,
this he said to me:
The greatest thing you'll ever learn
is just to love and be loved in return."

Oliver met her eyes as he sang the last line under his breath. Dinah's heartbeat sped up, her cheeks flushed red. And suddenly she found herself fighting the urge to pull him toward her, to—

The second bell rang, jolting her out of the moment. They were officially late. Oliver cleared his throat.

"I guess we'd . . . we'd better go," he said.

They walked the rest of the way in silence. Just before they reached the classroom door, Dinah blurted out, "So who do you think you're going to ask now?"

He lifted his shoulders.

"I don't know." He gave her a half smile. "I guess we'll have to see."

As she followed him to their seats at the back of the room, his voice echoed in her ears.

The greatest thing you'll ever learn . . . is just to love and be
loved in return.

And she wondered, with a sharp pang, what possibilities might have just passed her by—now that she'd had to say no to a date with Oliver Queen.

That afternoon's training session with Sandra couldn't have come at a better time. As Dinah recounted the events of the previous night, Sandra's dark eyes flashed with indignation.

"Those bastards," she muttered, before motioning Dinah to her feet. "Come on. Let's use that anger as fuel."

The two circled each other in the living room turned fighting ring, and Sandra threw the first punch. Dinah blocked her strike and jumped into a side kick, her foot swiping Sandra's raised fists.

"Tell me again how it felt when they tore your room apart," she called, baiting Dinah. "What did you want to do to them, right in that moment?"

"It felt like I was burning," she answered, "and I wanted them to burn, too."

She picked up speed and launched into a backflip, landing right behind Sandra and trapping her in a judo clinch. Sandra jabbed her with knees and elbows, making Dinah's eyes sting from the pain—but for possibly the first time ever opposite her teacher, Dinah was in the dominant position. She gripped Sandra's waist from behind and, utilizing every ounce of strength and muscle she possessed, lifted and threw her to the mat in a takedown.

"Did I just do that?" Dinah blurted out, staring at Sandra in awe.

Sandra rolled over, a glint of respect in her eyes.

"Nicely done. Now get up and show me that wasn't just a lucky break."

"If only I'd whipped out that move on the Owl Guards last night," Dinah said, her moment of triumph turning to frustration. "I just froze. I was useless."

"Well, if you had, you very likely would be dead right

now," Sandra said flatly. "Suffice it to say that it's better you froze up."

"So how do I know when I'm supposed to actually *use* what you're teaching me?" Dinah complained, for what must have been the hundredth time in their years of training.

Sandra paused.

"When you're directly in the space between life and death. And trust me—when that moment comes, you will know."

CHAPTER ELEVEN

The Patriarch's Ball fell on a grim, rainy Saturday, as though Gotham City was lamenting the same anniversary the Owls were celebrating. While Dinah's big plans for the night consisted of vegging out in front of the TV, she still headed to Mandy's house that afternoon to help her friend get ready. She perched on Mandy's bed with a bowl of popcorn, calling out her opinions as Mandy tried on the different dress options her mom had borrowed for the occasion.

"I'm so jealous of you right now," Mandy grumbled as she hiked up the bodice of a truly uncomfortable-looking sheath dress. "I wonder if there's a way I can get out of tonight, too."

"Well, you can't leave Ty in the lurch," Dinah reminded her. The two were going as each other's friend-dates. "Besides, I'm sure you'll get some good stories out of it."

"Yeah," Mandy agreed. "Like finding out who Oliver Queen's mystery second-choice date is."

"Yup." Dinah fell silent. She'd asked him just the other day if he had found someone to take her place, knowing full well that it would probably be the easiest task of his life.

Half the school was clamoring to go out with him. Oliver had nodded, yet he hadn't told her who he ended up inviting, and Dinah was too proud to ask. But that hadn't stopped her from wondering.

"Okay, last dress. What do you think of this one?"

Mandy posed before her in a blush-pink gown with lace sleeves, the color highlighting her beautiful brown skin and dark eyes. Dinah's heart swelled at the sight of her friend looking so radiant.

"That's the one," she declared. "Although those creeps in the Court don't deserve to see you in that dress."

Mandy laughed and flopped onto the bed next to Dinah, smoothing out the dress underneath her.

"I really wish you were coming, D." She paused. "Promise not to get in any trouble while we're all out, okay?"

"Well, I can't promise," Dinah said with a grin. "But I'll certainly try."

Dinah hugged her dad goodbye as he left for the ball, where he would serve as one of the cops keeping watch over the event, and shuffled off to her room to change into her favorite cozy pajamas. She was just settling in on the couch for a night of solitude ahead, when she heard the knock at the door.

She sat up in surprise. Nearly everyone she knew was on their way to the ball right now . . . so who could be outside her apartment?

And then it hit her. *Owl Guards* . . . or worse, *Talons*. They must have waited until her father was gone, till she was alone and vulnerable. Dinah's heart hammered in her chest as she glanced frantically around the room for some type of weapon. The closest thing she could find was her dad's letter opener on the coffee table, which would be a joke in the face of Talons, but she grabbed it anyway. Her eyes caught on the window, open a crack—enough for them to get through. She jumped off the couch to close it, when she heard—

"Dinah?"

She nearly slammed her finger in the windowsill in shock. *No way.* This had to be a bizarre dream, or a trick. He wasn't actually *here.* But just in case, she made her way to the door to check through the peephole, still clutching the letter opener in her hand.

There he is. Oliver Queen was standing on her front stoop—dressed in a tux and holding a single rose.

Dinah spun around, clapping a hand over her mouth. *What is happening?*

"Dinah Lance," he called out, a note of amusement in his voice. "I can hear you in there. Will you let me in?"

She glanced down at her knit tank top and pj pants, but there wasn't exactly time to freshen up. Dinah could feel her cheeks turning bright red as she opened the door.

"I wasn't expecting anyone, as you can probably tell," she said, gesturing to her outfit. She was too self-conscious to meet his eyes, but she could feel him looking at her, his gaze lingering on her bare shoulders and collarbone—two areas that girls always kept hidden in public. Dinah cleared her throat. "So, were you just . . . dropping by on your way to the ball, or what?"

"Nope. I'm springing you out of here and taking you with

me." He grinned, pulling a long garment bag out from behind his back.

Dinah's mouth fell open.

"Wh-what do you mean? I thought you asked someone else. I'm banned, remember?"

"Can I just come in already?" Oliver asked with a chuckle, and Dinah opened the door wider, stepping back to let him inside. He followed her through the door, and she felt another wave of self-consciousness as she looked at their modest two-bedroom apartment through his eyes. He'd probably never set foot in any home this small before. But to his credit, he didn't look too out of place as he plopped down on her couch. Dinah blinked at the sight of him, still not fully convinced this was happening. And then her stomach flipped, as she realized this was the first time she'd been home alone with a boy who wasn't Ty.

"Once in a while, it's good to be a Queen. Like today." Oliver's grin widened. "I was able to pull some strings and get you re-invited."

"Wait. What?" Dinah stared at him in disbelief, and Oliver nodded proudly.

"That's right. You're back on the list."

She didn't know what to say, as a mix of emotions rushed through her. There was the spark of excitement that he was here, that he had actually done this for her, complicated by the fact that she knew she shouldn't go. Dinah was skating on the thinnest-possible ice with the Court; they clearly didn't want her there. Even with Oliver working his magic to get her back on the guest list . . . how could it possibly be a smart move for her to walk right into the lion's den?

"But—but *why* would you do that?" she finally said. "I thought you asked someone else."

"You're not really that slow on the uptake, are you?" Oliver gave her a teasing glance. "I never asked anyone else. I only wanted to go with you."

A warm glow spread through Dinah's chest at his words, driving her fears about the Court out of her mind. Was he—and was all of this—for real? But as she looked at him, so confident and polished in his formalwear, the doubt started nagging her again.

"But you barely know me. And you had practically the whole school to choose from."

"I barely know most people at this school," Oliver reminded her. "But so far . . . I like everything I know about you. I like the way you talk about music, how you're passionate about things. I like seeing you stand up for yourself. Your spark." He grinned. "You challenge me. And that's one more thing I like about you."

This time, Dinah couldn't hold back her smile. She could feel her protective shell starting to crack, wanting to let him in.

"I might like you, too."

They locked eyes. Dinah looked away first, suddenly shy, as she asked, "How did you manage it, anyway? The letter seemed pretty nonnegotiable to me."

"I should probably give most of the credit to my uncle," Oliver admitted. "He's practically a shadow member of the Court, and I got him to convince them that you'd realized the error of your ways and tonight would be a good opportunity for you to honor and swear your allegiance to the Owls. *And* that you were the only person I felt comfortable dancing in public with—that much is true, at least."

Dinah tentatively placed her hand over his. A shiver ran through her at his touch. But she still wasn't sure about going.

"I don't know if I can do that. Swear my allegiance to the Court, I mean." She looked him in the eye. "I hate them, just as much as they clearly disapprove of me. And while I do think you seem different, you're connected to them. Which makes all this . . . messy."

"I'm not as connected to them as you might think," Oliver said, appearing to choose his words carefully. "And . . . wouldn't this be a good way of sticking it to them? Showing up, and showing them you're not afraid?"

He did have a point there. Dinah looked into those green eyes, and her remaining resolve melted away.

"Okay."

"Really?" Oliver's face lit up, and Dinah laughed.

"Yes. There's just one problem. I didn't get around to buying a dress."

"That's where I come in." Oliver grabbed the garment bag hanging over the back of the couch. "I had my butler go to the store and get a few different options for you to try. Don't worry, he says he's into fashion."

"Really?" Dinah cocked an eyebrow at him. "That's awfully fairy godmother-y of you."

"C'mon, go try them on. We've got to be out of here in thirty."

Dinah jumped up and took the garment bag from Oliver, smiling the whole way to her room. This was the kind of thing that happened in fairy tales published hundreds of years ago, not in real life. Not to *her*.

There were three dresses inside, all of them nicer than

anything she'd ever owned before, made of rich silks and delicate lace. The simplest of the three was her favorite: a light blue chiffon gown with embroidered lace sleeves and a tiny silver bird motif on the shoulder. Dinah slipped it on, praying for it to fit. It zipped up easily, and when she looked in the mirror, she almost didn't recognize the girl behind the glass. She had always thought of herself as reasonably attractive—cute enough, but never one of the "Gotham City Beauties," as some of her peers were called in the *Gazette*. Tonight, though, for the first time, she felt truly beautiful.

She only had time to run a brush through her hair and dab on some lip gloss and mascara, and then it was time to go. She slipped on the one pair of heels she owned and took a deep breath before returning to the den to make her appearance.

Oliver's eyes widened at the sight of her, his cheeks flooding with color. He rose to his feet.

"You look . . . wow. Amazing," he murmured.

Dinah beamed and couldn't resist giving a little twirl.

"Thanks to you. This dress is something else."

"Especially on you," he said with another admiring glance. He offered his hand, and this time Dinah didn't hesitate before taking it. "Let's go."

As Oliver drove over the Gotham City Bridge, leaving the urban sprawl behind them and crossing into the ritzy suburbs, their flirty banter faded into a nervous quiet. It was one thing to get caught up in the thrill of Oliver's attentions at home, but now that she was minutes away from having to face her enemies—from within the Court as well as from school—her second thoughts were creeping up again.

"Did you go to a lot of these things growing up?" she asked, glancing warily out the window.

"Yeah. They kind of all blurred together," he said, steering his convertible around a curve as they exited the bridge. "Except for the events thrown by the Owls. Those were always different. More . . . ceremonial." The way he wrinkled his nose, Dinah could tell he didn't mean it as a compliment.

They turned onto the recently renamed Cobblepot Road, winding past a long trail of trees that served as a red carpet leading up to the star attraction: Cobblepot Manor. It was a Gothic vision, rising from the top of a bluff—a castle of turrets, towers, and flying stone gargoyles, bordered on all sides by wrought iron gates. The overall effect was meant to dazzle, but Dinah knew that beneath the fantastical facade was a place of nightmares—nightmares that began with the first owner of this house, the man who called himself the Penguin.

Oliver joined the line of cars pulling into the circular driveway in the mansion's front courtyard, and Dinah felt suddenly dizzy with nerves. They were walking straight into the fire. *Maybe I should tell him I don't feel well, ask him to drive me home*, she thought with a gulp. But . . . she didn't want to be a coward, either. And so she stayed quiet, watching silently along with Oliver the parade of entrances happening through the window in front of them. One after another, couples and groups, dressed in lavish clothes and dripping in jewels, stepped out of their cars and trotted up the marble front steps. Dinah's stomach churned at the scene.

"Hard to believe all this pageantry is in honor of us losing our voices," Dinah grumbled.

Oliver shifted uncomfortably in his seat.

"It's probably more about marking the mayor and the Owls' rise to power than anything else."

"And how did they secure that power?" Dinah gave him a pointed look. "The Silencing."

Before Oliver could respond, the valet motioned them forward. It was their turn to hand over the keys and walk up the grand steps.

The two of them climbed out of the car and into the starless night. Oliver took Dinah's hand before heading up the steps, where they found a liveried footman on one side of the double doors, checking names off a list, while another handed out masquerade masks to the guests. Naturally, the masks were designed to look like owl faces, with large, beaked noses and tufts of feathers at the temples.

"Gentleman's name?" the first footman asked Oliver, paying no attention to Dinah. He did a double take when he heard the name *Queen*.

"*Ah*, yes, of course. Oliver and Guest, welcome." He ushered them toward his colleague, who handed them each a mask before pulling open the heavy double doors. Oliver slipped his mask on while Dinah kept hers in the palm of her hand, not sure she could bring herself to wear anything affiliated with the Owls. And then they stepped into a strange, dark wonderland.

Hundreds of masked figures swept through a long marble hallway lined with macabre statues into a multilevel ballroom, lit by chandeliers and adorned with dark oil paintings and walls of climbing black and blood-red roses. A trio of stone-carved balconies ran parallel to the ballroom, each flanked by gargoyle statues, their mouths open wide in a silent scream. In front of a raised platform, a sixteen-piece orchestra played operatic selections, each musician disguised with an owl mask. Artificial fog floated through the room, curling itself around each guest, so that everyone had a ghostly look about them. Dinah shivered.

"Where are they?" she asked Oliver nervously. "The Owls, I mean?"

"They usually make their big entrance later in the night. But they're always watching." He glanced up, and Dinah followed his gaze to one of the paintings above them—a rare portrait of two of the earliest Owls, unmasked. From history class, she recognized the pale, pinched face and long hooked nose as belonging to Thurston Moody, a Grandmaster of the Court in the early eighteen hundreds. He leaned on a sloping black cane in the painting beside his eldest son, a young man with a wavy pompadour and a proud smirk.

Dinah looked away from the nauseating portraits of the historical figures and peered across the sea of gowns and tuxes, trying to pinpoint Mandy's blush dress or her dad's uniform. Her throat turned dry at the thought of how he would react if he saw her there—the last place he wanted or expected her to be. Not to mention, she definitely wasn't supposed to be spending any more time with Oliver. The only positive about the owl mask in her hand was that it would disguise half her face—and hopefully keep her dad from recognizing her.

Just then, a man who looked like he'd arrived straight from the court of Louis XIV grabbed Dinah's elbow, pulling her and Oliver aside. It took a few moments before Dinah recognized him as the mayor's costumed deputy secretary, Mr. Ruben.

"There you are! We're about to officially open the ball with the quadrille d'honneur. Come join the others backstage. And I must insist you both don your masks."

There was no escaping now. Dinah took a shallow gulp of air as she set the mask on her face, muttering to Oliver, "I'm pretty sure I just blanked on all the moves."

"The good news is that in ten minutes, it'll all be over," he said, though he looked like he wanted to bolt as much as she did.

They followed the deputy secretary to a velvet-covered vestibule just off the ballroom, where their six classmates stood waiting, dressed to the nines. Dinah's arrival was like a record scratch in the room, cutting off conversation and drawing gaping stares. Zed Cobblepot looked especially dumbfounded.

"That's not Dinah *Lance*, is it? Who knew you'd clean up like that?"

"Thanks," Dinah said drily.

"I thought you weren't coming," Natasha Wycliffe said, her eyes flickering between Dinah and Oliver.

"I wasn't. But someone convinced me otherwise." She looked up at Oliver with a small smile.

Suddenly, the music from the ballroom faded to silence. A hush fell over the room. And then they heard Mr. Dwight's voice echo through the speaker.

"Welcome, prized citizens of Gotham City, to our landmark Patriarch's Ball! Tonight is a *truly* special event, honoring two anniversaries of note—the Silencing, which marked the end of the war and the Court of Owls' victory, and the beginning of Mayor Cobblepot's reign. Yet we also look back even farther, to the origins of the Court as a secret society made up of Gotham City elite in the eighteenth century. In a spectacular merging of the new guard with the old tradition, we've invited four of Gotham City's most notable young gentlemen and their chosen dance partners to officially open the ball with a quadrille d'honneur, danced exactly as it was for the first Patriarch's Ball nearly three hundred years ago."

Dinah turned to Oliver as a wave of nausea hit. Everything about this was wrong. She was in the house of the enemy—and now she was about to put herself on display for him. For all of them.

"You sure you don't want to invite someone else up?" she whispered.

Oliver just squeezed her hand.

"You'll be fine."

"And now for our first guest of honor," Mr. Dwight boomed. "Mr. Desmond Clark, accompanied by Miss Camila Orchard."

The two of them sauntered out the side door of the vestibule that led onto the ballroom floor, swinging hands like this was just another fun night out for them. Dinah couldn't help envying how carefree they seemed. They clearly didn't have bloodthirsty Talons to worry about.

"Mr. Thom Elliott, accompanied by Miss Natasha Wycliffe!"

Natasha fixed a smile on her face, taking Thom's arm and following in Desmond and Camila's wake.

"New to Gotham City but hailing from an impeccable family respected by the Court—we have Mr. Oliver Queen, accompanied by . . . DinahLaurelLance." Mr. Dwight mumbled her name, running the syllables together, as if he hoped to muffle Oliver's unsuitable pick from the public. It might have worked for the older crowd, but the Gotham City High students knew exactly who he meant. Their rumblings and whispers were almost as loud as the applause that had followed Desmond's and Thom's names.

"Here goes." Oliver offered his arm with an attempt at a smile that looked more like a grimace. The two walked out together, blinking under the spotlight beaming down on the pairs. While Mr. Dwight waxed on and on about the last and most important of the honored guests, Dinah scanned the audience, both afraid and anxious to see who was in the crowd. She finally spotted his blue uniform at the edge of the room by the terrace doors, where he stood frozen in shock, staring at her. *Dad.*

I can explain, she tried mouthing at him across the ballroom. But he just looked at her like he didn't know her anymore, and Dinah winced with regret. She really should have thought this through better, instead of getting swept up in Oliver.

Dinah heard a familiar voice cheering her name, and she turned to see Mandy, elbowing her way through the crowd to get a closer look, with Ty right behind her. His mouth was hanging open in astonishment, while Mandy looked as if she might jump out of her skin in excitement. Dinah managed a slight smile in their direction.

Once Zed and Maya took their places, the owl-masked orchestra launched into a jaunty waltz. Half her mind was consumed with trying to keep up with the steps, as the stodgy voice of the Culture Enforcer echoed in her memory: *Forward and back, cross over, chassé!* But the other half was hyperaware of the hundreds of eyes focused on them—like the Owl Guards, who seemed to be homing in on her in particular. Hooded eyes of the mayor and the Owls, whom she knew were watching from somewhere unseen. *One wrong move tonight, and everything could come crashing down.*

Dinah felt on the verge of throwing up throughout the whole routine, but luckily she managed to hold it in. And then, at last, the music reached its finale and she could breathe normally again. The four pairs took their bows to polite applause, and one particularly high-pitched wolf whistle that Dinah knew belonged to Mandy. She caught Mandy's eye across the room, where she was giggling into Ty's shoulder. Clearly the dance had looked as ridiculous as she figured it would.

"Well, no one can accuse us of being great dancers," Dinah said with a laugh. "But we survived."

"Thank goodness it's over," he replied, throwing an arm around her shoulder. Dinah leaned in closer as something fluttered in her chest. She looked back out at the crowd and spotted Mandy staring at her agog and mouthing, O-M-G.

Mr. Dwight invited the rest of the guests to join them on the dance floor, and soon Dinah, Oliver, and the others were swallowed up in a rush of masked, waltzing figures. It was the perfect time to break away and try to smooth this over with her dad . . . except the crowd had hidden him from view.

"I'll be right back," she told Oliver. "I just need to—to find someone really quick."

He nodded, getting pulled into another conversation of his own with Desmond and Thom. Dinah weaved her way through the crowd of stiff, overdressed dancers, making it halfway across the ballroom floor, when the music came to an abrupt halt.

The candlelight flickered. A solo trumpet began to play from somewhere unseen, a dark and brooding melody. And then the crowd parted, clearing a path for the marching military drummers, their snare drums striking the beat of fear as they moved in a uniform line across the ballroom floor. The orchestra joined in from the front of the room, launching into a song that never failed to send a sick shudder through Dinah's body: "Hail to the Court of Owls," Gotham City's new nationalist anthem.

The guests surrounding her raised their palms in the air, the men forced to sing along and the women to recite the lyrics out loud, whether they agreed with them or not. The pit in Dinah's stomach grew heavier as she mouthed the words.

Now Gotham is ours, ours alone.
The Court of Owls took back our home!

Right on cue, the Owl Masters strode into the room, long black cloaks sweeping behind them. The gathered crowd chanted their names like a twisted prayer as the men stepped up to the raised dais.

"Wycliffe. Powers. March. Elliot. Moody. Greaves."

They formed an identical line, six tall and slender figures moving with the same chilling gait, their faces a mystery preserved behind owl masks of priceless porcelain. And then, following in the Owls' wake, came their chosen mayor and figurehead. He sauntered forward, a crimson velvet cape draped across his stocky frame. Chester Cobblepot was the only Owl allowed to show his face, and Dinah trembled with loathing as she looked upon it—the face responsible for the Silencing.

As soon as Cobblepot joined the other Owls on the raised dais and the line was complete, the guests in the ballroom burst into fervent applause. Dinah felt bile rising in her throat as she was forced to clap along.

"Welcome, valued citizens," Mayor Cobblepot began, flashing the smile that had always struck Dinah as venomous—an expression more befitting a snake than a man. "I am deeply proud to be celebrating the historic length of my tenure with you all this evening. Additionally, tonight we remember the key victories that returned the Court of Owls to the forefront of power—and Gotham City to its rightful role as the most influential city in the world." He paused for effect. "I am, of course, alluding to the cleansing that took place right here—when the last vigilantes were defeated, and we as a people made the triumphant return to tradition and strong moral values."

As he spoke, a line of tuxedo-clad waiters filtered into the room, carrying trays of champagne and sparkling cider. They passed out drinks one glass at a time as Mayor Cobblepot continued his sickening speech.

"The Silencing was the day justice was served to those who misused their voices," Cobblepot said, raising his own. "It also served as an important warning to the world: flouting rules, conventions, and authority only leads to punishment and pain. And now, thanks to the events of twenty years ago and the rebalancing of power that followed, we gather tonight in a time of great prosperity and renown for Gotham City. Join me in raising a glass."

Dinah's rage seared through her, so strong she could

barely see straight. As she reached for a glass of cider from the waiter's tray, she was near certain the force of her anger would send it shattering. So when she heard the deafening crash—when she saw the flying shards of glass—Dinah's first instinct was to think she had somehow caused it. Until she turned, following the sound. And that's when she saw the bodies . . . leaping through the broken window, one after another.

There must have been ten of them, women and men, all of them dressed in their unsanctioned blue jeans and black shirts. *The Resistance.*

As the bodies leaped to the floor, the walls lit up, bursting to life with eye-popping projected images. The visuals played in rapid succession for the stunned crowd, a montage of costumed crime fighters of the past, their autographs scrawled underneath each image. Dinah could barely breathe as she stared, watching the iconic shadow of Batman give way to an acrobatic vision of Nightwing, before segueing into a trio of women warriors in black leather who were called the Birds of Prey. Above each image, bold red letters spelled out, RETURN OUR HEROES—REMOVE THE COURT.

It was the Resistance staging their biggest protest yet. But they had only a moment's head start.

Gunshots rang out from somewhere on high—as if an invisible sniper was hidden above them, poised for just this moment. Dinah ducked behind one of the ballroom's pillars, watching in horror as a bullet flew right into the chest of a woman from the Resistance. Screams flooded the room, just as the Talons, hidden in the eaves, swooped down from the shadows. Their yellow eyes glimmered, their gloves sprouting blades at the fingertips. And before Dinah's mind could even process what was happening, the Talons flew into motion, sinking their blades into the protesters' chests. The Resistance began to fall just as quickly as they'd burst in, blood spurting from the bat shirts that were meant to symbolize hope.

A gut-wrenching scream tore through Dinah's ears, and it took a second to realize the scream was coming from her, as the nightmare played out in front of her in slow motion. Shouting guests stampeded away from the dance floor as bodies slammed onto it, demolished by the claws of the Talons. Some Resistance fighters stumbled back up to wield their defense weapons and continue the fight, only to be sliced apart by the Talons' blades before they had a chance. Dinah's eyes burned, and she knew this terrifying scene would be emblazoned in her memory forever. *I have to do something—anything.*

Guards swooped onto the dais to shield the Owl Masters and Mayor Cobblepot, while guests charged for the doors and cops flew onto the scene, trying in vain to control the chaos. Dinah darted out from her hiding place behind the pillar, crawling on her hands and knees to disappear into the crowd and avoid being hit. Everyone was a stranger in this blood-spattered room. The red streaks soiled gowns and suits and spilled across masks and faces, making the crowd look like a mob of monstrous clowns. Weaving through the panicking, shoving throng, Dinah agonized over what to do next. *Help the Resistance?* She didn't have any weapons on her, but she had her jujitsu. *Just get my friends out of here and run?* She would need to find them first. Oliver, Mandy, and Ty had all disappeared in the mass of bloodied faces.

And then the lights gave one last flicker, the chandeliers blazing in one final burst. The ballroom plunged into sudden, silent darkness—and that's when something in Dinah snapped.

The world is a dangerous place, not because of those who do evil, but because of those who look on and do nothing. She had read that once in a book from her father's library, a volume so old the pages were nearly crumbled, but the Albert Einstein quote had remained clear. As the message returned to her mind now, a shivery sensation ran across Dinah's skin. Her breath quickened. And then her eyes closed as something far bigger than herself took over.

"No more staying quiet when our world's gone wrong.
There's no time for silence when they steal our song.
So, ladies, let's stand up and find our own way.
Our time to be heard begins today."

But this time she wasn't just speaking or whispering.

The voice that filled the ballroom was like honey, soft and tender, strangely familiar. And as disbelief turned to certainty, Dinah's voice gathered strength and power—until the notes soared above the cacophony, like she'd been doing this her entire life. Like she was born to sing. And she realized then why her voice sounded so familiar.

It was *her*—the singer she thought she'd overheard when she was eight. It was Dinah all along.

She just never believed that it could be.

In a flash, her mind returned to that day, nine years ago. When young Dinah Lance had been in so much pain from losing her mother that she couldn't speak, couldn't do anything but let out the massive wall of emotion through the only medium big enough to convey it: music.

It had stunned her when she began to sing, just like it was stunning her now—so shocking that she had convinced herself it was someone else she'd heard. Convinced her body, her voice, that they were incapable.

Until now.

CHAPTER TWELVE

"*. . . One day soon our winning bells are going to ring.
Play them loud when the Black Canary sings!*"

Dinah's voice worked like a spell, freezing the scene, as even
the bloodthirsty Talons couldn't help but pause in dismay.
How, in this day and age, was a female able to *sing*?

The backup lights started to flicker when Dinah reached
the end of the chorus, jolting her back down to earth. She
cut herself off in the nick of time, just as someone pushed
through the crowd to get to her.

"Run," his familiar voice whispered in her ear. *Oliver.*
Even in the dark, even from across the room—somehow he
had guessed it was her. *How?*

Before she could follow his warning, a wash of artificial
light flooded the ballroom, casting the blood-battered space
in a harsh yellow glow. Dinah instantly noticed a change in
the scene surrounding her. Before she'd begun singing, the
protesters had all been scattered on the ground, a devastat-
ing heap of motionless figures in black and blue. But now, a

half dozen of them were crawling back up to their feet, the spark of fight returning to their eyes.

The Talons snapped back into action, too, lunging toward the Resistance members on the ground. Dinah held her breath at the sight of a petite, middle-aged woman, dressed in the blue denim pants that only men were allowed to wear, scrambling to reach two knives buried under one of her dead comrades. She looked so small and slight, easy as an insect for the Talons to squash. And there was one Talon in particular who was inching closer to her, his finger blades flexing menacingly.

Dinah yelped out a warning no one could hear above the noise, but it didn't matter. The woman had a plan of her own. Instead of succumbing to the Talon, she spun around to face him with a wild yell—and drove her knives deep into his abdomen.

The Talon's gruesome face froze in openmouthed shock. He staggered backward against a marble bust of Mayor Cobblepot, and the two came crashing to the ground together in a pool of blood and marble shards.

No one moved, no one breathed. The Talons were supposed to be indestructible—just like women weren't supposed to be able to sing. But both of those truths had come undone, in the same amount of time it had taken for Dinah to sing her mother's song. And for the first time, when Dinah looked up at the Owls on their dais, she didn't see unimpeachable power—she saw panic.

Their faces were even whiter than normal behind their owl masks, and instead of the usual eerie calm, they moved at a frenzy, shouting commands and questions above the din. Only one of the Owls, the Grandmaster, remained still, his body language giving nothing away. Until, suddenly, he drew himself up to his full height and raised his arms skyward. His hands curled into fists as he made a strange gesture, like he was drawing an invisible *something* toward him. And then Dinah saw it. They all saw it.

The massive gray hood seemed to materialize in the middle of the ballroom, a towering figure cutting its way through the crowd, until it reached the woman who had dared to strike a Talon. The hood fell away, revealing another sharp-clawed assassin underneath. Only . . . there was something about this Talon. He moved differently than the others, like he was more wind than flesh. He showed more of his face through the mask, too, revealing a hooked nose and waxy pale skin—almost familiar.

He swung his cane straight up into the side of the heroic woman's skull. It took only three seconds for her to die. It was quick and simple—over. Dinah was too stunned, too horrified, to scream.

As this new Talon tore his way through the remaining Resistance, the terrified guests stampeded for the doors. Dinah fell into step with the rush, her heart hammering in time with the Talons' heavy, stalking footsteps. But then she turned around, eyes scanning the surreal scene for a glimpse of her dad. She hoped Ty, Mandy, and Oliver were running for the exit along with her, but the one person she knew wouldn't be was her father. He would never leave an active crime scene when there were people still there to protect. It was something she admired about him, but for the first time, Dinah found herself wishing that her father was the type of man to walk away, to shirk his duty—just so she wouldn't have to be left wondering if he would make it home tonight alive.

At the sheer force of hundreds of bodies pushing against the locked ballroom doors, they finally weakened and burst open, the guests flooding through. As Dinah followed, the last thing she heard was the ice-cold voice of one of the Owls on the dais above her, hissing: *"Who was she? Who was the singer?"*

Dinah shrank back, letting the crowd elbow and slam into her on the way out the door. Oliver had seemingly guessed the truth, but if anyone else did . . . then she would be in just as much trouble as the Resistance fighters killed in this room.

A mass exodus flooded the marble halls and spilled out onto the front courtyard, the surge of guests nearly knocking the stunned valet staff to the ground. Dinah whipped her head around, searching through the chaos for a familiar face. And then she saw a flash of a torn pink gown, heard a familiar sob.

"Mandy!" Dinah screamed, running to her friend. They threw their arms around each other. Dinah peered past Mandy's shoulder for a sign of Ty.

"Where is he?"

Mandy shook her head, guilty tears pooling in her eyes.

"I don't know—I started running and I thought he was right next to me," she choked out. "I was too fast. I should have held on better."

"It's . . . it's okay," Dinah murmured, even as dread formed a giant pit in her stomach. *What if he didn't escape? What if he's in the grips of a Talon right now?*

She was just gathering the courage to run back inside, when a hand grabbed her elbow.

"Come on!" Oliver Queen appeared beside her, a long,

jagged cut running down the length of his cheek. "I can see my car up ahead—let's go!"

"Wait." Dinah stayed rooted in place. "Our friend Ty might still be in there, and my dad, too—"

"The police are inside right now, trying to control the situation," Oliver interrupted. "You can't do any more than they can. The only thing going back in would accomplish is drawing attention to yourself." He gave her a pointed look. "And that's the last thing you can afford. Now, come *on*."

No one spoke the first several minutes of the drive, all three of them shell-shocked by what they had just lived through. By the time they reached the bridge, the only audible sound in the car was Mandy's muffled sobs coming from the back seat. And then Dinah whispered, "All those people . . . dead." She clapped her hand over her mouth, fighting the bile rising in her throat. "I've never seen anyone die before."

"You don't forget it," Oliver said numbly. "It stays with you, haunts you—until you figure out a way to live with it."

Dinah turned to stare at him. So then . . . this wasn't the first time he'd seen someone die? But before she could ask, Oliver murmured in a voice low enough for only Dinah to hear, "How did you do it?"

"Do what?"

"*Sing.*"

Dinah swallowed hard, turning her gaze to the passenger-seat window to avoid his eyes. She thought about denying it, which would clearly be the safest move, but she waited a beat too long. Instead she asked him, "What makes you think it was me?"

"Because before I even moved to Gotham City, I heard there was a girl here who could do things that others couldn't. Someone who could fight as well as she could sing, someone who was impervious to Cobblepot's curse. The day I met you and saw you try to fight Zed—I knew it. I just knew it was you."

He glanced at her with such admiration, it crushed Dinah to disappoint him. The pieces were falling into place now, his unexpected interest and pursuit of her finally making sense. Oliver had thought she was someone different. Someone more special than just Dinah Laurel Lance.

"You're thinking of somebody else," she said. "No one's talking about me or what I can do, because I didn't even know what I could do until . . ."

Oliver glanced at her, unconvinced. And suddenly, a thought—a theory—started brimming in her mind. Maybe there once was someone like the exceptional girl Oliver just described, and while it wasn't Dinah, what if it was—

"What are you guys talking about?" Mandy's voice behind her yanked Dinah from her thoughts. "I was on the phone."

"Oh, nothing," Dinah fibbed. "Just . . . wondering what's happening back there."

"I'm going to try Ty again," Mandy said nervously, and Dinah held her breath as Mandy dialed his number. But there was no answer.

"What if . . . what if he didn't get out?" Mandy's voice broke, and Dinah twisted around in her seat to squeeze her friend's hand.

"If he's still in that ballroom, then my dad is there, too, watching out for him," she said, silently praying for them both to be okay. "I know it."

"Yeah," Mandy whispered. They lapsed back into near silence for the rest of the ride home, until Oliver turned onto Mandy's street. Before getting out of the car, Mandy leaned forward. "You want to come with me, Dinah? I know at least my mom is there, so we wouldn't have to be alone right now. . . ."

"Thanks." Dinah forced a smile. "I just—kind of feel like being at home right now, if that makes sense."

"Okay. I obviously won't be sleeping tonight, so call me or come over no matter what time it is, especially when you hear about Ty. Your dad will be on top of it—he'll make sure to find him, won't he?" Mandy hugged her arms against her chest, shoulders still trembling, as she looked pleadingly at Dinah.

"Of course. And I—I'll call you the second I hear." Dinah's stomach lurched. "It's going to be okay." *It has to be.*

Dinah and Oliver waited for Mandy to disappear inside the house, and then Oliver pressed on the gas, heading for the Lance apartment.

"You ask me all these questions about myself, but . . . how am I supposed to trust you?" Dinah blurted out as they drew closer to home.

Oliver gave her a quizzical look, and she continued, "I know your parents were in the Court's inner circle, and I know they helped the Owls rise to power all those years ago. So how can I trust that you're not loyal to them? That you're not about to turn in . . . the singer?"

Oliver took a moment to reply, weighing his words. And then he said, "The connection between my parents and the Court is complicated, and there are some things I can't talk about—but I'm not one of *them*, if that's what you're thinking. I've never been." He gave her a sidelong glance. "And if I was planning to hand 'the singer' over to the Court, wouldn't it have made a lot more sense for me to do it then, the second I heard you? Why would I be driving you home right now?"

Dinah had to admit he had a point there. She felt her shoulders start relaxing a smidge. But she still wasn't ready to confirm out loud that she had been the one singing. She remained silent.

"You know the answer, don't you? I like you. It's as plain and simple as that."

A shiver ran through her at his words. *I like you.* Who could have guessed that one little phrase would make her feel suddenly light-headed . . . in the best way?

"There's something else I want to ask you." The car slowed to a stop. Oliver turned in his seat to face her.

"Okay."

"Can I kiss you?"

"You're . . . asking me?"

He nodded, smiling shyly. And as she gazed back at him, it was like the sun broke through the dark, and all she could see and feel was light.

He asked me. He didn't just assume, like every other boy or man in Gotham City, that she was there for the taking. Oliver Queen was different. He wanted to make sure she was okay with it.

In his own way, he was subverting the Court alongside her.

"Yes," she whispered. "Definitely."

Oliver reached for her cheek, and she could feel her heart speeding up, her skin tingling from his touch. He tilted her chin toward him, and just as her mind started scrambling to process what was about to happen—her first real kiss—his lips brushed against hers. And her stomach swooped with the rush of a roller coaster, the kind she never wanted to end.

He pressed his forehead to hers, his fingers running through her hair, and Dinah closed her eyes, forgetting everything but this moment. Their lips met again in a kiss as tender as it was passionate, a kiss she could lose herself in. She had a flash of guilt at the fact that she could feel anything this good after what she'd just witnessed at the ball, but she couldn't help it. There was an electricity between them, a chemistry ignited that she couldn't deny anymore.

They kissed again and again, tangled in each other's arms, until she finally murmured, "I should go." Not because she wanted to, but because every passing minute made it that much more tempting to stay.

"Of course," he said, a longing in his eyes that gave her a thrill. "Call or text me if you need anything, okay?"

"Okay. Thank you. It was a . . ." Dinah trailed off, lost for words. How could she even attempt to describe the evening they'd just experienced together? "It was a night," she finally said.

"Yeah. It was." He stroked her hair one last time, and Dinah leaned in for another kiss, her body melting against the seat at the feel of his lips.

"Good night, Dinah Laurel Lance."

"Good night, Oliver Queen."

Her head was spinning as she stepped through the door to the apartment. Dinah felt like she was coming back an entirely different person from the girl who left with Oliver just hours ago, so different that when she glanced in the hallway mirror, she half expected to see someone else. But it was still her own face staring back at her.

Dinah tried calling her dad and Ty again, but both numbers went straight to voice mail—and the brief burst of happiness she'd felt in that moment with Oliver started seeping away. Worry coiled her stomach, along with terror-inducing flashbacks of the violence at the ball. She paced up and down the entryway, trying to think of something to do, some way of getting through the unbearable silence. And then she remembered the theory brimming in her mind during her conversation with Oliver. Now was the time to investigate.

She hurried into the master bedroom, which retained the same floral curtains and bedspread from when her mom shared this room, too. Larry had done little to change it, and stepping inside often felt like entering a time capsule.

Dinah dragged her dad's desk chair over to the closet so she could reach the top shelf—the place where Larry kept the three boxes containing her mother's valuables and mementos. These were Dinah's to inherit one day: her mom's wedding ring and veil, the photo albums from her youth in pre-Owls Gotham City, the silver and china passed down from her own parents. And maybe, if Dinah's suspicions were right . . . something else?

The first box held the expected keepsakes, including what looked like a stack of love letters between her mother and father, a sight that made Dinah's heart ache. But it was the second box that revealed the first clue of her mother's double life.

She found it folded up in quarters, wedged into the side of the box—sheet music, once again in Dinah Drake's handwriting. But this was a new song, and instead of a title, there was simply a message: Happy Birthday, B. Dinah's pulse sped up as she read.

In every story that I read,
there's one thing our hero needs.
She searches for an ally who
is unconditional and true.

Through all of life's ups and downs,
you've kept my world turning round.
My best friend, birds on a ride,
always there, right by my side.

'Cause you're the gold standard.
You're a prayer answered,
a living example
of fighting fear with love.

Yeah, you're the gold standard.
You're a prayer answered,
a living example
of fighting fear with love.
As birds, we soar above. . . .
You're the gold standard.

Dinah stared at the lyrics, tears prickling in her eyes as she realized who this song was written for. Barbara Gordon was right—they had been best friends. And just like with her mom's first song, all it took was a glance at the musical notes and Dinah could *hear* the melody, playing in her mind. This one was catchy, infectious—and she was dying to hear it sung.

She cleared her throat and took a deep breath, standing in the very room where her mother might have written these words. And when she opened her mouth, she heard the glorious, soaring tone from earlier tonight, the sound that felt more like a superpower than a voice. She had dreamed about singing all her life, but the magical reality of it was even better—like jumping off the edge of a precipice and discovering you could fly.

She could have easily spent the rest of the night focused on the song alone. But there was still one box left to uncover, one more chance to prove her growing suspicion. And that third box was where she found it.

Tucked at the bottom, hidden beneath a pile of photo albums, was an outfit of black leather—the polar opposite of the modest skirts and sweaters Dinah had seen her mom in when she was alive. This black leather bodysuit, with its matching pants and cropped jacket, was the kind of outfit that would instantly land a woman in jail nowadays.

When Dinah spotted the black domino mask underneath the clothing, she gasped in amazement. The mask was the final confirmation, the finishing touch . . . the proof of who her mother was.

She was holding the costume of Black Canary—one of the founding members of Birds of Prey.

Dinah's hands shook as she unzipped her ball gown and let it fall to the floor. She stepped into the black bodysuit and pulled the straps over her shoulders, marveling at the perfect fit. She zipped up the leather pants, imagining her mom in this same pair, fighting and taking down Gotham City's most evil. Now it was her turn.

She slipped on the black cropped jacket, which somehow, incredibly, retained a faint smell of her mom's perfume. Dinah closed her eyes, wrapping the jacket tighter around her, like an embrace. And then she slid the mask over her eyes.

Staring back at her in the mirror was that someone else she'd been looking for, someone powerful. She had been there, hiding in her DNA, all along.

There was one more surprise waiting for her in the box: a long and slender black baton, similar to the martial arts weaponry she'd seen on Sandra Wu-San's table. Dinah was just turning the baton over in her hand, figuring out how it worked—when she heard the cry.

It was her father. Larry Lance stood frozen in the doorway like he'd seen a ghost, his uniform battered and bloodied from the carnage at the ball. And as he looked at his daughter in the costume, he blinked back tears.

"The Black Canary," he whispered. "It's you."

CHAPTER THIRTEEN

Dinah had never seen her father cry before, not even when her mother died. It was almost like his fury at losing her kept the real, deeper emotions at bay. Larry had worn a permanent scowl in that first year, always on the verge of lashing out, until single fatherhood had forced him to soften. He often said that it was Dinah who healed his heart, but as he looked at her now, with those shocking tears pooling in his eyes . . . Dinah had the sinking feeling that she might be about to break it.

"How—how did you—?" Larry sputtered, barely able to speak. He took a breath, and when he regained his voice, it was the rough, angry tone she'd heard him use on others, but never her. "Go to your room and take that off, right now. I don't want to see you like that—not ever."

"Why not?" Dinah challenged him. "Why can't I be like her? It's so clear who I'm supposed to be. The Black Canary—"

"Is what got her *killed*!" Larry shouted. "It's the last thing your mother would ever want for you. She was desperate for you to be normal, to stay out of trouble."

"Are you talking about Mom, or about you?" Dinah raised her eyes to meet his. "Because if I'm supposed to be so 'normal,' then how come I can do this?" She took a deep breath.

"In every story that I read,
there's one thing our hero needs."

Larry sank into a seat, the color draining from his face.

"It's impossible," he whispered.

"It's a miracle," Dinah said. And then her heart soared as she realized, "Oh my god. I can sing *anything* I want now! Every song I ever loved and wished I could—"

"No!" Larry jumped up, seizing her hands in his. "You can't. You have to keep this quiet. Didn't you see what happened tonight? Your singing . . . it might have just started a war."

"What?" Dinah gave an incredulous laugh. "That's a stretch, don't you think?"

But Larry's intense expression didn't waver.

"You emboldened the Resistance tonight by revealing a flaw in Cobblepot's scheme—the fact that you are somehow immune to it. You saw that woman stab a Talon, right there in front of everyone. It was after she heard you."

Dinah was speechless. It had never occurred to her that she could have been the catalyst—that her voice could have had such a dramatic effect. She could feel her hands starting to shake as Larry continued, "The Owls are enraged, and they'll be merciless in going after *anyone* perceived to be disloyal to them," Larry continued. "And the 'mystery singer' of tonight is number one on that list."

Dinah gulped.

"Did . . . did any of the Resistance survive tonight?"

"No," Larry said flatly. "Ten deaths in all."

Dinah covered her mouth with her hand, sickened.

"Who were they?" she whispered. "What were their names?"

"We're still working on identifying all the victims," he answered, looking almost as miserable as she felt at the thought. *Dead and nameless.*

Larry wrapped his arm around her shoulder.

"It's not your fault. You didn't put the Resistance up to their foolish plot tonight. But I'm afraid you've now given them a reason to keep fighting. Whether you meant to or not, your voice has become a sort of . . . symbol."

Dinah pulled back, staring at her dad.

"You say that like it's a bad thing."

"We can't have another war." Larry picked up the Black Canary domino mask that had dropped to the floor during their argument, and a pained expression crossed his face as he held the dark fabric in his hands. "Your mother would still be here if not for the last one."

"How did she die?" Dinah's voice lowered to a whisper. "All these years, you told me a lie."

Larry shut his eyes.

"I had no choice. You were just a little girl, and I was so angry. I didn't want that pain for you. But the truth is that she . . . she wasn't just part of the Resistance. She was one of its leaders."

Dinah gasped. She'd guessed it after reading her mom's lyrics to "The Black Canary Sings," but hearing her dad confirm it was stunning. Her chest constricted, and underneath the ache was another emotion. *Pride.*

"There was a fight on the Gotham City Clocktower," Larry said numbly. "Every fighter is invincible until the day they're not, and . . . and that's what happened with your mother." He gave her an entreating look. "It's why I'm so desperate to protect you, to prevent you from following in her footsteps."

"But she would hate that," Dinah insisted. "If Mom died for the Resistance, that means there's no *way* she would want us to just roll over and give in to the Owls. And if I've somehow given people hope, a reason to keep fighting . . ." Dinah looked up defiantly. "Well, then I want to keep that hope alive."

"It's a fight we can't win!" Larry exploded. "Didn't you hear me earlier? *Ten people* died on the Resistance side, to only one Talon."

"But until tonight, the Owls had never even lost one," Dinah reminded him. "So maybe—maybe the tide is turning, and we finally have a chance."

Larry narrowed his eyes at her, recognizing Barbara's words.

"What exactly did you do, Dinah? How did you know your mother's song?"

"I . . ." Dinah hesitated, nervous for the first time this whole conversation. "I went to see her at the library. Barbara Gordon."

The look of betrayal on her father's face was worse than any punishment.

"So you lied to me. Again."

"It wasn't a lie. It was more of a . . . withholding of information," Dinah said, trying to justify what she'd done. "But if you hadn't hidden so much from *me*, I wouldn't have had to go see her! You gave me no choice."

"One of these days, Dinah, you will realize I have been doing everything in my power to protect you," Larry said heavily. "And instead of appreciating that, you are undoing it all."

"Well, maybe I don't want to be *safe* if it means having no freedom!" Dinah shot back. "I know you're on my side, but . . . you'll never understand what it's really like."

Larry's head snapped up, his eyes full of alarm.

"What?" Dinah asked. "What's that look for?"

"Dinah—your mother." Larry swallowed hard. "She said the same thing, not long before . . ." His voice trailed off, not wanting to finish the sentence. *Before she died.*

"She said she wasn't worried about her own safety, that there were things that mattered more," he said bitterly. "More than you and me, apparently."

Dinah stared at her dad, seeing it for the first time—something else beneath his grief. He felt abandoned by Dinah Drake. And now he was afraid of losing her, too.

"Mom would still be here if those monsters at the Court were no longer in control," she said gently. "That's the real enemy. Not her Black Canary persona, or Barbara Gordon, or anyone else."

He didn't answer. And in the silence that followed, Dinah remembered with a flash of guilt—*"Ty! Please tell me you saw him!"*

Larry gave her a bemused look, surprised by the conversation's sudden turn.

"Yeah, I think I saw him running out of the ballroom with his parents, same as everyone else. Why?"

Dinah let out a long exhale.

"So he made it out, then. Thank goodness."

The only question left was . . . why wasn't he answering their calls?

"There was—something else about your singing tonight," Larry said, refocusing the conversation on Dinah. His eyes were troubled as he studied her. "Did you notice what happened to the ceiling?"

"Um, what?" Dinah gave her dad a flabbergasted look. "I was a little too preoccupied with all the blood and horror to pay attention to the ceiling!"

"Maybe it's because I knew to look for it," Larry said, more to himself than to her. "After you started singing, there were these . . . cracks forming in the plaster right above me. Cracks that weren't there even a minute before." He lowered his voice. "Was it you?"

The hairs on the back of her neck started to rise.

"I . . . I don't know."

$3 MILLION REWARD OFFERED FOR SINGER'S IDENTITY

10:00 a.m. EDT—As of this morning, the Court of Owls have announced a handsome reward for the first person to correctly identify the mystery female singer whose actions last evening threw the Patriarch's Ball into violence and chaos. As soon as this individual is located, the Court will have her examined to see what other anomalies she may possess, before taking the appropriate steps to ensure she will never be a harm to our community again.

If you have **any** information whatsoever,
please call the tip line below immediately. Be
aware that the Court will be thoroughly vetting
all tips, so any pranks or false information
will be traced to the caller, who will be duly
punished. However, now is a time to keep your
eyes and ears wide open. An ordinary, humble
citizen could find themselves a millionaire by
morning if they discover the truth—and learn
the name we are all searching for.

Dinah's hands shook as she stared at the article on her phone, the words swimming together before her eyes. She'd gone to bed certain the public would be far more concerned about the new, overpowering Talon summoned by the Grandmaster of the Court, and experiencing grief for the ten who had died, than the much more trivial question of *Who was singing?* But with the media fixating their news cycle on the singer, the Gotham City residents followed suit.

It was all anyone could talk about: the mystery singer, the Bloody Ball. From the *Gotham Gazette* to the radio and TV news, there was round-the-clock coverage, all of it painting the Resistance as bloodthirsty criminals, the Court of Owls as innocent victims, and the mysterious singer as some kind of dangerous witch—how *else* could she be immune to Cobblepot's Silencing gas? And now, with a $3 million bounty on her head, Dinah was beginning to realize just how much danger she was in. She'd been planning to tell Mandy and Ty the truth as soon as she could, but it hit her now that she couldn't say a thing. The fewer people who knew, the better. Which made it that much more nerve-racking that of the two people who did know it was her, one was the guy she had only just started going out with. She cringed at the thought of what her dad would say if he heard what happened with Oliver. *Nope.* That was one more secret she'd have to add to her growing pile. At least she didn't have to worry about Oliver being tempted to sell her out for the prize money.

When she padded into the kitchen for breakfast, she found her dad staring into space with a frown, absently cutting his toaster waffle into dozens of tiny pieces.

"Okay, Dad, I think you can put the knife away," Dinah joked. "I'm pretty sure that waffle knows who's boss."

Larry glanced up, startled. It looked like new worry lines had sprung onto his skin overnight, and Dinah felt a pang of guilt.

"You read the article, didn't you?"

He nodded. "You're going to have to keep a seriously low profile from now on," he warned. "No more doing anything even *remotely* controversial. Do you understand? Put one foot wrong, and it'll be that much easier for them to figure out it was you."

"I know," Dinah sighed.

"In fact, it might be best that you don't leave the apartment for anything other than school for the foreseeable future," he continued. "You can always have your friends over here—"

"Dad, I'm going to the library. I need to see Barbara Gordon."

Larry's mouth fell open.

"You didn't just say that."

"Come on, Dad. There's hardly anything controversial about the library," she pointed out. "At any given time, you'll find a couple girls from my school studying in there. No one will think anything of it if they see me talking to a librarian. Not even the slowest news day could make that interesting."

"Barbara is the one who started this mess by giving you that song," Larry said through gritted teeth. "Why would you go back and invite more trouble into your—*our*—life?"

"Because there's so much I need to know that only she can tell me." Dinah gave her dad a pleading look. "I'm trying to do what you asked and be honest with you . . . but if I'm going to trust you, I need you to trust me, too, and not try to keep me under lock and key."

Larry didn't speak, and Dinah continued, "You said it before yourself, that acting like you have something to hide is the fastest way to prove your guilt. The Court and the Owl Guards are probably banking on the 'mystery singer' to be hiding out at home today. Doing something as mundane and normal as going to the library makes *me* look normal and like less of a suspect."

"Fine," Larry said grudgingly. "But I'm coming with you. I may not be able to keep you inside, but I'm not letting you go *anywhere* alone right now, especially with the city under even stricter martial law since last night."

It wasn't ideal, but at least he wasn't trying to stop her. Before they left, Dinah tried calling Ty again, for what must have been the fifteenth time. The call went straight to voice mail yet again, but right after she hung up, Dinah heard the ping of a text message. It was a group text, from Ty to her and Mandy.

> Sorry, sorry! My phone battery died and then it
> was so late by the time we got home, I passed out.

Crazy night. Out with the family now but let's talk
soon—so glad you're both okay.

Dinah stared at the message, rereading it twice. There
was something about the words that just seemed . . . off.
Crazy night was the way to describe a party where a few too
many drinks were had, not an evening of violent bloodshed
with ten casualties. The Ty she knew would have been just
as shaken up about it as she and Mandy were.

Dinah dropped her phone into her purse without reply-
ing. She would figure out Ty later. But first . . . Barbara
Gordon.

Larry drove Dinah to the Gotham City Public Library in his
cop car, something she would have normally balked at. The
glare of police lights had proven to be a friend-repellant in
the past, especially with the sons and daughters of the Court
spreading their parents' disdain for the GCPD. But today
the bulletproof car was a relief. Through the window she
could see an influx of armed guards on each passing street,
stopping to interrogate every woman or girl who walked by.
Dinah shuddered at the sight.

She and Larry climbed the grand stairway up to the library together, his steps heavy beside hers. As they moved
through the revolving door, Dinah saw a haunted expression
cross his face. It occurred to her then that he must have been
here before, with her mother.

The library was a ghost town inside, not a patron in sight.
Larry turned to give her a pointed look.

"As I predicted. Everyone's staying safe at home after last night. Come on, let's g—"

"Wait!" Dinah gasped at the sight of her. Barbara Gordon was sitting right underneath the CHILDREN'S LITERATURE sign, her body still and her eyes closed, as if she was in the middle of a meditation. But then her eyes snapped open, and she greeted them with a nod that betrayed no hint of surprise. It was as though she'd been expecting them.

Dinah felt a rush of emotion as she ran toward her, knowing now who Barbara really was—and the song she once inspired.

Larry was the first to speak, an awkward grimace on his face. "Barbara. About the other day—"

She put a finger to her lips.

"Not now. We have company up here. . . . Follow me."

Barbara wheeled toward the other end of the children's wing and led the way into a service elevator, swiping her key card for access to the underground level.

"So, I—I'm here because of last night," Dinah began, unsure of how much was safe to say. The elevator gave a sudden lurch before shuddering two stories down, and Larry swore under his breath.

"I know," Barbara said simply. "It's the reason for where I'm taking you."

The elevator doors slid open, and Dinah's jaw dropped.

Instead of a storage space for books, or anything else library-related, they were standing in a room filled with next-generation touchscreen computers and surveillance cameras, all arranged in a semicircle surrounding . . . an actual *fighting ring*. It was the last thing she would have imagined finding down here. And there was someone inside.

Dinah stared at the woman warming up in the ring, dressed in a black leather jacket and pants strikingly similar to her mother's Black Canary costume, but with a crimson bodysuit. A vision of last night flashed through her mind—the image of the Birds of Prey, splashed on the wall in a desperate bid by the Resistance. And that's when it hit Dinah like a lightning bolt. She was looking at another Bird in the flesh.

When she turned around, Dinah's heart nearly flew out of her chest.

"*Sandra?*" she cried, racing toward her. "What are you doing here?"

Sandra Wu-San broke into a rare smile at the sight of her longtime pupil.

"All these years later, you're finally going to meet the real me." She drew herself up to her full height, a flicker of pride in her eyes. "It's been a long time since I've used the name—but here in this ring and in this room, I am Lady Shiva."

"You were one of them," Dinah breathed as the years of training suddenly took on a new, profound meaning. "A superhero . . . like my mom."

The three adults exchanged a look.

"No," Sandra said flatly. "I'm no hero. In fact, when Dinah and Barbara first met me, I was on the opposite side—a hired killer for the League of Assassins, serving Rā's al Ghūl."

"What?" Dinah gaped at her, struggling to process the idea of her mentor as a . . . villain. "But—"

"Rā's helped me avenge my sister's murder, and for that, I would have been loyal forever," Sandra continued. "But then the League was overtaken by the Court of Owls and their Talon army, and the second they moved in, I was out. 'We have no use for a female' were the Court's exact words." She laughed bitterly. "Remember when I told you, Dinah, that I wasn't invincible against the Talons and their electrum? The reason I know that is because they were seconds away from killing me . . . until Batgirl and Black Canary showed up." Her expression twisted at the memory she was clearly loath to remember. "Even among all three of us, we couldn't defeat them—but we did get away. The Birds saved my life." She lifted her chin. "And so I owed them."

"Wait. Did you say Batgirl?"

Sandra and Larry both glanced at Barbara. Dinah stared at her in astonishment as she nodded.

"Yes, that was me. A long time ago, anyway." Barbara fell silent for a moment before continuing, "Your mom had been telling me for months about a Lady Shiva, who was rumored to be the best martial artist in the world. When I heard that she was on the outs with Rā's al Ghūl, I thought we might be able to bring her over to our side. With Lady Shiva on our team, Dinah and I were sure we could be unstoppable. So that was the deal we made: if Sandra joined the Birds of Prey, we would help her take down her enemies in the League of Assassins. And for a time, we were—unstoppable."

"A *very* short time," Larry interjected, glaring at the two of them. Dinah had almost forgotten he was still there. "Please. Let's not romanticize this for my daughter."

Sandra met his gaze head-on.

"You don't need to remind me," she said sharply. "It's one of my great regrets that I arrived too late that night at the clocktower—that I couldn't save her."

Dinah was just starting to feel moved by her words when, in classic Sandra fashion, she quickly pulled back the emotion.

"Not because I was particularly close to your mother," she added, arching an eyebrow. "I won't pretend we had a bond like her and Barbara. We were too different, Dinah with her traditional family life and all those attachments, and me with no interest in any of that."

"So if it wasn't Mom you cared about, then what was it?" Dinah shot back.

"Honoring my debts," Sandra answered. "It's something I take pride in. But I was never able to repay her, and after what happened to Barbara—well, for a long while, it looked like the Birds were done."

"What do you mean?" Dinah looked questioningly at Barbara.

"I wasn't always in this chair," Barbara said simply. "The same year we lost your mother, I tried and failed to stop a shooting between Owl Guards and the Resistance at the top of the Old Wayne Tower. When I got hit, the bullet left me paralyzed from the waist down."

"I . . . I'm so sorry," Dinah whispered. The words felt wholly inadequate.

"It's all right. Really," Barbara said. "I thought the bullet meant the end of my superhero career, but to my immense surprise and relief, I found a new identity—as the one-woman information network. Oracle." She gestured at the tech and spyware around the room, her face lighting with a smile. "I loved every thrilling, dangerous minute of being Batgirl, and I'll continue to miss it. But I've found something just as rewarding now. Maybe even more so."

"Before she died, your mom told us she sensed the Canary power within you—that it showed the potential to be even stronger than her own," Sandra revealed. "So we've been waiting for you to grow up, to see if she was right. To see if you will take on her role as Black Canary."

"And," Barbara added in a low voice, "if you could be the one with the power to bring down the Court."

"*Me?*" Dinah's voice came out in a squeak. She stole a glance at her dad, whose face was frozen in shock.

"It's the reason why Barbara first asked me to train you all those years ago," Sandra explained. "And why I said yes."

"You've settled your debt, then," Dinah said.

"Yes. And I expect it to pay dividends," Sandra quipped.

"Wait just a minute." Larry turned to her with a thunderous expression. "*I* asked you to train her, for the sole purpose of teaching my daughter self-defense, nothing more—"

"After I planted the idea in your mind," Barbara said, raising an eyebrow. "Don't you remember our last conversation?"

"I never would have agreed to it if I'd known this was what you had in mind!"

"Last night proved we were right," Barbara continued, a spark of excitement in her eyes. "And now it's time to escalate your training to the next level, Dinah. Starting with your greatest weapon. Your voice."

"That's it." Larry grabbed Dinah's arm, pulling her toward him. "I brought you here like I said I would, but now it's time for us to go." He directed his fiery gaze at Barbara and Sandra. "This isn't Dinah Drake we're talking about here. This is my seventeen-year-old daughter. I will not see her getting roped into some sort of junior-league Birds of Prey, just as I *won't* let her follow her mother to—"

Dinah wriggled out of his grasp, and as the adults in the room bickered back and forth, they didn't notice Dinah slipping away from them, climbing into the fighting ring. And then she thought of the one way to silence them.

> *"You're the gold standard.*
> *You're a prayer answered,*
> *a living example*
> *of fighting fear with love.*
> *You're the gold standard. . . ."*

Her voice rang out across the room, casting a spell, freezing the three of them in place. Larry gaped at her with equal parts awe and fear, while Sandra's dark eyes grew wide with wonder. But it was Barbara's reaction that Dinah would never forget. Her hand flew to her chest, and she stared at Dinah with silent tears streaming down her cheeks. In that moment, Dinah saw a sudden glimpse of the young woman she used to be—a daughter, a best friend, a Batgirl, with the world at her feet. Barbara was trying to find her way back . . . just like they all were.

Dinah climbed out of the ring and stood before her.

"Mom wrote that for you, didn't she?"

Barbara managed a smile through her tears. "Yes. I was so sure I would never get to hear it sung out loud again."

Dinah turned to her dad, taking his hand. "You saved this song for a reason. You could have thrown the sheet music away, but you didn't—because you knew how important Barbara was to Mom. Which makes her important to me." Dinah took a deep breath. "I'm not leaving. Now that I've found this missing piece of Mom—of *me*—I'm not letting go."

Larry gazed down at her sadly.

"I never wanted this for you, Dinah. It's the whole reason I didn't tell you who your mother really was. Being the Black Canary comes with more danger and risk than you can imagine, and it's not worth the price."

Dinah could feel her heart twisting at her dad's plea. But there was no going back.

"I have to do this, Dad. She gave me this voice—and I'm going to use it."

CHAPTER FOURTEEN

By the time Larry and Dinah turned onto their street, the sun was already setting over Gotham City, adding a splash of neon orange to the gray skyline. Larry hadn't said more than two words since they got in the car, but Dinah barely noticed, her mind too busy replaying the highlights reel from her very first Birds of Prey training. She couldn't hide her smile as she remembered how it felt to spar with Sandra in the ring, to hold a baton just like her mom's and learn how to wield it, and most of all—to *sing*. Dinah still couldn't figure out how her voice could possibly serve as a weapon, but she was grateful for any excuse to practice in the library's soundproofed basement. It was the only place she could sing without fear of being caught.

"You've got to be kidding me."

Dinah glanced up at the sound of her dad's outburst, and her heart jumped. Parked outside the building was an all-too-familiar convertible . . . and seated on the front stoop was none other than Oliver Queen.

"My blood pressure can't take any more surprises, Dinah," Larry grumbled. "What's he doing here?"

"I don't know," Dinah admitted, biting her lip to contain her smile. "But let's not forget, he's the reason Mandy and I made it home safely last night."

"Hmph" was Larry's response to that. "Did he forget how to work a phone?"

Oliver rose to his feet as soon as he saw Larry and Dinah climb out of the car, flashing Dinah a grin that made her stomach flip. His deep green eyes locked on hers, and she could tell, somehow, that he was thinking the same thing as she was. *His lips on my lips, his hands in my hair, on my skin—*

The sound of Larry clearing his throat next to her brought Dinah crashing back down to earth. She could feel her face flushing bright red as they approached the front stoop, and Oliver extended a hand to her dad.

"Detective Lance," he said, looking at Larry with just the right amount of deference. "It's good to meet you. I'm Oliver Queen."

Larry paused and then shook his hand.

"Nice to meet you," he said grudgingly. He glanced from Oliver to Dinah and back again. "Did you and my daughter have plans for tonight I was unaware of?"

"No," Oliver said sheepishly. "I just . . . wanted to talk. Is it okay if I come in?"

Larry narrowed his eyes at Oliver.

"You two stay in the living room. No closed doors. Got it?"

"Dad! So embarrassing!" Dinah groaned, her face turning a distinctly tomato shade of red. But Oliver just laughed.

"Nah. He's looking out for you."

Larry's eyebrows shot up in surprise.

"That's right. Hear that, Dinah?"

He led the way into the apartment, and as they followed, Oliver and Dinah exchanged a smile. The training session had her feeling bold, and Dinah reached for his hand, interlacing her fingers in his behind Larry's back. His smile grew, but then he quickly dropped her hand as Larry turned.

"All right, Dinah, I'll expect you in the kitchen for dinner in an hour." He glanced warily at Oliver. "Are you . . . joining us?"

"No, thank you, Detective," Oliver replied. "I'll be out by then."

Larry nodded and then moved awkwardly toward the hall. "I'll just be . . . in my study. But around."

"Okay, bye, Dad!"

They waited for him to go, and then Dinah ushered Oliver toward the couch, giggling under her breath. As soon as they were alone and she saw him looking at her with that magnetic smile, she couldn't help pulling him toward her. His hands snaked around her waist, and she could feel his heart beating against hers as he leaned down for a kiss.

"Hi," he murmured.

"Hi," she whispered back. "This is . . . a surprise."

She wasn't just talking about his unexpected visit, but about him. The two of them. And the way he was looking at her right now, she could tell he understood.

"I need to talk to you about something," he said quietly, drawing her toward the couch.

"Okay." She sat down, a nervous flutter in her stomach. Were they going to have the whole DTR talk—"define the relationship"—that she'd heard so much about since starting high school? Was it too soon? Did she *want* to put a label on it? She felt her lips lift into a dreamy smile as her thoughts began to swirl with the possibility of being Oliver Queen's girlfriend, with all the joy—and danger—it might bring her—

"It's about Cobblepot. I saw Zed today, and he said . . . well, he said he's never seen his dad more furious in his life. Which is an unsettling thought." Oliver swallowed hard. "The Owls are planning to declare war on anyone who 'fails to conform to the rules of the Court.' And you can probably guess who they consider enemy number one at this point."

Dinah shifted uncomfortably in her seat. So much for the dating conversation. She did her best to push it out of her head and ventured forward carefully.

"I've seen the headlines, the reward money being offered. But . . . the Cobblepots don't suspect anyone, do they?" Dinah was still careful not to admit out loud that she was the mystery singer everyone was searching for. There was always the possibility that Oliver wasn't completely sure. She decided to play coy.

Oliver gave her hand a reassuring squeeze.

"No, I haven't heard any names come up. But you're going to have to be more careful than you've ever been. As much as I loved that voice . . ." He smiled grimly. "We can't have a repeat performance." He caught her eye meaningfully. Yeah—there was no doubt he knew. She gulped and hoped that she could trust him to keep her secret safe.

"I know. My dad already gave me the whole talk about keeping a low profile." She scooted closer to him, so ready to be done with this buzzkill of a conversation. "Was that what you wanted to talk to me about?"

"That, and one more thing." Oliver paused. Dinah could feel herself growing warm with anticipation again.

"Zed also told me the mayor's gotten it in his head that the existence of a female singer could be tied to a possible return of the superheroes. Like . . . maybe they weren't all destroyed in the last war."

Oh, come on! It took every fiber of her being not to roll her eyes in frustration. She let her body go still as a statue.

"I don't know anything about that."

Oliver peered closer at her, and she forced herself to meet his eyes.

"Are you sure?" Oliver asked, his head tilted.

"Yes," she lied. She breathed in deeply and looked away from Oliver's imploring face. "I can somehow sing, but that's it. There's nothing more to it."

She couldn't explain, even to herself, why she was lying. Oliver already knew her most dangerous secret—what was the harm in telling him the rest? Especially considering the fact that he was someone she trusted—at least, enough to make out with him. But something about his line of questioning, and the curiosity in his eyes, made her uneasy.

"My turn to ask a question." Dinah shifted on the couch to face him. "When you were spending all this time with Zed Cobblepot today, did you happen to tell him about . . . this?" She gestured to the two of them.

Oliver didn't answer. Dinah could feel her face turning hot as her old suspicions about Oliver Queen came crashing back.

"I mean, he obviously knows I . . . I like you." Oliver's face smoothed into a smile. "I wouldn't have asked you to the ball otherwise. The only thing I didn't tell him is that we might be—a thing."

"Okay. So if we *are* maybe a thing, do you still plan to hang out with the people who would like oh-so-much to have me killed?" Dinah folded her arms across her chest and internally cursed herself. This is *not* how she envisioned having the "are-we-or-aren't-we" conversation, but she couldn't stop herself. She knew she might be coming off a bit aggressive here, but she had to know if she could trust him. And his mixed signals certainly weren't helping things. She felt her eyebrows draw together as her frustration bubbled to the surface.

Oliver looked taken aback.

"Well, I mean . . . if I suddenly cut them off, won't that make it obvious we—you—have something to hide?" *So we aren't a we?*

"Not necessarily! You could be cutting Zed off for simply being an ass to me from the beginning." *If he chooses the Cobblepots over me . . .*

Oliver raked a hand through his hair, his expression torn.

"I get where you're coming from, Dinah, I do. But trust me, there's nothing good that will come out of me making enemies of the Cobblepots. It's better for both of us that I keep them close."

"How do I know you're not saying something similar to them?" Dinah jumped up from the couch, about to raise her voice, and had to remind herself to keep it down—the last thing she needed was for Larry to come barreling in to protect her. "What if you're suckering me in and keeping me close so you can get information for *them*—"

Oliver sprang up to join her, an indignant look on his face. He held her shoulders and looked into her eyes.

"You really think that of me, after last night?"

"I don't know." Dinah bristled. She knew she wasn't being fair. She didn't want her mistrust to get in the way of her developing feelings for Oliver, but she had to be careful. He was set to become well integrated into the Court—and the Court had made her an enemy. She had to be strategic.

She paused before she responded. "I don't want to think it. I just . . . don't see how you can like me for real and also be able to stomach the Cobblepots."

He shook his head. "It's hard to explain."

"Well, try," Dinah urged. She *had* to understand where he was coming from, why he insisted on maintaining a good face with the Court. But he just stood there, gazing at her as if he could convey the truth only through his eyes. And then he dropped his arms and took her hand, his shoulders stooped. He leaned in and gently kissed her cheek. It was the wrong kind of kiss, a resigned goodbye instead of the giddy passion of earlier.

"I'll see you tomorrow, Dinah."

She watched him go, tears pricking at the back of her eyes. He was hiding something, and she wasn't going to be made a fool of. She was going to get the truth out of him—no matter what it took.

The first morning back at school after the Bloody Ball had Dinah shaky with nerves, preparing for the acting performance of a lifetime. It took three tries for her to button her school blouse with trembling fingers, and she could barely swallow a bite of breakfast. How in the world was she supposed to get through the day without giving herself away?

Larry kept eyeing her nervously as he drove toward Gotham City High, where the Owl Guards lining the streets seemed to multiply the closer they got to school.

"Are you sure you don't want to call in sick today?"

"You know I can't," Dinah said, dabbing her cheeks with blotting papers to try to hide her nerves-induced sweat. "I can't give anyone a reason to wonder about me."

Larry didn't respond, and she could guess what he was thinking. If she continued acting this jittery, she'd be giving them reason indeed.

"Don't worry," Dinah said as Larry paused the car in front of the main entrance. She leaned over to give him a hug. "I'll be fine. I'm sure everything will feel a lot more normal once we're all in class."

"Good luck," he called after her, his forehead creased with worry.

Dinah held her breath as she climbed the steps, where cloaked Owl Guards loomed in wait on the top stair. She tried to smooth her expression into a poker face, but her heart was hammering with every step, beating out the truth no one was supposed to hear. *I'm the one you're looking for.* And as the Owl Guards sharpened their eyes in her direction, Dinah said a silent prayer for no one to sense her nerves, to guess her secret.

One of the Owl Guards lifted his long, spindly arm and pulled the backpack from her shoulders.

"All bags and belongings will be checked from this point on," he announced.

Dinah nodded, not trusting herself to speak. Thankfully her mother's sheet music was tucked under her mattress at home, so there was nothing for the guards to find but the usual textbooks and class binders.

The guard tossed her backpack at her with a nod, and Dinah hurried past them and through the double doors to school, relief filling her lungs. *One hurdle down.*

She glanced up at the clock in the main hall. There was just enough time before class for her to stop by Ty's locker. And when she saw him there, digging out his homework from under an avalanche of books and discarded projects in his locker, she felt a wave of fondness for her friend.

"Hey, stranger."

Ty jumped at the sound of her.

"Jeez, Dinah! I didn't see you there."

"Sorry," she chuckled. But her smile faded at the sound of marching footsteps: another pair of Owl Guards bursting through the double doors, guns at their sides as they stalked the hall, their eyes surveying each student they passed. Dinah and Ty exchanged an uneasy glance.

"This is crazy," Dinah whispered when they were no longer within earshot. "Can you believe all this?"

"No." Ty slammed his locker door shut. "But I guess it's to be expected, after the bloodbath the other night."

"How come you never called us back after that?" Dinah pressed as they started walking.

"What do you mean? I texted back in the morning."

"Mandy and I both called you like a hundred times," she reminded him. "A weirdly casual text wasn't really the right response." *Why is he being so shady?*

"Sorry," he mumbled. "My parents have been . . . let's just say more overprotective than usual. They barely let me out of their sight yesterday, to the point where I thought I might not even be able to come to school. So I didn't have much freedom for phone calls."

Well, that made sense. If Meg Carver had been a helicopter parent before, the Bloody Ball would make for an easy excuse to tighten the reins that much more.

"That sucks," she said, putting a sympathetic arm around him. "You must be glad to get away, even if it's just here."

"Yeah, tell me about it." He glanced at her and lowered his voice. "I've been thinking of you so much, though—especially after the *singer.*"

Dinah froze. "What do you mean? Why would that make you think of me?"

Ty gave her a funny look.

"Uh, isn't it what you've always wanted your whole life? To be able to sing? And another female just *did it!*"

"Right." Dinah nodded, trying to fix an appropriately wide-eyed expression onto her face. "It's unbelievable, isn't it?"

"I can't stop wondering who it was," Ty continued as they made their way down the hall. "Any guesses?"

It felt so wrong to lie to him. *But I have no choice*, Dinah reminded herself. If Ty ever accidentally let her secret slip to his uptight parents . . .

"I wish I knew," she sighed. "Whoever it is, they're lucky."

"No," Ty said grimly. "Whoever it is . . . she'll be dead as soon as they catch her."

Dinah could feel Oliver's eyes on her the moment she stepped through the door to history class. She slid into her seat in front of him, determined to avoid his gaze—but of course she slipped, glancing at him out of the corner of her eye about three seconds before sitting down.

I'm sorry, he mouthed.

Dinah's stomach did another involuntary flip at the sight. His green eyes were so intent on hers, his eyebrows knitted together in concern, that it seemed impossible for him to be toying with her the way she'd suspected he might be last night. But . . . what was he sorry for, exactly? Had he realized his mistake in trying to have it both ways, dating her while staying put in the Cobblepots' inner circle? Or was he sorry that he couldn't cut them off, and that it would never work between him and Dinah? She dropped her eyes back to her desk.

"Good morning, class." Mrs. Pritchard sounded like a deflated balloon, drained of her usual hyperperky energy. Her face looked shaken as she surveyed the students. "This . . . was not the Monday morning I had planned. We were supposed to spend our first hour recapping the highlights of the ball, but instead, I'm afraid we must discuss a deeply serious subject instead." Her eyes narrowed. "Treason."

Dinah held her breath as the teacher's gaze swept the room. *She has no clue. There's no way she's talking about me.* But whether it was paranoia or something more, Dinah could have sworn Mrs. Pritchard eyed her a second longer than everyone else.

"The Court of Owls took a wayward city and a floundering generation, and turned us into a righteous, prosperous people of proper values," the teacher said crisply. "To go against them in *any* way is an unforgiveable act. Which is why the ten people who sabotaged the ball lost their lives."

Dinah's hands clenched into fists beneath her desk. She always knew Mrs. Pritchard was brainwashed, but this was yet another low.

"We also witnessed something that can only be attributed to a form of witchcraft. I am talking, of course, about the female voice you heard singing. The voice that contributed to such chaos."

A storm was going on inside her, but Dinah didn't move, didn't blink.

"Gotham City High has agreed to cooperate fully with the Court's search for the mystery singer—which means all of our female students will be examined by both the doctor on staff and the choir teacher, with the Owl Guards present."

Dinah felt the ground falling beneath her. She gripped the edges of her seat, struggling to breathe through her panic. *What kind of examination?* Would she survive it? What if there *was* something visible that marked her as the one? Ty's words echoed in her mind. *She'll be dead as soon as they catch her.* She had to think fast. Could she sneak away? Stage a distraction? How could they force her to sing?

Dinah heard a sharp intake of breath and turned to see Oliver leaning forward in his seat, his jaw clenched, green eyes darkening with fear. And in that one look, she saw just how much he cared. Something tightened in her chest as Dinah realized she might have been in the wrong last night.

She would talk to him, try to pick up where they left off before the argument. *If* she survived the examination.

CHAPTER FIFTEEN

It happened on their lunch break.

Dinah was just setting her tray down across from Mandy and Ty, finally able to exhale after three tension-fueled classes, when the dreaded footsteps came marching toward the cafeteria. Dinah's drink slipped from her grasp, crushed ice and water tumbling to the floor, as the Owl Guards entered. The boys' choir teacher, Mr. Ward, and the school district's medical chief, Dr. Vaughn, followed close behind, both of them walking with an almost comical dose of swagger. These two, unaccustomed to being the key players in any room, were clearly relishing their moment in the spotlight. If Dinah hadn't been so terrified for herself, she would have had a good laugh over the ridiculousness of it all with Mandy and Ty. But instead, she sat frozen.

"Girls, we'll be calling you in for your examinations in groups according to your last name," Mr. Ward announced. "If your last name begins with the letter *A* through *G*, you're up first. Please follow us through these doors to the auditorium."

A quarter of the girls in the cafeteria slid out of their seats, and Mandy and Dinah exchanged a nervous glance.

"Well. This is going to be weird," Mandy said under her breath. "What kind of exam can determine whether or not you can sing, anyway?"

"Maybe the person they're looking for has, like, a bulging vocal cord," Ty guessed. "Or maybe they'll try to *trick* the person into singing."

"Hold on, guys." Mandy's voice switched to a conspiratorial whisper. "I see Oliver Queen coming this way, probably to sweet-talk our very own Dinah Lance, in three . . . two . . ."

Dinah twisted in her seat, smiling in spite of herself. *He wants to make it right between us, too.* But then—

"O-*kaaay*. Never mind, then," Mandy said as Oliver brushed right past them, dumping his lunch tray and moving quickly for the door. Dinah felt the foolish smile slip from her face. There was no way he hadn't seen her there, looking at him.

"Trouble in paradise already?" Ty asked through a mouthful of food.

"We never got to paradise," Dinah muttered back.

"But you guys were so cute the other night—" Mandy started protesting, until Dinah gave her a Look.

Twenty minutes later the *A–G* girls reentered, and Dinah felt the cold pit of fear return to her stomach. Her legs were already wobbly under the table, and she wondered if she would give herself away as soon as she stood up.

"Surnames beginning with *H* through *L*, please!" Dr. Vaughn called out. Dinah and Mandy glanced at each other.

"Well. At least we're up together," Dinah said, making an effort to sound unruffled.

"Good luck!" Ty called out, blissfully unaware of how much Dinah would need it.

She stood up, taking a deep breath. Mandy looped her arm in Dinah's, and as the two followed the other girls in their surname category to the cafeteria doors, she caught the look on the doctor's face—the pompous, puffed-up pride of a man being given authority to examine dozens of girls' bodies today. And suddenly, Dinah's fear disappeared, replaced with a crackling rage. She lifted her chin as they walked down the hall to the auditorium. What she would give to wipe the smirks off *all* of these men's faces, to show them that not only could she sing, but she could also clinch them in a choke hold, throw them against the floor—

"Line up in a row, please."

Dinah and Mandy stood together at the end of the line, watching as the doctor and the music teacher studied each girl one by one, with the Owl Guards closely surveying the scene. The girl with the misfortune of being first in line was sweet, quiet Lindsey Hinton, and Dinah felt bile rising in her throat at the sight of Dr. Vaughn reaching his bare hands under the collar of her shirt, feeling her chest bone and clavicle, his fingers climbing up her throat. *I could stop this,* Dinah thought desperately as mortified tears sprang to Lindsey's eyes.

"Open wide," Dr. Vaughn ordered, holding a rounded wooden stick up to her mouth. Dinah cringed as the doctor held down her tongue with the stick, peering into the back of her throat with a flashlight.

Standing beside them, the choirmaster played a note on his pitch pipe. "Lindsey, I'd like you to copy this note exactly. There is no need to be afraid—if you can do it, you will be rewarded."

Dinah and Mandy exchanged an incredulous look. Did he think they were all complete idiots? But Lindsey had nothing to hide. Her attempt at singing the note came out like a half yell, half croak, and Mr. Ward laughed snidely. "Well, we certainly know it wasn't you!"

As the men continued down the line, Dinah's mind was racing a hundred miles a minute, trying to figure out a way to stop these disgusting exams without getting herself killed in the process. The Black Canary wouldn't stand for this—and she couldn't, either.

This was her fault. Her power. She couldn't let the other girls pay the price. She had to do the right thing . . . even if that happened to be the scary thing.

She stepped forward out of the line. Mandy yanked her sleeve, pulling her back with a hissed "What are you *doing?*" And Dinah had a flash of fear—of what would happen to her, and to her friends, her *dad*—after she was found out. Was there more that she could do in secret as the Black Canary, rather than giving herself up now?

But what if someone else were to somehow take the fall? She could never let that happen, either.

Dinah moved forward again, clearing her throat. Opened her mouth, felt the air fill her lungs. She could feel the music on its way, her voice readying for the rush of sound. There was a murmur among the line of girls, and then the Owl Guards, the choirmaster, and the doctor all turned away from the pupil they were examining, their attention shifting to Dinah. Until a scream filled the room.

The arrow appeared with no warning, materializing in the air and flying in a perfect arc. Dinah stared, her mouth hanging open—until she realized it was coming straight toward her.

Mandy grabbed her hand and the two scrambled back behind the drum kit, but not before the arrow grazed Dinah's shoulder. Then came the swish of another flying arrow, this one landing with a *smack* right in the center of Dr. Vaughn's throat—the same part of the girls' bodies he'd been so freely "examining."

The auditorium devolved into chaos as the arrows soared one after another, snaring the choirmaster by the leg, snagging the backs of the girls' blouses as they ran. The Owl Guards spun into a rage, searching for the invisible archer as arrows rained down from overhead, missing them by less than an inch. For the briefest of moments, all of them—male and female alike—were dodging the same threat. Until the bell rang.

The arrows scattered across the floor. The sound of running footsteps echoed on the other side of the wall, and the Owl Guards swept out the door in pursuit.

"Go on," the choirmaster told the girls, his voice shaking as he waved them toward the exit. "Just go!"

Mandy seized Dinah's hand as all the girls from *H* to *L* took off running from the room.

It was only when they were in the relative safety of the locker hall, gasping for breath, that Dinah realized . . . those arrows had just saved her life.

The students were trapped in their next class, unable to escape for so much as a bathroom break, while the Owl Guards combed the school for evidence. It wasn't just the mystery singer they were hunting now, but the anonymous archer, too.

Dinah kept her head down, heart hammering in her chest, as classmates whispered their theories of who the "secret rebels" could be. It felt like the truth was written across her forehead in neon letters, but thankfully, no one was paying attention to her. The names she heard murmured between the desks were girls who had already proven to be, in some way, exceptional. Girls like Alanna Rodriguez, who had the highest test scores of anyone in school and was rumored to be a genius; and recent graduate Rose Liu, who was brave enough to unsuccessfully petition the school board last year for females to be allowed to play sports. And though it was a relief to know her identity was safe, Dinah's stomach churned at the possibility of someone else paying the price for her actions. It was something she could never let happen . . . which meant the clock was ticking on her secret.

Of all classes for them to be stuck in for an indefinite stretch, it *had* to be home ec. Dinah's fingers kept slipping as she returned to the dreary cross-stitching project, where each student had been assigned a different virtuous slogan to sew. Dinah's was "Honor thy elders," though she was tempted to correct the statement with what she knew her teacher really meant. "*Male, straight, upper-class* elders."

When the bell rang for the day, the teacher didn't move. The door remained locked, and Dinah swallowed hard. They weren't going anywhere—not until the Owl Guards got what they wanted.

One hour dragged into another, with Dinah finally making it past the word *Honor* in her cross-stitch when they heard the furious rap at the door. She dropped her sewing needle as the teacher, Mrs. Loewe, sprang into action, rushing to let the Owl Guards in. •

Their stone-faced expressions let Dinah know they

hadn't found what they were looking for. The first-in-command strode to the front of the room, his gaze darkening as it swept across the all-female class.

"We've just been informed that Mayor Cobblepot has signed a new decree, in response to the incendiary actions of the Resistance—both at the ball and here today at this school." His eyes narrowed. "Effective tomorrow, all female students will be barred from attending school. Gotham City High will transition to a males-only learning institute."

Dinah recoiled in her seat. He wasn't serious—*couldn't* be serious. Gotham City High was the furthest thing from perfect, but still, it was all they had. It was their last reprieve before submitting to a future that held no options, their final tie to the past generations of girls who were given the chance to learn and become something. And now the mayor was taking all that away . . . because of her voice?

"This could change, however, *if* the individual we are seeking turns herself in," the guard continued, surveying the room. Dinah held her breath. "Once we're certain we've cleansed this school of destructive influences, Mayor Cobblepot has indicated he would be inclined to allow female students back in. Until then . . ." He gestured to the door.

The rest of the class looked as stunned as Dinah felt. Mrs. Loewe's voice wavered as she thanked the guards and then turned to face her students—for possibly the last time.

"All right, class. I'm afraid this is goodbye. Please pack up your things from your desks and lockers."

It was like a fog fell over the room. The students moved in slow motion, gathering their sewing materials and emptying their desks. And then they filed out the door in silence, numb with disbelief.

The guards were still at their posts outside the school entrance when the now ex-students came flooding through the double doors. There could be no commiserating among them, no railing against their lives being upended this way—not as long as the Owl Guards were watching. All the girls could do was make their final walk down the front steps with as much dignity as they could muster.

When she reached the bottom stair, Dinah heard a familiar voice behind her. It was Mandy, coming from the second home ec class that had let out just minutes after Dinah's. Her face was stricken as she grabbed Dinah's hand.

"How can they do this?" she whispered.

Dinah lifted her shoulders helplessly.

"The same way they've done everything else."

A trio of school buses lined the driveway, waiting to deliver the girls home for good. Living a twenty-minute walk away from school meant that Dinah rarely had to take public transport, but as she remembered what today was, she changed direction, heading toward the bus bound for Old Gotham.

"Where are you going?" Mandy asked under her breath.

"The library," Dinah replied, and Mandy's eyes lit with curiosity. She was still unaware of the true significance of Barbara Gordon and was clearly wondering what the rush was for Dinah to see her now. "I'll tell you more later," Dinah promised, giving her friend a quick hug before stepping up onto the bus.

"Declare your destination," the driver ordered while she handed over her fare. And as she answered, the realization hit her: this could very well be her last time accessing the library. After all, if girls were now barred from attending school . . . the library could easily be next.

Dinah swallowed the nauseating thought and slumped into the first available seat. One conclusion was becoming clearer in her mind with every ticking minute.

The mayor and the Court had to be stopped. And she was willing to do whatever it took, using every resource and bit of power at her disposal, to make it happen.

CHAPTER SIXTEEN

In the dim light of the library basement, Barbara and Sandra listened, thunderstruck, as Dinah told them everything. By the time she'd finished with the dark recap, Sandra looked like she wanted to take her fury out on the furniture, while Barbara had to turn away, muttering a string of expletives.

"Every time I think they can't get any worse . . ." Barbara shook her head in disgust.

"I have to do something," Dinah said, even as a shiver of fear accompanied her words. "I can't let the Court keep punishing every girl in Gotham City, when it's only me they're looking for."

Sandra and Barbara exchanged a knowing glance.

"Your intentions are honorable," Barbara said carefully. "But revealing yourself won't stop the Court from their despicable crimes—it will simply change their target to you, and those closest to you." She gave Dinah a meaningful look, and Dinah gulped as she realized just who Barbara meant. *Dad.* And Mandy, Ty . . . *Oliver.*

"What am I supposed to do, then?" Dinah exhaled in frustration.

"We can still use the tools in your arsenal to fight back," Sandra said slowly. "*Without* exposing your identity."

Dinah nodded, goose bumps prickling across her skin at the change in Sandra's tone. In all their years of training, this was the first time she had ever alluded to them actually preparing for something real.

"What about the archer?" Dinah asked. "Do you have any idea who it could have been? Because part of me is wondering . . . well, was there ever a superhero who used arrows?" Her heartbeat sped up at the thought of another superhero from the past, returning to help them, but Sandra shook her head.

"I've never heard of one, and I had to keep close tabs on all superheroes back when I was in the League of Assassins," she said. "What you're describing was probably just a skilled hobbyist, who—in your case, at least—happened to be in the right place at the right time."

"Yeah. Maybe," Dinah said. But at the memory of the arrows, flying so expertly toward their targets, it was hard to imagine the archer being anything other than a professional.

"It might have been someone from the Resistance," Barbara said. "I thought I knew all the core members, but perhaps there's been a new addition—or someone who's discovered a new talent." She wheeled up to the ring. "All right, you two. Let's get started."

Dinah nodded, her pulse racing in anticipation. She climbed up the side of the ring and jumped over the edge, landing on her feet in front of Sandra, who quickly unleashed her kusarigama weaponry. While Dinah threw out jabs and kicks, Sandra swung the weighted chain in a circle above her head, before whipping it forward to ensnare Dinah by the legs. But just as the kusarigama made contact with her foot, Dinah leaped into a back handspring, freeing herself from its grip in the nick of time.

Dinah and Sandra continued to exchange punches and swipes and kicks until both were covered in sweat and nearly out of breath.

"Nice, Dinah," Barbara called from the corner of the ring where she'd been watching carefully for the last hour or so. "Now, this time I want you to try something else."

Dinah watched as Barbara and Sandra exchanged a nod, and then Barbara wheeled closer.

"This might sound like a strange request," she began, "but it will be your most powerful weapon by far once you learn how to use it." She paused. "The next time Lady Shiva goes on the attack, I want you to fight back using only . . . your voice."

Dinah stared at Barbara, certain she'd misheard.

"Uh. *What* was that?"

"The same power that allows you to sing gives you the power to do something else entirely with your voice. Something verging on deadly." There was an almost hungry look in Sandra's eyes as she described it. "Whenever your mom managed to pull out this trick, she *demolished* her opponent."

"We called it her Canary Cry," Barbara said softly. "You've inherited so much of your mother's . . . I have to believe you've inherited this, too."

"Canary Cry," Dinah echoed. "So what exactly is it? How would I do it?"

"Well, that's the rub," Barbara said. "We . . . don't know how. It was just something that came flooding out of her lungs, like that beautiful voice you two share—only with the Canary Cry, it was a scream. The kind of scream that can break bones and melt metal."

"Um . . ." Dinah side-eyed the two of them, wondering if this was the hazing portion of Birds of Prey training. Was she really supposed to believe that her mom took down enemies with just a *scream*? They had to be messing with her. But Sandra wasn't exactly known for her sense of humor, and from what she knew so far of Barbara, neither was she. As the two looked back at her with dead-serious expressions, Dinah realized they actually meant what they were saying. She would have to try.

She moved uncertainly back into the center of the ring. Sandra lunged toward her, starting with a series of leg kicks, then an uppercut to the jaw. And Dinah just stood there, trying to gather some mysterious force within her for a mythical scream that she wasn't even sure existed. Of course, nothing came out.

"Come on, Dinah!" Barbara shouted. "Let's see some fight in you!"

Dinah bristled at that. If she hadn't already proved how much fight there was in her—

"Go on, try it," Sandra called from the other end of the ring. "Scream like your life depends on it—like Mayor Cobblepot and those guards from today are right where I'm standing, and you have a chance to knock them out with your loudest, most powerful cry."

Dinah took a deep breath and bent down, hands on her knees. And then she lifted her head, narrowing her eyes and picturing those snakes in Sandra's place.

"*ARGHHHH!*"

Well, it was a lot more impressive in her head. Barbara and Sandra didn't even flinch.

"Okay," Barbara said delicately. "That was a reasonable first try. How about for the next one, though, let's try a little less 'Halloween ghoul' and more, you know—killing your enemies with a powerful scream?"

Dinah slumped back against the wall of the ring.

"I just don't . . . feel it." And as she said the words, she felt a twinge of worry. What if this was proof that she *wasn't* following in her mother's footsteps after all? What if she had the voice, but not the power?

"Maybe you just need a little vocal warm-up," Barbara suggested. "Why don't you start by singing a few bars of something high-energy, get your vocal cords ready before transitioning into the scream?"

"Uh. Okay."

Dinah straightened her stance, took a deep breath. And then, as she opened her mouth to sing, she felt something electric start coursing through her, followed by the flutters of excitement when her voice soared out into the air.

"Hey, ladies, coming out the other side,
now we know just what it takes to survive.
One day soon our winning bells are going to ring.
Play them loud when the Black Canary sings."

"Now!" Barbara called.

Dinah clenched her hands into fists, squeezed her eyes shut.

"AHHHH—"

She gasped as the room around her began to *move* with her scream, tilting on its axis. Barbara and Sandra faded to fuzzy background figures as her vision blurred, and then the scene before her turned black. She couldn't see, couldn't feel—the only sense she had left in this moment was her hearing. And it had never been stronger.

As the scream continued to echo through the space, a new cacophony of sounds filled her ears, sounds that went far beyond this basement. She could hear the crisp voice of a library patron upstairs, the slam of a car door outside, the laughter of children on the elementary school playground across the street. But even more astounding were the conversations—dozens of them, playing in her ears at different hums and pitches. She squinted, trying to differentiate them, honing in on different snippets.

"For the millionth time, Cassidy, quit picking on your sister!"

"The client call was postponed to Tuesday. Timing is tight, but we'll make it work—"

"Where are you headed, miss? This isn't your usual stop."

"I'm looking for a book on electrum."

She took a gulp of air, quieting the voice that she hadn't even realized was still echoing from her lungs. And with the quiet, the world shifted back into place. The dizzying array of sounds faded to stillness; her vision cleared. She sank to her knees on the mat and found Barbara and Sandra staring intently at her.

"I did it—didn't I?" Dinah managed a weak smile.

To her surprise, Sandra shook her head.

"No, that wasn't the Canary Cry . . . but something else clearly happened. It was almost like you . . . *went* somewhere."

"That's how it felt," Dinah whispered. And as she recounted what she had heard in those surreal moments, Barbara darted behind one of the computers on her desk, rewinding the library security footage.

"I'm looking for a book on electrum."

There it was, just as she'd heard it. The three stared at each other in astonishment.

"How is it possible?" Sandra asked, turning to Barbara for answers. "This basement is soundproofed and too isolated to hear anything from upstairs, so how on planet Earth could Dinah have detected *exactly* what that random person was saying three floors above us?"

"It must be another power derived from her sonic vibrations," Barbara said, gazing up at Dinah reverently. "A power not even the original Black Canary knew about."

"Whoa." Dinah's hands shook as she held them up to her face—hands that seemed somehow alien now, along with every other part of her. But before she could ask another one of the endless questions racing through her brain, their conversation was cut short by an alarm's high-pitched wail. Beams of red light flashed a warning from Barbara's array of computers, and she wheeled quickly up to the nearest screen. Sandra darted over to look with her.

"Robinson Park again?" she asked Barbara under her breath.

"What?" Dinah stared at the two of them. "What about Robinson Park?"

But they were too fixated on the screen to answer her. Dinah jumped out of the ring and squeezed between them in front of the computer. And as she followed their gaze, she drew in a sharp breath.

They were watching a live camera feed of the *opera house*. It looked just as it had when Dinah tried entering weeks ago—a decaying, abandoned relic that still somehow retained hints of its old beauty.

"How did you—*why* would you set up a hidden camera over there?" she asked Barbara. The answer came to her almost as soon as she'd spoken the words. "It's about the vault, isn't it? The Vault of Voices supposedly hidden inside?"

Barbara and Sandra both looked up sharply.

"You really are your mother's daughter," Barbara said, eyeing her closely. "Nothing could get past her, either."

"So is it true? Or just one of the old Gotham City myths?"

"That's what both sides are trying to find out, isn't it?" Sandra said, lifting her shoulders.

"There's a theory that someone working for Cobblepot, who was actually an undercover Resistance agent, preserved and stored something related to the stolen voices in a vault," Barbara explained. "Something that could potentially help return those voices to their owners . . . and negate Cobblepot's Silencing gas."

Dinah's mind swirled, trying to make sense of this revelation, as Barbara continued, "So just as the Court is desperate to prove the rumor false, the Resistance has the deepest reasons for believing in it."

"What do you mean?"

Sandra and Barbara exchanged another one of their inside glances.

"You haven't figured out who the leaders of the Resistance are yet, have you?" Sandra asked.

"They're the people among us who bravely oppose the Court, without regard to consequence," Dinah said, looking at Sandra in confusion.

"That's just the textbook definition," Barbara spoke up. "Think. Who has the most reason to fight back, and the least to lose?"

Dinah looked from the two of them to the opera house on-screen—and then it hit her with a jolt.

"It's the *singers*," she whispered. "Of course. Like the women whose pictures hung on my wall, who lived for their music. It's *them*, isn't it? They're in charge of the Resistance."

"Yes," Barbara said. "It's them."

Dinah felt a swell of emotion like a tidal wave about to break loose. She had only known what it was like to sing for a matter of days, but even with that short amount of experience, she couldn't fathom the pain of waking up to learn she'd lost her voice. And that's what these women had to contend with, along with so many other injustices, every single day.

"You're trying to find the vault, too, aren't you?" Dinah asked hopefully.

"And to make sure the wrong people don't," Barbara replied. She stiffened as a rustling sound echoed through the computer speakers. "Someone's coming."

Dinah leaned forward—and as the hazy figures on-screen came into focus, her heart nearly fell into her stomach.

Oliver Queen and Zed Cobblepot crept into the frame, moving deliberately toward the opera house. Dinah's mind struggled to process what she was seeing as the two ducked under the police tape and marched up to the door. Barbara zoomed in on the live footage as the boys attempted to break off the rusted lock.

"Doesn't look like anything special." Oliver's voice crackled faintly through the speakers, and a fist pressed into Dinah's chest. He peered through the first-story window. "I still don't see why we're bothering with this."

"I told you. If we—*I*—find the vault, Dad said he'd finally have the confidence to name me successor in his will. Is that not a good enough reason for you?" There was a sharpness to Zed's voice, and yet he sounded younger than Dinah was used to—like a lost boy desperate for approval.

"I'm pretty sure he was being facetious," Oliver said drily. "I mean, how are you supposed to find something that doesn't exist?"

"Stop with the big words and just help me, okay, dude? It's not like you have something that much better to do." He paused. "Oh wait, sorry—am I keeping you from another hot date with Dinah Lance?" Zed snorted with laughter, and to Dinah's disbelief, she heard Oliver laughing, too. Her cheeks burned and a sickening sensation roiled in her stomach as the awful truth dawned. He'd been playing her this whole time. *Lying* to her. He'd never wanted to date her after all—it was just a sick joke to provide entertainment for the children of the Court. She wanted to vomit.

Barbara squeezed her arm in empathy, but the gesture only made Dinah feel worse. Now there could be no deluding herself that she'd heard wrong or misunderstood. Her humiliation was that much more real now that someone else had acknowledged it.

"You'd better hurry up and finish that whole Dinah experiment already," Zed added as they started picking the lock. "Maya told me today that Natasha is, in her words, 'done with Thom and wants to get a piece of Queen.' Didn't you say she was the hottest chick in Gotham City?" He gave Oliver a crude smile, and Dinah flinched as though she'd been slapped. "Hey, the lock is moving."

Zed turned the doorknob, and suddenly Dinah wasn't thinking about Oliver or anything else except *what was inside* the opera house. But just as they were about to enter,

Barbara pressed a command on her computer. A deafening *bang* shot through the night, with curling smoke following the sound. Oliver and Zed both jumped.

"What the hell was that?" Zed yelled above the noise.

Oliver stepped through the smoke, scanning the weeds fronting the opera house.

"Looks like . . . firecrackers. Someone else is out here."

"Firecrackers?" Zed scoffed. "Pathetic. C'mon, let's go in."

"Let's see if you call this pathetic," Barbara muttered, pressing the command again and sending another burst of sound and smoke exploding between the two boys. This time, the firecracker landed close enough to knock Zed off his feet. He swore loudly as he hit the dirt, and Sandra laughed at the sight.

"More," Dinah urged through gritted teeth. "Chase those jackasses out of there."

"Happy to." Barbara's fingers moved in rapid fire, detonating one firecracker after another with a tap of the keys. The explosives erupted on all sides of Oliver and Zed, just missing the opera house itself. And as Oliver's laugh from before echoed in her ears, the sound twisting her insides, Dinah had the fleeting urge to see him get hit. Until she remembered.

"The Talons." She stared at Barbara. "This is going to summon them."

"They're already here." Barbara tapped the corner of the screen, where gathering shadows were beginning to form. "Anyone with the last name Cobblepot doesn't need to fear them, of course—but triggering a Talon appearance should be enough to deter these boys from returning to the opera house anytime soon."

"But what about you? If the Talons find out—"

"They won't trace any of this back to me," Barbara said calmly. "The Oracle always covers her tracks."

Back on-screen, Oliver and Zed were dodging one mini explosion after another, covering their ears from the piercing sound while coughing in the smoke. And then the shadows in the background started to grow, taking shape as they moved to the center of the screen. She heard Oliver's surprised yell, and then a grotesque new face filled the frame. One with a jagged beak for a nose and a dark hood shading his yellow eyes.

"Come on!" Oliver yanked Zed's elbow and pulled him toward the park gates. "This is Talon territory, and we're clearly not supposed to be here. Let's go!"

For once, Zed didn't argue. The two sprinted away from the opera house, away from the Talons, with Barbara's firecracker blasts lighting the ground behind them.

When they'd finally disappeared from the screen, and all that was left were Talons stalking the premises, Dinah turned away, her composure on the verge of breaking.

Both Barbara and Sandra were looking at her like they somehow knew what she was feeling, and Dinah dropped her gaze to the floor.

"He played me." Her throat felt like sandpaper as she spoke. "He's been pretending to like me, probably because he guessed that I was the one who could sing!" She broke off as a memory of their kiss filled her mind, and a crushing, confusing wave of longing mixed with regret washed over her.

"You don't know that for sure," Barbara said gently, and Dinah struggled to hold back the tears pricking at her eyes.

"You heard what they called me—an *experiment*," Dinah

said bitterly. "Oliver's master plan must have been to hand me over to the Court as his discovery, to boost his own position by selling me out. And I was stupid enough to fall for it."

"You are far from stupid," Barbara insisted. "And you're not the only person in this room to be betrayed by someone you cared about. It comes with the territory, unfortunately, when you open your heart. Sometimes the bad finds its way in, along with the good."

"Well, from here on out, consider my heart closed," Dinah declared. "I am so done—with Oliver, and all guys in general."

"That would be a shame to close yourself off altogether," Barbara said. "Not everyone is like Oliver Queen."

"But, speaking of him . . ." Sandra cleared her throat. "What do we plan to do about everything he knows?"

"That's the one thing that doesn't make sense," Barbara said. "He knows Dinah is the voice, so why hasn't he turned her in to the Court? What's he waiting for?"

"Maybe he's just a sadist who likes drawing out the punishment," Dinah grumbled.

"Whatever the reason, it seems you'll need to be prepared to assume the Black Canary mantle sooner than expected," Sandra said, her dark eyes intent as she looked at Dinah. "Step up your martial arts training at home, okay? In the meantime . . ." She glanced at Barbara. "We'll keep protecting the opera house until we can find the vault."

Suddenly, as Dinah looked from Barbara to the computer screen, the realization hit her with a gasp.

"*You saw me*. You were watching me that day when I tried to get into the opera house."

Barbara gave her a slight smile.

"How do you think your father showed up so fast?"

"Thank you," Dinah whispered.

"It's also how I knew you were ready," Barbara added. "I saw you fight those Talons, and I knew . . . your time as Black Canary was drawing near."

Dinah met her eyes, a shiver of anticipation running through her.

"I won't let you down."

CHAPTER SEVENTEEN

The entire bus ride home, there was a song in her head.

She didn't know where it had come from—it was certainly no melody she'd ever heard before. And yet she could hear it now, playing as clearly in her mind as one of her mother's old records: a wrenchingly beautiful minor chord progression, paired with an infectious up-tempo beat. An electric guitar riff, powering the chorus like an exclamation point. And most of all, a woman's voice. *Dinah's* voice.

She glanced furtively around the near-empty bus, half expecting the strangers sharing this ride to hear it, too. The song was growing louder in her mind, vibrating beneath her skin . . . calling out to be written. And as she squeezed her eyes shut to the twist of a knife—the memory of Oliver's lips on hers—the words came flooding in.

When we first met, I wasn't that impressed,
but somehow you distanced yourself from the rest.
Our very first kiss, that dark night,
all of these feelings, I just couldn't fight.

And you . . . you surprised me.
An unexpected spark to light my world.
Then you . . . you betrayed me.
No more can I be that innocent, trusting girl.

'Cause you're my shattered fairy tale.
You're my broken dream.
I thought we could have everything,
then pain came on the scene.
Never saw how this would fail.
We were supposed to be a team. . . .
Now you're my shattered fairy tale.
Oh—oh—oh.

Dinah felt like she could burst out of her skin from adrenaline as the song thrummed within her, demanding to be sung—to be remembered. She was afraid to speak, to do anything until she could be alone with the song and put the words and notes to paper, committing it to memory before it slipped away as mysteriously as it had arrived.

Finally, the bus pulled up at her stop. Dinah had to employ her amateur acting skills once again, plastering a bland expression on her face for the bus driver and pretending there *wasn't* a whole symphony going on inside her right now. She kept her pace slow as she walked the few blocks home, her head down, desperate to avoid any second looks from the Owl Guards lining the streets. In this moment, nothing seemed more important than getting home and completing the song.

Her hands shook with anticipation as she turned the key in the lock, and then she was home—she could breathe again. And with Larry still at the police station for another half hour, there was no one to warn her against singing.

She practically flew to her room, grabbing a notepad and pen and flopping onto her bed to scrawl everything she could remember of the song. And as she quietly sang along to her own words and music, she felt a rush and a thrill unlike anything she'd ever known—combined with bursts of fury as she poured her emotions out on the page. She could still hear Oliver's laughter ringing in her ears, along with Zed's stinging remarks about Oliver and Natasha. And then she had her second verse.

Now I'm all alone with this feeling of dread,
while you've got some other girl in your head.
How can this be? It's like the whole world's gone wrong.
I never imagined this would be our song.

And I . . . was the right choice,
the one who could bring out a different side of you.
And you'll . . . realize when you hear my voice,
every mistake you'll soon wish that you could undo.

"You're my shattered fairy tale, you're my broken dream," Dinah whispered, her pen flying across the page. But then an image entered her mind unbidden—Oliver's deep green eyes gazing perceptively into hers, a slow grin spreading across his face as he showed up at her apartment door. How was it that *that* memory felt so much more real than what she'd seen today with her own eyes?

She flipped the page, starting to hear a new variation on the main melody. *I know what this is,* she realized, remembering all those long-ago days of listening to music with her mom. It was the bridge of the song.

Now I must control my feelings,
must contain the longing.
Those few happy memories
haunt me like my enemies.
I know I deserve better,
so how could I miss us together?
The world's gone dim, turn on the light—
find a way to end this night. . . .

Reaching the final chorus, Dinah couldn't help but leap to her feet, singing louder than she should, modulating to a higher key. And then, as she held the last note, she raised her eyes to the ceiling with a smile.

"I'm a songwriter," she whispered. "Just like you, Mom."

Dinah could tell from the way her dad slammed the door behind him that his day hadn't gone much better than hers. Larry trudged into the kitchen, grumbling under his breath, but his face softened when he saw Dinah there, throwing together a salad on autopilot.

"I heard what happened today. I'm so sorry, sweetheart."

"Which part?" she asked as her dad pulled her into a hug.

"School," he said, his mouth setting in a firm line. "This might be the one time I'm actually grateful your mother isn't here. She wouldn't be able to stand it—seeing all of you lose your chance at education."

"It wasn't much of an education," Dinah said. "But it

was something. What are we supposed to . . . *do* now?" Her heartbeat sped up with panic. "They're not expecting us to go into one of those 'female vocational institutes' now, are they?"

It was another one of the Court's cruel jokes. While the boys got to attend actual university, the girls were relegated to two-year training programs where they would learn a sanctioned "female-appropriate" skill: dressmaker, midwife, or—if you were lucky enough to make it up the hierarchy— teacher of the Court's curriculum. Dinah was supposed to have plenty of time left before she even needed to think about it, but now she could feel that bleak future speeding toward her, chasing all the air out of the room. She struggled to take a normal breath as Larry put a comforting arm around her shoulder.

"Don't worry. I won't make you go to one of those. We'll . . . we'll figure something else out. Besides"—he swallowed hard—"I'm hearing at the station that the Owls are planning to implement more female restrictions, as part of their counterattack on the Resistance. So let's first just make sure you can safely leave the house before we worry about what's next."

Dinah stared at her dad.

"What kind of restrictions? What's even left for them to take?"

"I don't know. But what I do know is that the best thing you can do right now is stay under the radar," Larry said firmly. "Hold off on training with Barbara and Sandra, on singing, or doing *any*thing that flouts convention. It's the only way we can keep them from discovering you—and keep you safe."

Dinah's thoughts flew to the notebook in her bedroom,

filled with her defiant words and transcendent melody. Music had turned her heartbreak into triumph, and now that she'd discovered her abilities . . . she couldn't give them up.

After dinner, Dinah's phone lit up with a group video-chat invitation from Mandy. She clicked *Accept* and curled up in her desk chair as Mandy's face filled the box on-screen.

"Hey," she greeted Dinah. "Hold on, let me get Ty."

The screen froze and then another box entered the frame, with Ty blinking at the two of them behind his glasses. His face looked pale, almost disoriented, as if they'd just woken him up.

"You okay, Ty?" Dinah raised an eyebrow at him.

"Of course he's not okay. His best friends and half the student body were just expelled from school. No wonder he looks like a zombie."

"Gee, thanks," Ty said drily. "I just feel run-down, that's all. And yeah—knowing I won't be seeing you guys at school again obviously feels crappy. Plus my mom said—" He cut himself off. "Never mind."

"What did she say?" Dinah pressed.

Ty hesitated, and Mandy said, "You don't get to just drop that little nugget and then not tell us. C'mon!"

Ty sighed heavily, and it occurred to Dinah then that he didn't look tired so much as miserable.

"She said that war is coming, and I need to make it clear I'm on the 'right side,'" he said, using air quotes and rolling his eyes. "Basically, my parents want me and my brother behaving like loyal Court subjects so we don't wind up in trouble, too. They said no more spending time with anyone who's ever been on the wrong side of the Court. Which would mean . . ."

"Me," Dinah finished, prickly with irritation. Who did Meg Carver think she *was*, anyway? And what about her friendship with Dinah's mom? Did that mean nothing now?

"I guess you'd better get off the phone, then," she said shortly. "We wouldn't want your mom hearing you talk to *this* bad influence, who she's only known forever."

"It's not my fault," Ty protested. "I obviously don't agree. I'm just telling you what she said. So unless I want them to cut me off, I have to get creative when it comes to us hanging out and talking. Like right now is a good time, because they're all in front of the TV."

"Oh good, I'm so glad we're safely hidden," Dinah replied, though neither of them seemed to notice her sarcasm.

"I wonder if this is going to become our new normal," Mandy said grimly. "Instead of seeing each other every day at school, will 'hanging out' become just talking at each other through these screens?"

"Maybe it's only temporary," Ty suggested. "I mean, if whoever that voice at the ball was could just turn herself in already, this might stop."

Dinah stiffened. "You believe that? You really think they'd just limit the punishment to one person and spare everyone else?"

"I don't know. Maybe." Ty shrugged. "But doesn't it seem kind of selfish of that singer-person to let the search for her continue and watch things escalate for everyone else when there's a chance it could all stop with her?"

Dinah's heart started beating faster, the truth hovering

on her lips. *What if I tell him—right now?* If she started singing for both of them, right here on this call, would Ty still say the same? Or would he change his tune and want to protect her identity? *Was* she being selfish by keeping herself hidden?

Before Dinah could formulate a reply, her phone beeped with another call. Her stomach dropped when she saw who it was.

"Um. Oliver Queen is on the other line," she blurted out.

"Oh!" Mandy's eyebrows shot up. "Okay, go on. We'll talk later."

"I'm not so sure I want to—"

"I've got to run, too," Ty said, glancing at the door. "Let's do this again tomorrow, though, after school." He winced. "It's going to be so weird there without you."

"Good night, guys." Dinah clicked to end the call, sending Oliver straight to voice mail at the same time. But she must have done something wrong—because she could hear him now, his voice echoing through the phone.

"Dinah? You there?"

The sound of his voice gave her an unexpected pang. Dinah dropped the phone in surprise and then had to scramble to find it under a heap of books on her desk.

"What do you want?" she answered coolly.

"Um." Oliver sounded taken aback by her tone. He cleared his throat. "I just wanted to see if we're okay? After last night, I mean."

If Dinah had been thinking clearly, there were so many things she could have said to shut him down *without* revealing what she'd seen and heard. But she never had been one to think clearly when the fires of emotion were stoked.

Maybe it was even that characteristic that marked her as an artist from the very start. And so, Dinah turned Oliver's question around on him.

"Why do you care? Aren't I just an *experiment* to you?"

There was a bewildered pause on the other end of the line.

"What are you talking about?" he asked with a nervous laugh.

"You've been on their team this entire time—working for the Cobblepots and the Court. Haven't you? *That's* why you were asking me all those probing questions last night. And why you pretended to be so interested in me." Every word felt like poison in her throat as Dinah said it. How could she have let herself be so *duped*? How could she have confided her secrets in the enemy?

Oliver let out a resigned sigh, and Dinah's stomach twisted at the realization that he wasn't surprised. Because it was true.

"It's not like th—"

"I don't want to hear another lie," Dinah said, shutting him down. "Save your breath for Natasha Wycliffe. Didn't you say she was the hottest girl in Gotham City?"

The stunned silence lasted a beat longer this time, and a small part of Dinah wondered if she had gone too far. Now it would be obvious that she had been spying. When was she going to learn to keep her mouth shut?

"Where did you get all this from?" Oliver asked suspiciously.

"It doesn't matter." Dinah lifted her chin. "It's true, isn't it?"

"Trust me, none of that is what you think. And I will explain everything to you. But I need to tell you something now. It's important."

"Convenient change of subject." Dinah folded her arms across her chest, glaring even though he couldn't see her.

"Just listen. Things are about to get . . . more dangerous," Oliver said. "Don't let anyone in your house unless you're sure they're supposed to be there. Even if it's someone you know. Got it?"

"Someone like you, you mean?" Dinah couldn't resist getting in one last dig. "And why would I believe your warnings, anyway, when you've clearly only been leading me on so you can lure me straight into the Court's hands?"

Oliver paused, and when he spoke again, his voice was barely above a whisper. "Ask yourself why I haven't yet." He took a deep breath. "Good night, Dinah."

"Goodbye, Oliver."

As she hung up, Dinah could feel the wall of anger that had held so strong during their call start to crumble—leaving her with just the sting of sadness.

CHAPTER EIGHTEEN

Dinah tossed and turned through the night, weaving in and out of fitful dreams that changed shape as quickly as they began. She saw flashes of features: her mother's long-missed smile, her father's furrowed brow. Snippets of sound weaved their way around the images—Mayor Cobblepot roaring her name, the scratching of Talon claws. And then she heard a slow violin waltz, the scene changing in step with the music, placing her inside a memory.

"... *Many a heart is aching, if you could read them all.*
Many the hopes that have vanished, after the ball ..."

Six-year-old Dinah and her parents were crowded around an old gramophone in Rags 'n' Tatters, listening intently to the two-hundred-year-old male voice warbling through it. The gramophone was Rory Regan's latest find, and when he proudly showed the Lances the two aged discs that came with it, he let Dinah choose which one to play first. She had gone with "After the Ball," expecting to hear a cheery tune about the joy of parties. Instead, the song was all about hearts broken on the dance floor.

"Why are the words so sad when the music sounds happy?" Dinah wondered, glancing up at her parents.

Dinah's mother crouched down, looking at her in that serious way she always did, as if they were on the same level.

"Sometimes sadness hides, or it shows up in unexpected places," she said quietly. "A song is a perfect reflection of that."

"Do you ever feel sad, Mommy?" Dinah asked.

Larry shot his wife a cautionary look, but she ignored him, brushing a lock of unruly hair from Dinah's face.

"All the time. Because I wish you could have seen the world I knew before."

"You mean when you were little, like me?"

"Yes." Dinah Drake smiled and then held her daughter close. "But it's okay. Something tells me you'll make the world that much better on your own."

She could feel the present pulling her forward, up and out of her dream, but she clung on to the scene. "Don't go," she whispered, holding herself in her mother's arms. "I need you. I can't do this alone. Please—stay with me this time."

But the scene was fading, her cruel consciousness tearing her away from her mother and back into her bed, alone, in a world even darker than the one Dinah Drake left behind.

The wave of grief that crashed over her upon waking was so intense, the only way to get through it was to scream into her pillow. Except—she'd forgotten what her scream could do.

As Dinah expelled the sound, her bedroom walls started to sway, her vision becoming a blur of spots. And then she heard the singular voice—a man's slow hum, coming from blocks away, yet sounding as clear as if he were right behind her.

He was humming the same waltz from her dream. "After the Ball."

Dinah froze, all her senses shut down except for her hearing, as she tracked the sound wave of the humming man. *He's coming closer.* She could hear the firm footsteps accompanying the voice, the snap of a twig beneath his boots, and with every step—the jangle of metal. *Knives.*

And suddenly Dinah knew exactly where he was going.

She took a gulp of breath, covering her ears and waiting for her other senses to return. Once she could feel her limbs again and see the outline of furniture in the dark, Dinah jumped out of bed and threw open the door.

She burst into the master bedroom and found her dad snoring softly, looking years younger without the worry lines that so often creased his face while awake. Dinah knelt at his side, shaking him until he blinked his eyes open. Larry scrambled upright.

"Wh-what's wrong?"

"Someone's coming," she whispered. "I can hear them."

"What are you talking about?" Larry peered sleepily at her. "Who did you hear?"

"I . . . I don't know. I just know that whoever it is . . ." Dinah swallowed hard. "They're coming for us."

Larry fumbled on the bedside table for his phone, swiping to open the Home Security app. He held up the screen to show her.

"Look: no alerts or security weaknesses here in the apartment. You must have just been dreaming, sweetie."

"No, I—"

The sound pierced the stillness, right on cue—blades scratching glass.

Larry leaped out of bed, grabbing Dinah's arm and ushering her into the closet.

"Stay right here and don't move," he ordered her.

Dinah watched, heart in her throat, as Larry flung open a chest of drawers, using his phone as a flashlight to unlock the safe tucked in the top shelf. And just as he pulled out the handgun, came the crash of shattered glass.

Dinah clapped her hand over her mouth to keep from crying out. Larry took a shallow breath, turning to give her one last look. Then, holding his gun aloft, he crept out the door in pursuit.

She squeezed her eyes shut, tuning into the sounds around her. There were her father's footsteps, light and cautious, as he ventured toward the living room. And then there was a loud creak as heavy boots hit the ground, the swish of a knife freed from its sheath. The intruder was inside.

She couldn't just stay here. There was no way.

Dinah scrambled to her feet in the darkened closet, even though she knew just what her dad would say. *I'm a cop, for heaven's sake. I know what I'm doing. This is my domain. Your job is to stay safe.*

But what was the point of all her training, her skills, if she hid in the closet?

A loud pop of gunfire rattled the walls. Dinah held her breath. *Did Dad get him?*

A second gunshot followed—and then her father's agonized yell.

Dinah tore out of the room, heart clanging in her chest. She felt her way through the darkened apartment, her skin soaked with fear as she covered her mouth to muffle her breathing. Tiptoeing toward the sound of her father's cry, she saw a glint of metal flashing in the dark—and now she couldn't breathe even if she tried. She heard the creak of approaching footsteps and darted around a corner, crawling under an end table as one word echoed on repeat in her mind. *Please—please—please.*

She peered out from her hiding place, scanning the darkness. And then, just when it seemed safe to climb out—

A hand gripped her shoulder, seizing her from behind. Dinah jumped in terror, a scream rising in her throat, but the hand clamped across her mouth, silencing her. When Dinah saw the gold wedding ring, she knew who it was. *Dad.*

She spun around, weak with relief, until she saw the gunshot wound. Blood spurted from Larry's arm, dripping onto the floor. And something was missing—his gun. The intruder had been skilled enough to disarm a cop.

Dinah wriggled out of her dad's grasp, searching for something to stem the bleeding. He shook his head.

"*Just—go!*" he choked, his face contorted with pain. He used his uninjured hand to point shakily to the door. "Go to the police sta—"

"Are you kidding me? I'm not leaving you like this!"

"The gunshot went right through him, and nothing happened," Larry hissed, his eyes wide with terror. "Whatever this is, you shouldn't be—"

Larry broke off as the *creak-creak* of footsteps returned. He grabbed Dinah's hand and the two shot forward, away from the sound, into the kitchen. Larry reached behind him for the knife block on the kitchen counter, slipping a serrated blade into her palm before arming himself with the chef's knife. Dinah could hear both their hearts thundering with nerves as they gripped their makeshift weapons, listening. And then—

The footsteps grew more urgent, insistent, as they drew closer. Metal clanged against the dining table just outside the kitchen, sending dishes clattering to the floor. Dinah heard cabinets flung open, chairs upturned, and she realized the intruder was looking for something . . . just like the Owl Guards who had torn their home apart weeks ago.

Suddenly the kitchen flooded with light—and Dinah realized the intruder was no man. He was a monster. A hulking, towering figure in black armor, his face a mask covered in leather scraps, with only the eyes visible through the fearsome disguise. Eyes that were strangely familiar, even with their unnatural yellow glow.

He wore the telltale steel gloves with claws for fingernails—a Talon, but unlike any she'd seen before. And as he lunged toward them, he swiped Dinah's eyelid with his claw, sending blood trailing down her cheek like tears.

Larry roared with fury, charging at the Talon with his knife, but the blade barely made a dent in the Talon's armor. With one claw, the Talon seized Larry in a choke hold.

Dinah leaped up onto the Talon's back, punching him in the arms to loosen his grip, then using her elbow to jab the side of his head—the exact spot Sandra had said would create a punishing gash. But the Talon pried her off his back in one swift move, throwing her down onto the hardwood floor, knocking the wind from her lungs.

For a moment, everything went black. But then she crawled back to her feet, her breath and voice returning.

"What do you want?" she shouted hoarsely. "What have you come here for?"

The Talon wasn't budging his grip around Larry's neck. She could see her dad's eyes rolling back, consciousness slipping away. And at the thought of losing him—all Dinah could do was scream.

She screamed with a fury she'd never been able to conjure before. It was shrill, raw-sounding at first—then it escalated into a higher plane. Otherworldly. The floor and ceiling shuddered, the room convulsing like an earthquake just hit. The framed photos lining the walls tumbled like dominoes, crashing into a heap on the floor. And then she heard the howl of an animal as the Talon dropped Larry, using both his hands to grip his head—as if her scream had hurt him somehow.

While the Talon writhed in pain, Larry grabbed a knife off the floor. He reached up—and stabbed the Talon right in his wide yellow eye.

The Talon slumped onto the floor, head twisting with a crack as it hit the hardwood. Larry and Dinah stayed frozen, watching, waiting to see if the Talon would jump up again. After a few minutes, Larry finally lowered his arm. He and Dinah stared at each other with mirroring expressions of shock, relief—and terror. The Talon was dead.

In killing him, Larry and Dinah had put their own lives in jeopardy. No one got away with killing a Talon. No one ever *had*. Any danger they had escaped tonight would only follow them tenfold.

"Why . . . why is there no blood?" Dinah asked, finally finding her voice again, as she backed away from the body. *What if it springs back to life?*

Larry placed his hand on the Talon's neck.

"No pulse," he confirmed. He leaned forward, slowly peeling back the scraps of leather from the Talon's face— and scrambled back, crying out.

"What? What is it?" Dinah bent down beside her dad, following his gaze to the uncovered face. She clapped a hand over her mouth, bile rising in her throat.

"Rory Regan," she whispered.

It was impossible. *Impossible.* The kindly man she grew up visiting could never align himself with the Talons—it was almost as unthinkable as her own father joining them. Not only that, but how could the elderly, delicate-looking Rory she encountered just a few weeks ago have turned into . . . *this?* It couldn't be him, and yet it was. His face was unmistakable behind the leather scraps, complete with the crescent-shaped scar beneath his eye.

"But he was—he was already dead." Larry stared at Rory in disbelief. "I saw his body with my own eyes, last week."

"What?" Dinah's head snapped up. "You're saying you've known for a week that Rory Regan was dead, and you didn't *tell me?*"

Larry lowered his eyes, his expression guilt-ridden.

"You had enough to worry about. The last thing I wanted was to give you one more. And besides, I . . ." He took a shaky breath. "I blamed myself. I knew Rory was in trouble if the Court found out who he was, and when they did—"

"Wait, wait," Dinah interrupted. "What do you mean, who he was?"

Larry paused, a sad smile crossing his face.

"He was a superhero, from Before—like your mother. He called himself the Ragman." Larry laughed softly. "It was a play on the suit he wore while fighting crime. It looked like nothing more than patched-together rags, but those rags were charged with electric currents that gave him extraordinary powers. When the suit was stolen during the war against superheroes, Rory was never able to regain his full powers. He stepped into the background, into his 'normal' identity, just like your mom."

"So his store was a cover," Dinah realized, taking a sharp breath. "Like Mom's flower shop."

"There was a reason their stores were on the same block." Larry's smile faded. "And also like your mom, he couldn't hold himself back from joining the Resistance. When I found out the Talons had caught Rory, there was a moment I might have done something for him, only . . . I had to pretend to be on the opposite side. I was supposed to be working for them, remember?"

Because of me. Dinah's stomach lurched at the reminder of why her father had made that despicable deal.

"So if Rory Regan died a week ago . . ." Dinah's voice shook. "How did he show up here tonight, in the form of a Talon?"

"The Court," Larry murmured after a beat. "I've been hearing that they're experimenting with electrum and other chemicals, to create some mysterious new serum. And Rory Regan has just given us our biggest clue into what that serum is."

Larry carefully pulled at the ammunitions belt that was strapped across Rory's armor, dumping the array of knives and swords onto the floor between them.

"We might need these."

And then a look of surprise crossed his face as he pulled a scrap of paper from one of the weapons compartments. Dinah peered over his shoulder to look.

It was a list, written on Rags 'n' Tatters stationery—a list of all the customers who had received music from the shop over the last thirty days. The half-dozen names before hers had all been crossed out, with *Dinah Lance* the final name.

"That's a suspect list." Larry's eyes filled with horror as the realization dawned. "The Owls were clearly looking into Rory's customers to narrow down who could read and perform music—to see who the female voice might be."

Dinah could feel her legs starting to tremble beneath her. "Which means they're onto me. They *know.*"

CHAPTER NINETEEN

Barbara Gordon picked up the phone on the first ring, even though by now it was almost 4:00 a.m. To her credit, her voice didn't so much as waver when she heard what had happened. She remained cool and calm, her instructions clear.

"Leave the apartment at once. Take your valuables and essentials, but not much else. When the Owls discover Rory never came back, you can be sure they'll send more Talons to your door. You can stay at the library as long as you need. I'll meet you there now. Oh, and, Larry—before you drop the body at the morgue, I need you to collect a blood sample."

Larry grabbed his emergency medical kit from the bathroom, and together he and Dinah managed to tend to his gunshot wound. Then, while he donned gloves and prepared to pierce Rory with a needle, Dinah raced to her room to pack for their sudden departure. She flung clothes and toiletries into her duffel bag, along with her mother's sheet music and her own notebooks, plus the two framed photos from her dresser. At the top of the getaway bag, folded carefully, was the Black Canary costume. She had a feeling she'd be needing it soon.

Lifting the body was the most excruciating part. Although stripping his armor shed plenty of weight, carrying Rory's large corpse between the two of them was like trying to move a boulder. But Larry had enough practice with this macabre task from years in the police department, and his muscles worked double time as they rushed the covered body into the back seat of the cop car, the dark curtain of night shielding their moves.

Neither of them spoke as Larry drove to the morgue. With gloves hiding his fingerprints and a hood covering his face, Larry hauled Rory's strangely inflated body out of the car and dragged it in front of the morgue entrance, leaving it for the undertaker to find. He jumped back into the car, and as he sped away from the scene, Dinah could see tears welling in his eyes.

"I'm sorry, Dad." Dinah squeezed his arm.

Larry nodded, his eyes trained on the road ahead.

"He was my friend." His voice caught on the last word.

"I know." Dinah swallowed the lump in her throat. "But it wasn't really him."

"No. That Talon was the furthest thing from Rory Regan."

When they crossed into Old Gotham, and the statuesque structure of the library came into view, Dinah was finally able to take a normal breath. The library was the one place in Gotham City where she felt safe.

Barbara let them in through the garage, and Dinah and Larry followed her inside, past the darkened, empty stacks and reading rooms, until they reached the secret passage in the Children's Literature wing that led to her basement domain. Dinah had never gone past the fighting ring and Barbara's office before, but farther beyond was a tiny bathroom and another alcove with a few beanbag chairs and blankets, just like the ones in the reading rooms upstairs.

"This is the best we can do in terms of sleeping accommodations," Barbara said, nodding at the beanbags.

"That's more than enough for me," Dinah said as a wave of exhaustion hit. It suddenly felt as if this night had lasted two lifetimes.

"Larry, did you bring me the sample?"

He nodded, opening his briefcase and retrieving the vial from its protective casing. A hush came over the three of them as they eyed the dark red blood, all of them wondering the same thing: What secrets of the Court would they find within it?

"I'll start the analysis tonight," Barbara said, closing the vial in her palm. "You two get some rest."

Dinah was back in her bedroom at home, standing before the closet that used to be her portal into the pre-Owls world. She slipped inside and sat with legs crossed, leaning against her mother's old trunk, keeping the lights off. There, in pitch darkness, she began to sing a slow, lush melody. She could feel the power rising within her as she sang, the vibrations from her voice taking on a form of their own, carrying miles beyond the darkened bedroom closet. And then she gasped as the song on her lips faded to the background—and she could hear something underneath. Something far away.

"They'll be ready soon. Talons beyond their wildest imaginings. A stunning number of them."

The voice was unmistakable. Mayor Cobblepot.

"You have enough serum to bring them all back?"

The second voice was harder to place, but it had the authoritative tone of someone equal in stature to the mayor. It had to be one of the Owls.

"Remember, Moody, it's not a matter of bringing them back. They won't be human anymore. They'll be something else entirely . . . and far more powerful."

"When?" Moody's voice rose in anticipation. "When do you begin?"

"Tomorrow."

Suddenly the scene opened up before Dinah's eyes. Instead of only hearing their voices, she could see them now, too, in all their sickening finery. The two men were standing in a drawing room at Cobblepot Manor, beneath a portrait of the seven original Masters of the Court. Dinah's gaze fell on the painted image of the Grandmaster with the hooked nose, the long black cane. Thurston Moody, circa 1880. As she looked into his pale, pinched face, her mind flashed back to the eerily similar Talon who wreaked such destruction at the ball. And the hairs on her skin stood on end, as the truth started to surface from behind the shadows.

Dinah woke up gasping, her forehead drenched in sweat. *Just a dream*, she told herself, shifting on the beanbag chair and trying to get comfortable again. *It's not real.*

Except . . . Dinah had never had a dream like that. A dream she could still hear and feel on her skin. A chapter she knew was still unfolding somewhere, instead of a closed book.

She glanced over at her dad in the beanbag opposite hers, watching the soothing sight of his chest rising and falling, before hoisting herself up to her feet. She tiptoed out of the alcove and down the basement hall toward Barbara's computers. Barbara was awake, too, studying one of the screens.

"Trouble sleeping, Dinah?" she asked, without even needing to see who it was.

"I just had this . . . weird dream."

Barbara swiveled her chair to face Dinah, her eyebrows rising as Dinah recapped the dream.

"Serum, you said?"

Dinah nodded.

"Because I just finished reviewing the preliminary results from Rory Regan's blood sample," Barbara revealed. "And what I've found is a high dose of another chemical in his bloodstream, in addition to electrum. A chemical that, until today, I wasn't sure even existed."

Dinah stared at her, goose bumps prickling on her skin.

"What is it?"

"Dionesium," she answered. "A liquid metal with the power to revive dead tissue—and bring the deceased back to life."

Dinah's jaw dropped. For a moment she was convinced she must be back in the midst of her dream.

"So . . . so that's how he's creating his 'next generation' of Talons? By reanimating dead bodies?"

Barbara nodded.

"But it's not only that. As you saw with Rory, the dead don't simply come back as the people they were before. Dionesium is a tricky, highly hazardous drug—one with a reputation for turning its users into deranged, vicious caricatures of their former selves. They lose their conscience, their emotions become heightened. They turn into killing machines."

Dinah froze.

"So if we don't want an army of the undead taking over Gotham City," Barbara continued with a shudder, "then we need to stop the Court before it's too late."

Sandra arrived in the morning with coffee and bagels, which seemed almost hilariously normal, considering the surreal conversation taking place in the library basement. The four of them huddled around Barbara's desk, filling Sandra in on the terror of last night and all they'd uncovered about the Cobblepots and the Talons. When Barbara revealed the dionesium discovery, Dinah expected to see disbelief in her dad's eyes. But instead, he wore a knowing look of fear.

"Did you have any idea about this?" Dinah asked, almost afraid to hear his answer. If he had, and hadn't told anyone . . . what would that say about the father she adored?

Larry closed his eyes, pressing his forehead against his fist.

"I . . . I knew the mayor wanted to keep the bodies of the Talons' victims. That was part of the deal I made that night in Robinson Park. To protect you." He took a shaky breath, and Dinah's stomach started to churn. *To protect you.* It was her fault.

"The GCPD may not have the power we need to end the Court's violence, but we always did our best to look after the victims' families, bringing the bodies home to them and making the arrangements for a proper funeral. It was the least we could do, after they were put through such horror. But these past few weeks . . . I didn't even try." Larry's voice dropped, shame creeping into his tone. "I let the mayor keep every one of the dead bodies from the Patriarch's Ball.

I thought it was just a sick ego trip, that they were his trophies. I should have known he was planning something far worse. I should have known it the second I saw that Talon at the ball—the one who looked like the second coming of Thurston Moody."

Dinah stared at her dad, guilt twisting her insides, as she realized just how much damage she might have caused with that forbidden trip to Robinson Park.

"We have to make this right," she said. "I know you were only trying to protect me before, but all it did was embolden Cobblepot. So . . . you have to let me fix this, Dad."

Larry frowned across the table at her.

"Let *you* fix it? What are you suggesting here?"

"I'm talking about going after him ourselves." The words came tumbling out before she had thought them through. But as soon as Dinah said them, she knew she was right. "No more of this running and hiding. Maybe we could use the same thing he's so intent on destroying—my voice—first as a lure to catch Cobblepot off guard and draw him out, and then . . . as a weapon."

Dinah had barely finished her sentence when Larry jumped in with his protests.

"You can't be serious. Even if I were reckless enough to let my daughter anywhere near Cobblepot, how do you expect to make it past the Owl Guards and the Talons? How do you suppose you'd make it back alive?" He eyed her intently. "The answer is no. We can come up with another plan. One that doesn't involve risking you."

Dinah squared her shoulders, steeling herself for the smaller battle ahead of the big one. It would be far from easy to convince her dad that she was ready for this—but she knew the only plan that could work was one with the Black Canary in it.

"I wouldn't be alone," she said, glancing at Barbara and Sandra. They were both looking back at her with approval, with pride . . . as if she'd just passed some sort of test. "Between all of us—Lady Shiva, the Oracle, and you, too, Dad—there's enough power here to make a difference. To stand up to the mayor and the Court, and maybe even win."

"She might be right," Barbara spoke up. "The key is getting to Cobblepot from the inside, in a more vulnerable setting, away from the full-scale security he has in public. Even with just a few minutes of a head start before the Talons are summoned to the scene, that could be enough to overtake him." She focused her gaze on Dinah. "Particularly because of what you can do."

A shiver ran through her, equal parts exhilaration and fear. She knew she was ready.

"I'll call in the leader of the Resistance to meet us here." Barbara didn't even wait to finish her sentence before reaching for her phone and starting to type out a message. "She'll want to help however she can, and can provide reinforcements—"

"What reinforcements?" Larry gave her a dubious look. "The Resistance is mostly . . . dead."

"It's true that they've suffered a great many losses. But the core members remain, and new, younger allies continue to join the cause," Barbara said.

Sandra pushed back from her chair and began to pace, plotting aloud.

"What if we turned the Court's strategy around on them . . . by staging our own middle-of-the-night ambush attack on Cobblepot Manor? We'll need to go as soon as possible, tonight ideally, because every minute that Rory Regan doesn't return to the Talons is one minute sooner they'll be coming after Dinah and Larry."

Dinah locked eyes with her dad. Sandra was right. They had no time to spare.

"We could catch him unawares, using our different strengths to get past the guards," Sandra continued. "Then, once we're close enough to our target, Dinah, you can let out the Canary Cry—"

"I just—I don't know if I can do it on cue," Dinah blurted out. It was one thing to stun everyone with her singing, but the Canary Cry was a whole other level of power . . . one she didn't feel remotely in control of yet.

"Of course not. You've done it only once. They can't expect anything like that of you." Larry shot Sandra a cold stare. "I came to you to train my daughter in *self-defense*, to keep her safe, and this is what you propose? What is she to you, a lamb out for slaughter?"

Dinah's face flushed with indignation at his words. She couldn't deny that she was afraid and unsure if she could do this, but the fact that her dad was so quick to write the whole thing off only kicked up her stubborn resolve.

"I'm not a *lamb*," she shot back. "I can do this, Dad. It's what *I* propose, and it's happening."

"Hold on a second." Larry gripped Dinah's arm. "I haven't said yes to any of this. You're not ready—"

"I am. I'm the reason we survived last night," she insisted. "Please, Dad. I don't want to go against you, so let me do this. For Gotham City, for the Resistance." She took a deep breath. "For Mom."

Larry looked at her for a long moment, his face torn. And

then, just when she thought he would keep holding on to her forever . . . he let go.

He steeled himself and nodded once. He knew Dinah was ready. She felt it in her bones. And she would do whatever it took to make this right . . . tonight.

Dinah stood in front of the bathroom mirror, watching the transformation take place as she slipped on her mother's Black Canary costume. With every piece she added, she felt stronger, more powerful—more like her mom, but also more like her true self. The black leather getup was her armor, the domino mask her smoke screen. And as she turned the fighting stick over in her hands, studying its dark, bladed edge, she had her defense.

"They're here!" Barbara called out from the hallway behind her. Dinah turned to see her wheeling toward the basement entrance while studying her phone, and she cleared her throat to catch Barbara's eye.

She glanced up—and at the sight of Dinah in full Black Canary costume, Barbara stopped still. She blinked rapidly behind her glasses, her face fighting to remain steady as she held back tears.

"The Canary is back," she whispered.

Dinah smiled, a warm glow spreading through her chest. "And she's here to stay."

The two of them moved forward together toward the elevator entrance, where Sandra, dressed in red as Lady Shiva, and Larry were already waiting. Dinah could feel her pulse starting to race in anticipation of meeting the leader of the Resistance, and she held her breath as the elevator door slid open.

The first thing she saw was a cloud of black hair, followed by the mesmerizing dark eyes she knew she had seen before. And as the petite woman stepped into the room, Dinah let out a gasp of recognition.

The opera singer. The same woman whose poster adorned Dinah's closet walls for all those years, like a beacon of hope. *It was her.*

"Mariam Noor," she whispered. "I've been looking up to you for so long."

She smiled, and her voice had a foreign lilt when she spoke.

"Merci. I am so happy to meet you. It's been years that I've been waiting for the return of the Black Canary."

Mariam clasped Dinah's hand, and as she came into the light, Dinah saw the lines of age. But while she was no longer the ingenue from the poster on Dinah's wall, age had made Mariam even more beautiful, like a queen from another time.

She stepped back, gesturing to someone coming out of the elevator behind her.

"I brought one of our strongest new allies with me today— a superhero for the next generation."

Dinah craned her neck, instantly curious. A returning superhero was one thing, even a daughter taking over her mother's mantle—but a new one was almost unheard of.

"I'm happy to introduce you all to the Green Arrow," Mariam said as a tall, muscular man with an athlete's build walked in, an archer's bow and a pack of arrows strapped to his back. And suddenly Dinah remembered in a rush—*the invisible archer from school.* The one who had stopped her vocal "examination" in the nick of time, whose bow and arrows had saved her. This must be him.

He wore a leather suit of dark green, with a heavy hood framing his face. Deep green eyes peered down at her from behind an olive-colored domino mask, and as the eyes crinkled upward and his lips formed a smile, Dinah let out an astonished cry. She would know those eyes, that smile, anywhere.

The stranger in front of her—the Green Arrow—was none other than Oliver Queen.

CHAPTER TWENTY

"*Oliver?*" she gasped. "Is this—for real?"

He grinned, rushing forward to close the space between them, until they were inches apart. Almost close enough to touch.

"You don't know how badly I've wanted to tell you."

"The Green Arrow has proven to be an invaluable asset to our Resistance efforts," Mariam said, looking out at the rest of them. "His alternate identity as Oliver Queen has given us the kind of access to Mayor Cobblepot and the Court of Owls that we've never had before—and he is the one I'm entrusting to help us on our mission today."

"'Nature Boy,'" Dinah whispered, staring at his bow and arrow. "You did try telling me . . . in your own way."

"Wait a minute." Sandra narrowed her eyes. "Aren't you that guy who hurt Dinah and tried to break into the opera house with Zed? What am I missing here?"

"You *hurt* Dinah?" Larry's hands balled into fists, and Dinah quickly jumped in front of him.

"No, Dad, not like that. I think I might have possibly

misunderstood . . . everything?" She stared up at Oliver, her mind reeling.

"By establishing a friendship with the mayor's son and getting into the Court's inner circle, Oliver Queen gave us a wealth of intel," Mariam continued, nodding at him in approval. "We've needed someone on the inside all this time, and he took on that role for us."

While everyone was looking at Oliver, his eyes were solely on Dinah. They could have been the only two people in the room.

"I wish I could have told you sooner—how we're so much more alike than you ever knew." His words poured out in a rush. "But every time I was about to cave, I remembered that I had to guard this role I'm playing. Does that make any sense?"

Dinah nodded slowly as she thought of the secrets she was keeping from her own best friends. She and Oliver had that in common: presenting a separate face to the world.

"I'm sorry I didn't trust you," she said, still stunned that this was real—a revelation far better than anything she could have dreamed up. "I guess I have a hard time trusting any male who isn't my dad, or Ty, and I misjudged you. I should have let you explain."

Oliver reached out to squeeze her hand.

"Who can blame you, in this city? During these times? I understand." He gave her a knowing smile. "But I'm on your side. I always have been."

Dinah's chest swelled at the magnitude and meaning of his words—of who he was.

She smiled up at him, and as he moved toward her, Dinah couldn't help noticing his rippling muscles in the Arrow suit.

He looked so much older suddenly—like he'd skyrocketed past high school and grown up ahead of her. But he was staring at her, too, his cheeks flushed, and it occurred to Dinah that he might be thinking the same of her right now, in the leather Black Canary costume.

"So . . . remember how you asked me about the possible return of superheroes?"

"Yeah?" he breathed.

"Well, you're looking at one. One in training, anyway." She grinned, gesturing to her costume. "Meet the Black Canary."

"The Black Canary. It suits you."

Oliver's appreciative gaze swept across her face. Dinah suddenly remembered the song she'd written about him and her cheeks burned.

"And now you know the reason I asked wasn't because I was trying to trap you," he said gently, "but because I wondered if we . . . we might be more similar than we knew."

Dinah reached for his hand, and he interlaced his fingers in hers.

"Ahem. You guys *do* know you're not alone, right?" Larry folded his arms across his chest.

"Sorry, Detective Lance," Oliver said, his face reddening under his hood.

"There's one thing I'm still not clear on." Larry gave Oliver a scrutinizing glance. "What would cause the son of *Robert Queen* to join the Resistance? You're about the least likely candidate I can think of for this group."

"My parents were wrong to support the Court's revolution." Oliver looked across the room at each of them as he spoke with conviction. "It took them longer to figure it out, but I knew the Owls were twisted from the beginning—especially after those summers we spent in my childhood 'vacationing' with the lowlife Cobblepots. I heard about every despicable thing they did to the people of Gotham City, especially the women. It was practically dinner table conversation." Oliver wrinkled his nose in disgust.

"When Dad sent me to a survivalist camp, thinking I must be too soft since I didn't act like any of them, it only crystallized my beliefs. I told myself, if I made it out of that place alive, I would become a person I could be proud of. I would do something good with the Queen name. And then something funny happened." He paused, and when he spoke again, his voice sounded different, like he was struggling to keep it steady.

"The last people I ever expected to change—my parents—actually *did*. It was my mom and her love of music that first opened her eyes to the evil of what the Court had done, and over time she got my dad to see more clearly, too. They finally cut all business ties with the Cobblepots . . . and that's when they wound up dead. So I guess you could say my reasons aren't entirely selfless." He tightened his grip on his bow and arrows. "I've been waiting to make the Owls pay. They took my parents from me. And I want to take everything of theirs in return."

Dinah squeezed his hand, thinking of all the things she wished she could say to him, to comfort him, if only they were alone. Meanwhile, Larry was nodding at Oliver with newfound respect.

"We have a few things in common."

Barbara cleared her throat from behind them.

"It's almost five o'clock. If we're going to make it in time to stop Cobblepot tonight—we need to get moving."

Dinah could feel the mood shifting in the room, like someone had lit a match beneath their feet. There was a jumpy, anxious, yet determined energy among the six of them as they gathered around Barbara's operations table to review the plan.

"Arrow, you'll lead us into Cobblepot Manor?" Barbara peered at Oliver from behind her glasses, and he stood up straighter, nodding.

"Zed is expecting me around seven."

Dinah couldn't hold back her smile at the thought of Zed opening the door to his "buddy" Oliver Queen and getting the shock of his life instead. She wondered which would stun him more: Oliver turning out to be a vigilante with the Resistance, or her—the Dinah Lance he'd always mocked and belittled—becoming the Black Canary, able to break him with her voice and her fists.

Suddenly a shrill, earsplitting signal broke through the walls. The sound drowned out every other noise, every thought, as it shrieked a continuous pattern. And Dinah froze as she recognized it—the signal of the Owls.

Phones lit up around the table in rapid succession, computer screens flickering to life all on their own. Dinah jumped as her cell phone vibrated in her pocket. She reached for it with trembling fingers, as if handling something explosive. And when she saw the image filling the screen, Dinah's legs buckled beneath her, the phone slipping from her grasp. Oliver reached his arm around her waist, keeping her from falling, but she hardly noticed. All she could see was Mayor Cobblepot's triumphant sneer, flooding every one of Barbara's computer screens, above the horrifying caption: MYSTERY SINGER FOUND, CAPTURED.

"Residents of Gotham City. It is with breaking news that

I interrupt your evening for this press briefing," Cobblepot began. He spoke slowly, drawing out the suspense, enjoying every word. "You will be glad to know that the would-be 'revolution' the Resistance was attempting has been stopped in its tracks. The war is won—before it could even begin." His lips curled up in a chilling smile.

"What is he talking about?" Mariam Noor's voice rose. "Dinah's right here—"

"The unseen singer who caused so much blood to spill at our Patriarch's Ball is anonymous no more. She will no longer sing, or speak, or sleep . . . not in her cell at Arkham Asylum."

Five faces turned to Dinah in fear, but her terror was on a whole other level. It was her worst nightmare: someone else being locked up for her crime. *Who is it?*

"The Court's belief that young females are particularly susceptible to corruption and danger was proven right today," Cobblepot continued. "The singer in question was a student at Gotham City High School."

Dinah's head snapped up, her eyes meeting Oliver's in alarm.

"Her name is Amanda Harper."

The world came crashing down onto her shoulders as her best friend's smiling face filled the screen. Every bit of air fled the room. There was nothing left to breathe.

They have Mandy.

CHAPTER TWENTY-ONE

"I destroyed my best friend. Just by singing."

Dinah could barely choke out the words. She could feel herself shaking uncontrollably, the tears frozen in her eyes. She turned her panicked face to her dad. "How could this happen? Why would they take *Mandy*?"

"The Court wants it to look like they have this under control," Larry said through gritted teeth. "They would rather lock someone up as soon as possible, even the wrong person, just to snuff out any flames of revolution that might have been building since we heard a female sing."

"The Harpers have been quietly supporting our cause from the beginning," Mariam said quietly. "That must be why they chose her."

And suddenly Dinah remembered where she'd first seen Mariam Noor's photo all those years ago—in the Harpers' attic. She and Mandy had just assumed it was a mistake, a lucky blunder on her parents' part, that led to that stack of magazines escaping the same fate as all other banned words and images. But what if it had been more than an accident?

"There are other, more obvious dissenters they could have chosen to punish, if that's all they were going off of," Barbara said, shaking her head. She glanced from Dinah to Oliver. "Did either of you see anything, at school or elsewhere, that could have made Mandy a target?"

It dawned on her then—a terrible realization that sent her heart plummeting.

"The examinations," she whispered. "When they were inspecting our throats to try to figure out who could sing, it was so intrusive, so disgusting, I was *this* close to coming forward and revealing myself." She caught Oliver's eye. "Until your arrows stopped me. But before you, Mandy saw me stepping out of line. She didn't understand what I was doing and pulled my arm back, tried to stop me from stepping forward. To an outside observer, she could have easily looked . . . guilty. There were daughters of the Court in that room with us, and one of them might have said something."

She knew it was true as soon as she voiced the thought aloud. Dinah dropped her head into her hands in disbelief. Her impulsive need to step in and save the rest of the girls had backfired so completely. Any good intentions she'd had were meaningless now that her best friend was in Arkham, facing a fate worse than death.

"We have to save her." Dinah lifted her tearstained face to the others. "Cobblepot can wait. We're going to Arkham. Now."

There was a beat of silence as the weight of her words sank in.

"Those who enter Arkham Asylum rarely make it out alive," Larry said, his voice low. "It's by far the most dangerous place in our twisted city. If we thought the old plan at

Cobblepot Manor was risky, well . . . that was child's play compared to this."

"I don't care." Dinah met Larry's gaze defiantly. "We're not leaving her there a second longer."

"Of course we're not," Larry said. "But *I* will be the one to go. Sandra, if you're willing, I think the two of us can take this one for the team."

Sandra nodded, tightening her grip on her belt of knives.

"He's right, Dinah. The training we've done so far isn't nearly enough to prepare you for the horrors you'd be facing at Arkham."

"No way. You're not going without me." Dinah crossed her arms against her chest, staring the two of them down and hoping they couldn't detect any fear in her expression. Truthfully, she was just as afraid as they were of what she would have to face at Arkham Asylum—but fear was beside the point. She had no time for fear.

"It's *my* best friend in there, and she's only there because of me. I'm not staying behind. And besides, whether you believe it or not, you guys need me. I'm the only one here with a weapon in my voice." She gave her dad a pointed look. "You saw with your own eyes what I did to that Talon."

"Yes, but that was one," he argued. "Arkham is *surrounded* by them. They guard all the prisoners."

"She'll have me there, too," Oliver spoke up. The words seized at her heart. And as Oliver slung a protective arm across Dinah's shoulder, she instantly knew—*this is it*. This was the start of the relationship she had never even dared to hope for. Or it would be—if they lived through tonight.

"My arrows are just as lethal as any other weapons at the asylum," Oliver continued, his green eyes intensifying.

"Especially my trick arrows. The Talons haven't seen anything like them."

"He's right," Mariam told them. She turned her gaze to Dinah and then Larry. "I know how frightening it is to send the person you love most in the world out into danger, but we can all see how strong and capable she is. And I can vouch for Oliver Queen. She's in good hands. And you'll need her powers to get in and out alive."

There was a long pause where Dinah could see the conflicting emotions playing across Larry's face.

"It is also possible this could be a trick," Barbara said slowly. "A ploy to bring the singer out of hiding, using the guilt tactic. It's working, isn't it?"

Dinah's head snapped up. She grabbed her phone off the floor, grasping at this sprig of hope, as she speed-dialed Mandy. But it went straight to voice mail without ringing, as if her phone had been abandoned long enough to be drained of battery. Dinah couldn't remember the last time Mandy had let that happen.

She swallowed hard and turned back to Barbara.

"It's not a trick. I would know if Mandy was safe, because she would have seen or heard that news update and texted me by now. Whether the Court thinks she's the real singer or not, we know she's innocent, and they've taken the wrong person." Dinah looked imploringly at her dad. "They could kill her! We *have* to go. I owe it to her. She's in this situation because of me, and if anything happened to her . . ."

"If we do this, you have to promise to follow my lead, to listen even if I'm telling you to run the other way." Larry looked at her firmly. "No going off-script. Do you understand?"

Dinah nodded quickly.

"So then the big question is how to get inside." Larry drummed his fingers on the table. "We're obviously not just going to go announcing ourselves at the front gates."

"We could go in disguise, like as Owl Guards?" Oliver suggested.

"Maybe, but we still can't get in that way," Larry said. "Trying to pass as Owl Guards without key cards or badges would give us away immediately. We need something else. . . ."

"The satellite Batcave."

They all turned to Barbara in amazement. The Batcaves beneath Gotham City were a source of legend, their existence a rumor passed down since the fall of Gotham City. No one had ever found evidence proving they were real. Until . . .

"You're saying the caves exist?" Oliver asked, his eyes widening.

"Bruce showed them to me," Barbara said softly. "He saw the Court's power starting to rise as he reached his elder years, and he feared they would take over the city after he died. So in those last years, he planted different satellite caves in strategic locations across the city, in case they were ever needed. He thought of everything." Barbara smiled sadly. "But he never imagined things getting this bleak. One of the satellite caves was beneath Arkham Asylum, with two different passageways leading in and out of the building. I haven't been there in years, but I'll always remember how to find it."

"Amazing," Larry said, a hint of a smile lighting his face. "That's . . . that's perfect. Though we just have to hope the Owls haven't discovered it in the time since."

"Bruce Wayne was miles more clever than all of them," Barbara replied. "So I have to believe they haven't."

"Okay, so we infiltrate Arkham through the Batcave, and while Dad and Sandra go looking for Mandy, Oliver and I will stay relatively hidden—and that's when I'll start to sing," Dinah said, thinking fast. "A distraction. That'll send the Talons away from the prison cells and on the hunt for me, so you guys will have that brief window to break into Mandy's cell and free her."

"And as soon as you get a signal from me that we have her, you and Oliver will exit Arkham through the Batcave immediately," Larry said firmly. "Got it?"

"Got it," Dinah and Oliver answered in unison.

"Speaking of a signal—I have something for all of you to wear on this rescue mission." Barbara reached into the desk drawer and retrieved four earpieces, along with four hidden cameras to clip into their collars. "This way, I can be in constant contact with you and track your whereabouts from the outside. And I managed to fashion the technology so it will protect your ears from the intense effects of Dinah's Canary Cry—if she can do it."

While the four donned their gear and gathered their weapons, Dinah watched from the corner of her eye as Barbara took out a pocketknife—and raised it to her forearm.

"What are you doing?" she blurted out in alarm.

Mariam knelt in front of Barbara, collecting drops of her blood into a small glass vial.

"You'll need the blood of a Wayne or a Gordon to enter the Batcave," Barbara answered as Mariam handed the vial to Larry.

Larry nodded solemnly, tucking it into the inside pocket of his jacket. And as the team set off for the elevator, Mariam stopped to give Dinah a hug of encouragement.

"Good luck, Black Canary. Go show them just how fierce we girls can be."

It took close to an hour to reach Mercey Island, the ironically named region on the outskirts of Gotham City where Arkham Asylum was built. Dinah could feel her heart beating faster with every minute that ticked past as Oliver drove them in the nondescript van he'd borrowed from Queen Industries, while navigating the stirrings of a growing thunderstorm. Fog clouded the windows and rain lashed at the roof, making it impossible for Oliver to drive nearly fast enough to soothe Dinah's nerves. Her mind tortured her with fears of what was happening to Mandy right this moment, and all she could do was close her eyes, willing Mandy to hear the message in her mind. *We're coming to get you. I promise.*

Finally, they crossed over the bridge that reached the sprawling, ominous island in the middle of Gotham Bay. A flash of lightning lit up a sign that read ARKHAM ASYLUM—1 MI, and a shudder ran down Dinah's spine. A canopy of twisted trees led them down a long, mud-slicked road, bare branches scratching at the van's windshield. And then it appeared in the distance—a towering, turreted castle on a hill. A Gothic pile in the middle of a modern city. Statues of hooded, faceless figures loomed from the north tower, the sinister sight illuminated by a smattering of stars, and Dinah shrank back in her seat. Arkham was already twice as creepy as she'd anticipated . . . and they hadn't even gone inside.

"Follow the signs to the Lookout," Barbara directed Oliver. "There—it's that winding road up ahead."

"You mean . . . Perilous Point?" Dinah gulped. That was the moniker locals had taken to calling the Lookout, after so many had died after a push or a jump from its cliffs.

"Yes. The entrance to the cave is after the jump."

"Um. *What?*" Dinah screeched.

"You do remember we can't fly, right?" Larry said to Barbara, a sharp edge in his voice.

"There's no need," Barbara said calmly. "No one has ever died from the fall itself. The tragic stories that gave Perilous Point its name are from those who hit their heads on the rocks lining the bottom—but that won't be you, especially since you aren't jumping to the bottom in the first place. There's a ledge jutting out from the cliff's midpoint, and *that* is where you will land—and find the entrance to the Batcave."

"How are we supposed to coordinate our fall like that?" Dinah asked, twisting in her seat to look at Barbara with alarm. "I'm starting to think that just charging through the front gates and taking our chances is a lot more survivable than . . . this."

"I must have done this jump a dozen times as Batgirl, and I promise you, it's infinitely safer than walking straight into a pack of Talons. Landing on the ledge really isn't hard when you know to look for it."

"Sandra and I are going first," Larry said grimly. "That way, if . . . if anything happens, you two know to stay behind."

With a wave of panic, Dinah quickly rolled down the passenger-side window, struggling to breathe. Oliver placed a comforting hand over hers.

"We're going to be okay," he murmured. "Barbara wouldn't steer us wrong."

She nodded, trying not to look at the steep drop in front of her as the van inched up the gravel to the peak of Perilous Point. And then, before she was ready, the tires came skidding to a halt. Oliver turned off the engine, Larry and Sandra threw open the doors, and Barbara began setting up her surveillance computers from the back seat. It was time.

Dinah had never known she was afraid of heights until she stepped through a jarringly cold sheet of rain to the edge of the cliff and looked down at the churning waters below. She froze, heart slamming against her ribs. She could hear Barbara saying something in her earpiece, but she couldn't make sense of the words. They just sounded like gibberish in her state. The only thing she could focus on was the fact that, in mere seconds, her dad and Sandra would be making a potentially fatal jump. And then she'd be next.

But it's for Mandy, Dinah reminded herself, taking in a gulp of air. No matter what could happen, it was worth the risk. She couldn't let Mandy stay in Arkham.

Before Larry and Sandra made the jump, Dinah threw her arms around them both.

"Thank you for doing this for her—and for me," she said, rain streaking down her cheeks like tears. "Please . . . please be safe."

Larry held her tight.

"We will. But I'm begging you—if anything goes wrong, turn back. Don't come after us." Dinah couldn't answer, and her dad looked past her at Oliver. "I'm counting on you. Please watch out for my daughter."

"You have my word," he promised.

As Larry and Sandra stepped forward, Dinah and Oliver seized hands. She held her breath, terrified to look but forcing herself to do so anyway as her dad and Sandra broke into a run—and leaped off the edge.

She heard a whoop, a scream, and then—the smack of feet landing on stone. Dinah rushed forward to look. *Barbara was right!* A ledge jutted out midway through the drop, and she could see Larry and Sandra there now, tiny upright figures far down below.

Oliver let out a long exhale.

"All right. Our turn."

Dinah felt her trepidation returning as she looked from him to the cliff's edge.

"Are you afraid? Not just about this jump, but . . . all of it."

"Yeah," Oliver admitted. "But only a little bit. Because I'm with the Black Canary." He smiled down at her. "I know I'll be safe with you next to me."

Dinah felt a swooping in her stomach, one that had nothing to do with nerves or fear. She smiled back at Oliver, and they squeezed hands.

"You ready?" he asked.

She took a deep breath.

"I . . . I think so."

"Remember, we're just arrows hitting that target below. Let's go!"

They counted down together, Dinah's adrenaline escalating to a fever pitch. As they raced forward hand in hand and leaped off the edge, it felt like Dinah's body and soul momentarily split. She was numb, felt nothing but pins and needles where her limbs should be, and at the same time it was as if she were somehow watching the scene from outside herself, could hear her screams mingling with Oliver's yells. And then the ground was rushing toward them, the ledge waiting to catch their fall. Oliver tightened his grip on her, shouted for her to bend her knees.

As their feet touched the ground, euphoria hit. Dinah could hear Barbara cheering in her earpiece, could feel Larry and Sandra rushing the two of them in relief, but they still seemed far away—like it was only her and Oliver in this moment.

Their legs buckled from the impact of the landing, and they knelt together on the stone, reaching for each other at the same time. Her arms circled his neck, he buried his face in her hair. Their eyes met, and this time it was Dinah who leaned in first. She brushed her lips against his, feeling her insides thrill as his lips responded, kissing her like she was all that mattered—like she was all that existed. It wasn't until they heard Larry's loud "A-HEM!" that they remembered where they were. They sprang apart, flushed and still grinning.

"I am going to pretend I didn't just see that," Larry said, shaking his head sternly at the two of them.

Dinah heard Barbara's faint laughter in her earpiece before she said, "Well done, all of you! Now, follow this ledge through a brick tunnel, past a bridge, and into an arched stone alcove. The northwest wall of the alcove is the entrance we're looking for."

The four of them launched forward with Larry and Sandra in the lead, Larry holding his gun in one hand and a flashlight in the other while Sandra kept a firm hand on her belt and kusarigama. They dodged loose, falling bricks and stones as they ran through the ramshackle tunnel, passing a rushing waterfall as they crossed the rickety bridge. And then they reached the circular alcove Barbara described, coming to a halt in front of a wall of stones.

"It's the third stone from the far right," she instructed them through the earpiece. "Push until it wedges loose."

"Uh, all right." Larry pressed his palms against the stone and shoved, but it wouldn't budge. "You sure this is the one?"

"Back up." Sandra swept in front of Larry, ramming the center of the square with her elbow and forearm until the stone at last began to move—sliding aside to reveal a fingertip-sized scanner behind it.

"Well. Okay then." Larry pulled the vial from his pocket and unscrewed the top, spilling drops of Barbara's blood onto the tiny scanner window. Dinah gasped as the surrounding stones started moving before their eyes, rearranging themselves. An interlocked opening in the wall started to form, and within moments, it was large enough for them to walk through.

"Awesome," Oliver breathed.

As they stepped through, the platform beneath their feet gave a sudden lurch—and then they were falling, clawing at rapidly vanishing walls while being dropped more than ten feet below. The four of them collided on the floor, where sewer water gurgled underneath a metal-grated trap door.

"You couldn't have warned us about that part, Barbara?" Larry shook his head in exasperation and glanced at the three of them. "Everyone okay?"

There was a chorus of slightly dazed-sounding *yeahs*, and then Dinah scrambled upright alongside Oliver and Sandra, finding herself in a compact, circular chamber. The room was empty, save for the ladders and power cords running from floor to ceiling—and the desktop computer at the center of the space, its large screen flashing the bat symbol. Dinah's hand flew to her chest.

"Unbelievable," Larry whispered, staring at the screen. "It's been decades since I've seen that sigil."

"This cave—it looks just the same as when we left it." There was a catch in Barbara's voice as she spoke through Dinah's earpiece. "It's hard to believe how long it's been . . . how much has changed."

A hushed silence fell across the room as the four gazed across the satellite Batcave in wonder. Sandra nudged Dinah, giving her a pointed look.

"Okay, Black Canary, give us the lay of the land. What can you hear?"

This was her moment. Dinah closed her eyes, and as she started to sing her mother's words for Barbara—it was Mandy she was singing for.

"Through all of life's ups and downs,
you've kept my world turning round.
My best friend, birds on a ride—"

She cut off in horror at the sound of desperate screaming ringing in her ears—a girl's anguished wail.

There was no way to tell for sure whether the screams were Mandy's, but the panic that gripped Dinah at the sound convinced her they were. She pushed her dad, Oliver, and Sandra toward the door.

"I hear her—she needs us *now*. We have to get to the cells!"

"Remember the plan." Barbara's voice rose through the earpiece. "Larry and Sandra will go alone, using Batman's secret passage within the wall to get inside the main building. Dinah and Oliver, wait for my signal before you make a single move."

Dinah was about ready to jump out of her skin with nerves as Sandra and Larry climbed up the long ladders, scaling the walls till they were just a few inches from the ceiling. Larry poured out a drop of Barbara's blood into another scanner, this one hidden behind one of the stones where the wall met the ceiling. The stones parted, revealing a dark tunnel into Arkham's interior.

Dinah's mind whispered a prayer as Sandra's body disappeared through the tunnel first, followed by her dad's. *Please let this work. Please let me see them—all of them—again.*

Barbara exhaled sharply and said, "They're inside. Dinah, if you can access your sonar hearing again, that'll be the best way for me to direct everyone while making sure to steer you as clear of the Talons as possible."

Dinah nodded, taking a deep breath. She leaned against the stone wall and began to sing as Oliver watched her in awe.

It was the same melody she'd been singing in the dream when she heard Cobblepot and Moody. And as she sang now, she could both hear it and feel it—a vibrational pull, a sound wave that drew her toward another approaching voice within this fortress. A muffled voice that was somehow, oddly, familiar . . . and coming closer. Not just a voice, but a low cry.

Dinah broke off abruptly.

"Are—are you sure no one else knows about this cave?"

"I never said I was sure," Barbara clarified. "But it would take a genius on the level of Bruce Wayne to find it."

Oliver peered closer at her. "What's going on?"

"I—I'm hearing a voice from the other side." Dinah pointed a shaky finger at the wall before them, opposite the stones Larry and Sandra exited through. "It's too muffled for me to tell who it is, but I also have just . . . the weirdest feeling. Like it's someone I know."

"Mandy?" Oliver asked, his eyebrows rising with hope.

Dinah shook her head. "If only."

She stepped forward, singing under her breath and trying to discern the snatches of sound she heard in her mind. It felt like a forgotten word was sitting on the tip of her tongue, a memory close enough to touch. . . . She could hear Barbara, too, her voice far away as she called through the earpiece for Dinah to stay put. But as Dinah focused on harnessing her sound wave, Barbara's voice faded into the background.

"How can we get to the other side?" she asked Oliver, nodding at the wall.

He gave her a sidelong glance.

"Aren't we supposed to wait for instructions here? Instead of going off-script?"

"Yeah, but I'm willing to bet that *this*—me hearing someone in trouble, who could be trapped on the other side of the wall and whose voice I feel like I know—is a worthy exception," Dinah persuaded him.

Oliver hesitated, and then reached into the quiver slung across his back. He pulled out a long, sharp-tipped arrow, positioning it in the bow.

"Let's give it a shot, then."

He drew back his bow, and as the first arrow sailed through the air with a swish, Oliver was already loading a second. Watching him in action, his eyes narrowing in concentration and muscles flexing as he hit a perfect target, Dinah felt goose bumps rise on her skin. He was incredible. And somehow, he seemed to think the same of her.

The arrows pierced the center of the brick wall, one after another, but nothing gave way. There were no retreating bricks, no new passageways. Oliver rifled through his quiver, as if searching for just the right arrow. And this time, when he drew back his bow, the single, slim arrow slammed against the bricks like a wrecking ball.

Dinah's mouth fell open as the wall caved in, bricks and stones tumbling to the ground in a mountain of rubble.

"What the—? *How* did you do that with just one skinny arrow?"

"It was one of my trick arrows, actually." Oliver grinned proudly. "Let's just say I learned a whole lot in my two years interning in tech and mechanics at Queen Industries. Not so much on the actual work front, but I did learn how to fashion an arrow into just about every kind of weapon."

"Okay, I am officially impressed," Dinah said, staring at the busted-open brick wall.

Oliver paused, hand on his earpiece.

"I'm glad you are, because it sounds like Barbara Gordon is in the middle of yelling at me."

Dinah winced.

"Sorry, Barbara," she called into her earpiece. "I just— I had to see what's beyond that wall. Someone's there. I can feel it, I can *hear* it, and I think they need—"

She broke off as the sound returned: the strangely familiar whispers, the wrenching cry. Dinah turned back to Oliver. "Let's go!"

The two clasped hands and climbed through the gap in the wall, stepping out into a dim, spiraling stone corridor.

"If this *isn't* an extension of the satellite Batcave, I wonder if someone else found out what Bruce Wayne built down here," Dinah said quietly. "And then made a point of building something of their own parallel to his?"

"He could have told someone besides Barbara about his caves," Oliver suggested. "It could be an ally. Like someone carrying the Bat torch . . ."

"Let's hope," Dinah muttered. She could see in his face that he believed that optimistic theory about as much as she did.

They reached the end of the short, narrow corridor, which was marked by a single arched door. Oliver and Dinah exchanged a glance.

"It's probably locked, right?"

Dinah turned the knob. And to her astonishment, the wall swung to the side, opening just enough to let the two of them through.

"What . . . the . . . ?" Oliver murmured as they left the dim corridor and entered a new room that was nearly blinding in its display of marble, from the gleaming floors and columned walls to the fireplace and gold-rimmed end tables. The lavish decor couldn't have been more out of place in the underbelly of Arkham Asylum, though the macabre artwork was a closer fit. An expansive mural painted on the ceiling depicted a cloaked figure, his mouth open in a scream, while porcelain figurines lining the mantel of the fireplace appeared to represent the various stages of death.

"What were they going for in here, exactly?" Oliver wrinkled his nose as they took in all the different horizontal marble slabs lining the perimeter. "A creepy indoor sculpture hall?"

"Um. Guys." Barbara's voice came crackling back through their headsets. "I . . . don't think those are sculptures."

Dinah blinked at the scene in front of them—and her hand flew to her mouth.

They were *coffins,* adorning the room like someone's sick idea of decor.

Dinah staggered backward as the gruesome rhyme of childhood nightmares returned to her mind.

Beneath the City's beating heart,
claws tear Owl enemies apart.
Their lair collects the bodies,
dead skin and bones for trophies. . . .

Is this it? Had the Court moved their underground labyrinth next to Batman's former domain, another dig at their greatest nemesis? And if so . . . how many seconds did she and Oliver have left before they were caught and killed on the spot?

"Turn around," Oliver whispered in her ear, the color draining from his face as he came to the same realization. "We need to get out of here."

Dinah nodded and tightened her grip on his arm, nearly tripping over her own feet in her haste to escape. She was just steps away from the collapsed wall separating the Batcave from the Owls' lair—when she heard it. The muffled, familiar voice that had beckoned her here in the first place was coming closer. It was *behind her.* A male voice, whispering words in Latin—the same words Dinah suddenly remembered her father reiterating to the Owl Guards the night he tried to pretend he was one of them.

Oliver drew back his bow and Dinah seized her knife. The duo hid behind marble pillars as the voice grew louder. *But wait*—she knew that voice. It was—

"*Ty?*"

The world stopped. Dinah's heart plummeted to the floor as she stepped out from behind the pillar to see her oldest friend, standing in the last place he ever should have been—the doorway of the marble room filled with coffins.

CHAPTER TWENTY-TWO

She lowered her weapon, shock radiating through her.

"What are you doing here?" she whispered to him.

"Dinah, stay back," Oliver called, a sharp edge to his voice.

Ty wasn't answering—*why isn't he answering?* He just stared at her behind his glasses in disbelief, his face even paler than usual.

"Say something," she pleaded. Her mind was scrambling, trying to convince herself that this wasn't what it looked like. It couldn't be. She would have known. "What are you *doing* here?"

"Dinah? I . . . I should ask you the same thing," he mumbled. He squinted, taking in her domino mask, her black leather pants and jacket. "What are you wearing? Don't you know you'll get in trouble for that?"

"Are you *kidding* me?" Dinah exploded. "Mandy is locked up there in a cell, and you're worried about what I'm wearing?" Her voice broke as she said Mandy's name, and then came a sudden, desperate hope. "Are you here—for her?"

It was the only explanation that wouldn't fly in the face of everything she believed about their friendship. But Ty just blinked rapidly, his mouth opening and closing like he was trying to formulate a response, too stunned by her appearance to follow through.

"Dinah." Oliver's urgent tone caught her attention, and she followed his pointing finger to a carved scroll on the marble wall: a list of names, etched beneath a bas-relief sculpture of an owl.

COBB

STAUNTON

BOONE

CARVER

Carver. Ty's last name.

"You're—you're one of *them*?" she choked out. "Since when—how—?"

Ty bent his head, and Dinah saw it then: the torment in his eyes.

"How is this even happening?" she cried. "Just weeks ago, you were running *away* from the Talons with me—"

"Because I didn't know," he said through gritted teeth. "It wasn't until the ball that I found out what we are."

"And what is that?" Dinah demanded. She could feel Oliver hovering beside her, his bow and arrow poised and ready just in case. It was unfathomable, to think he would have to consider using them on Ty.

"Shadow Owls," he said quietly. "Born to serve the Owls when our time comes. And it turns out our job, as Carvers, is to guard and . . . and prepare the bodies."

"The bodies of their murder victims." Dinah stared at Ty, aghast. "How are you *okay* with—"

"What's this?" Meg Carver's lofty, nasal voice preceded her entrance as she swept into the lair behind Ty. At the sight of Dinah and Oliver, she stopped in her tracks, eyes flashing—and then she threw back her head and laughed.

"Oh, did I miss the memo? Is it 'Dress Like a Dead Superhero' Day?" Meg said snidely. "Answer me, Dinah: Who let you in here?"

Meg tried to grab Dinah's arm, but she wasn't quick enough. Dinah seized both of Meg's wrists, pushing her into the stone, while Oliver drew back his bow, nailing her long platinum ponytail to the wall with one of his arrows. Meg shrieked in fury while Ty stood frozen, eyes darting between his mother and his once-closest friend.

"I don't understand," Dinah told him. "I'll never understand. Why—since *when*—are you guys part of the Court?"

"I wondered how long it would take you to figure it out," Meg said crisply, maintaining her attitude, even while she was still nailed to the wall from Oliver's arrow. "I've got to be honest, though. I'm a little disappointed in your poor dad. Shouldn't *Detective* Lance have guessed it first? It's not like family records are hard to access these days."

Dinah's insides pulsed with rage.

"No. He wouldn't have guessed, because he knows my mother would *never* have been friends with a supporter of the Court. Something's clearly happened to you. If you've been brainwashed by them—"

"I didn't know!" Ty burst out, chin quivering as he looked at Dinah. "You have to believe me. I had no clue until the night of the ball, when—when that girl went and broke the

laws of our world by singing. That's when Mom and Dad
finally told me we were born to a long line of Shadow Owls,
and now we'd been called up to service. I did what I—what
I thought I had to do. It's only today that I found out the
singer was Mandy, and now they're making me choose—"

"Enough!" Meg interrupted, her eyes blazing. Ty clamped
his mouth shut, his expression miserable.

Dinah felt her body start shaking as something cracked
in her chest. The betrayal seared into her soul—more than a
decade of friendship, tainted.

"They were wrong about Mandy."

She looked him dead in the eyes, and as her heartbreak
and fury mixed with shock, there were no words big enough.
There was only song.

"No more staying quiet when our world's gone wrong.
There's no time for silence when they steal our
    song. . . ."

Ty's eyes grew huge.

"No."

From Dinah's first note to her last, the scene before them
transformed. Meg Carver lunged at Dinah, hands grasping
for her neck, but Dinah spun into a side kick, sending her
mother's duplicitous, false friend careening into the wall.
Meg screamed for Ty to attack, and Dinah froze in shock as
he unearthed his hands from his pockets—revealing a set of
steel-plated gloves, complete with sharp claws.

He took a halting step toward her, and Dinah had the
surreal, crushing realization: she was going to have to fight
her oldest friend. But he didn't make it more than one step

before the strike of Oliver's arrow sent him reeling backward, clutching his arm in pain. Dinah gasped as Ty fell to his knees, the thump ricocheting through the marble chamber. Blood spilled from his arm as he withdrew the arrow, moaning in pain.

Oliver had done it for her—what he knew would have been agonizing for her to have to do.

She was just about to run past them when she saw Meg Carver break into a smile on the floor, heard Oliver's sharp intake of breath. Something was wrong.

Dinah's head snapped up at the scraping sound of metal and stone splitting apart—the ceiling opening up before them. Before she could even register what was happening, five figures shot down from the floor above, hitting the ground one after another in rapid succession: four armored Talons, their claws poised to strike, flanking the red-cloaked, wild-eyed figure of Mayor Cobblepot.

Dinah's heart lodged in her throat, the terror stealing her breath, her voice. She tried to reach inside herself for the Canary Cry, but her fear was too strong, her body shaking too hard to focus. Dinah glanced around wildly, searching for an escape route, but she knew better—they were in the Court's territory. There was no way out. And even if there was, the Talons would never let them get away. Dinah and Oliver would be dead in mere moments—they had no chance against the seven standing in front of them.

"Wait."

Mayor Cobblepot held up a hand to pause the Talons before stalking toward Dinah.

"Mayor! My son and I, we were the first on the scene to stop her." Meg Carver rushed up to him, her expression one of fawning sycophancy.

"Not much of a job you did, was it?" Cobblepot said coldly. "You two can go now."

Ty turned for one more look at Dinah as one of the Talons pushed him and Meg from the room. She had never seen her friend more conflicted, more lost. But she couldn't think about that now. The mayor was coming closer.

"So it was you," Cobblepot said in his cold, skin-crawling voice. "Detective Lance's girl. *How did you do it?* How are you immune to the Silencing?"

Dinah's mind raced, searching for something, anything, to say to buy more time.

"I—I don't know. It just happened. But as you can see, it was never Mandy Harper. Please, let her go—"

Her answer only enraged Cobblepot further. He grabbed her by the shoulders, shaking her so roughly that Barbara's earpiece tumbled to the ground. Two Talons lunged to grab Oliver behind them. Cobblepot's nails dug into her skin, his breath sour on her cheek.

"If you want to live," he hissed, "you'll tell us how you did it."

"I can't."

His despicable face was inches from hers, his fist closing around the collar of her jacket. And then, as she looked back at him, at those hateful, beady eyes, her fear fell away like a coat slipping from her shoulders . . . turning to anger instead.

She took a breath and then wrestled from his grasp, using her leg muscles to launch into a back handspring, kicking the mayor in the chest as she leaped. And at the fiery outrage in his eyes, Dinah knew—one faltering step and she'd be dead.

The Talons swooped down, their claws clamping onto her skin, sending tears burning in her eyes. And then, catching her off guard, the mayor tried a different tack. With one ruddy hand tight around her wrist and a Talon's claw gripping her by the neck, he shoved her forward, toward the row of coffins.

"See any familiar names?" he snarled in her ear.

Dinah tried not to look, knowing instinctively that what she was about to see would be too painful, too horrendous for what could be among her last moments alive. Her eyes darted in every other possible direction—to Oliver's hand trembling on his bow, the stray arrows scattered on the floor, the chasm in the ceiling.

"I said, *look*!"

Mayor Cobblepot gripped her cheeks and the Talon shoved her neck forward, so she had no choice but to read the names on the coffins. She hadn't finished reading the third name before an anguished cry filled the air. Her cry.

DINAH DRAKE

"You can have her back, you know." The mayor's voice turned low, almost silky. "The new electrum serum we've created will revive every one of the bodies in these coffins, creating an army of the undead to join the illustrious ranks of our Talons. Your mother will be one of them, and you can be with her again. All you have to do is tell us how you defied my curse . . . and then *join* us."

The words were more horrifying than any physical pain the Owls could inflict. The thought of the mother she ached for all these years coming back to life, but as a monster, someone she wouldn't be able to love—made Dinah sear with rage.

And when she opened her mouth to respond, something else came out instead.

A scream as sharp as a Talon's blades. A cry as weighty as thunder.

Dinah watched in astonishment as the sound left her body and moved into the world like a weapon. It created a visible *wave*, rippling through the space, sending the Talons, Oliver, and Mayor Cobblepot flying backward with the force of a hurricane. Cobblepot and the Talons covered their ears in agony, in pain, as the sound pierced the air like a blade.

For a moment she couldn't move, transfixed by the sight of what she'd just done. She locked eyes with Oliver, who was staring at her in openmouthed astonishment. Though the force of the wave had knocked him back with the others, Barbara's earpiece seemed to keep her promise of protecting his ears from the force of the Cry. Dinah motioned for him to follow her. And then she broke into a run—this was her one chance to get away while the Talons and Cobblepot were on the ground.

She was halfway to the wall separating the Owls' lair from the Batcave when she heard Mayor Cobblepot lurch to his feet, screaming, *"Resurgemus!"* And then a freezing-cold hand shot out, closing around her arm and sending her skidding down onto the floor. She scrambled backward on her hands and knees, dizzy with fear at the nightmare unfolding in front of her.

One of the gilded coffins was quaking, an arm snaking out from the closed casket. She recognized the silver TMM signet ring adorning one of the spindly fingers of the dead man's hand—the ring worn by the old Grandmaster of the Court, Thurston Moody, in all of his nineteenth-century portraits.

Oliver shouted suddenly. He drew back his bow and

Dinah turned in alarm. His arrow flew straight at Dinah. Her mouth fell open, the shock more piercing than any pain the arrow could inflict. But as the arrow grazed her skin, it retracted—releasing a *grappling hook line.* A long, zip-line-like cord stretched from her palm to Oliver's bow, and he tossed his hooked end up through the gaping hole in the ceiling, yelling, "Get on!"

Dinah didn't know what she was doing—*Will this even work?*—but she jumped onto the line, a rush in her stomach as her feet left the floor. Oliver leaped on to join her, and they sailed up toward the ceiling, while the reanimated Moody, Mayor Cobblepot, and the Talons thundered after them. But thanks to Oliver's trick arrow, they had a head start.

"Thank you," she gasped as they soared on the grappling hook line, landing on their knees in a dark, narrow corridor two floors up. "That was pretty amazing, what you just did."

"What about your scream?" Oliver marveled. "Now, *that* was something else."

But as the acute adrenaline wore off, reality sank in—the reality of what she just saw. And Dinah couldn't stop the tears.

"He has my mom," she whispered. "This whole time, she hasn't been at peace. And now, what if he—what if he does what he says—"

"We won't let him." Oliver held her close. "As soon as we get Mandy, we're destroying the mayor and his serum next."

Dinah managed a half smile.

"That's a whole lot for our to-do list, Oliver Queen."

Her smile slipped as the floor started jolting beneath their feet, as if someone were hacking at the ceiling below in pursuit of them. They stumbled forward, dodging the thumps underfoot, and nearly ran straight into a pair of Talons patrolling in their direction. Dinah grabbed Oliver's hand, the two shielding themselves behind a life-sized statue of Cobblepot, of all people, until the Talons passed.

Darting around corners and in and out of shadows, they hurried in the opposite direction, into an abandoned-looking hallway lined with empty cells.

"This must be an older part of the asylum that's no longer in use," Dinah said, nodding toward the broken doors. Arkham had been packed to capacity since the Court takeover—so where were all the prisoners?

"So, good news and bad news," Oliver whispered as they crept through the corridor toward an opening awash in harsh fluorescent lighting. "The good news is we're about to be reunited with your dad, Mandy, and Sandra. The bad news is . . ."

"We're now officially in the thick of Arkham Asylum," Dinah finished. "And being chased by the mayor and his personal security team of lethal Talons."

Oliver swallowed hard.

"Right. And—*look*."

The breath drained from Dinah's lungs as they crept toward the light.

They had reached the main prison floor—and it was a windowless, maximum-security panopticon. A *moving labyrinth*. A series of interconnected, solitary-confinement cells climbed from the ground floor to the top, with each cell stacked on top of the other, housing hundreds of prisoners. The cells rotated on spinning metal plates in the floor, while Talons climbed the bars and perched on stationary chairs set in balconies that encircled the cells—torturing prisoners who were too dizzy, too nauseous, to even attempt self-defense.

"No wonder they say Arkham turns people mad," Dinah whispered. "Imagine not even having the luxury of solid ground." Panic gripped her chest as she searched the faces below for Mandy, for her dad and Sandra. But while she couldn't spot them yet, she could see that the vast majority of the prison cells were filled with women. And suddenly she couldn't be still any longer.

She jumped to her feet just as Oliver cried, *"There she is!"*

Mandy's cell spun in their direction, and Dinah's heart stopped. She could see her best friend backing against the bars in terror, hear the agonizing cry bursting from her mouth, as a Talon loomed over her body, drawing his claws down her neck. On the floor beneath her cell, another Talon struck and pummeled Larry as he struggled to break free and get to Mandy. Staring at this scene of horrors, seeing the people she loved most so close to death or worse—Dinah knew what she had to do.

She clenched every muscle, closed her eyes, and thought beyond herself, beyond her own life. She thought of every girl who'd lost her voice, her freedom, her choice, her power. Dinah lifted her head back, eyes fixed on the metal prison bars, desperately hoping that she wouldn't harm the prisoners with her Cry. And for every girl who ever dreamed of raising their voice and hearing it sing, Dinah let out a scream powerful enough to shatter metal.

The sound exploded forth from her like a rushing swell of water. As the metal bars came crashing down, her jaw dropped, her scream fading to a stunned silence. The cells began to topple down over one another with a tsunami of force. And through the wreckage, the prisoners began to free themselves. They streamed out of their cells, whooping, shrieking, and rejoicing, and, just as quickly, the Talons dove into the crowds, slicing into the prisoners. In mere moments, the celebrations were streaked with red.

Oliver pulled back his bow and started firing arrows at the Talons while he and Dinah thundered into the chaos. And when they reached the center of the shattered open cells, Dinah and Oliver came face to face once again with Mayor Cobblepot and the undead Talon incarnation of Moody. Oliver shot an arrow into Cobblepot's stomach, turning just as Cobblepot lifted his gun, smiling sadistically before pulling the trigger.

"*Oliver!*" Dinah yanked him out of the crosshairs just in time—right as she heard her dad and Mandy screaming her name. Before she could react to their plea, the undead Thurston Moody dug his claws down the back of her neck, sending blood spurting across her skin.

The pain was dizzying, but instead of giving in to it, Dinah forced herself to stay upright—to use the pain as power for her scream. She let out another wild Canary Cry, the force sending Moody sprawling to the floor. She attacked another Talon with a spinning body kick, whipping her head around to keep tabs on her dad and her friends from the corner of her eye. She spotted Sandra choking one of the Talons with her elbows, freeing a young prisoner who had been under the Talon's grasp, while Oliver and Mayor Cobblepot fought their way across the floor, Oliver dodging his bullets and firing at him with arrows at lightning speed. Larry held Mandy under one arm, kicking and punching at Talons with the other. Suddenly Mandy darted out of Larry's grasp, sprinting into the crowd and yanking two young women to safety seconds before a pair of approaching Talons could sink their claws in. As she watched her brave best friend, Dinah felt a rush of warmth. Until a familiar face sprinted into the crowd—and her body turned cold.

Ty. He was back . . . and clearly here to fight against them.

In her moment of distraction watching him, she failed to notice the undead Talon creeping up behind her until Moody's claws were digging into her shoulders. He whipped her around, forcing her to look right into his terrifying masked face. His knife grazed her stomach, seconds away from plunging all the way in.

Dinah opened her mouth to scream and quickly discovered how much she relied on her entire body to produce the Canary Cry. With her mind distracted by the knife and her arms trapped in Moody's claws, she could barely make a sound. The cold shackles of panic gripped her body. She couldn't get out of the Talon's hold, she couldn't scream. *I'm going to die here tonight.*

Just then, another body hurtled forward, pushing Dinah away from the undead Talon. She tumbled backward onto the ground, covering her head to dodge the feet and fists of fighters as she struggled to get up. That's when she saw who it was, who had saved her. *Ty.* But because he pushed her out of the way, the knife that was meant for Dinah plunged into his own chest.

"TY!"

Dinah's heart split in two as Ty fell to the floor. His eyes rolled back, the knife lodged firmly into his body.

She sprinted toward them, so enraged that she unleashed

the earsplitting scream she'd been searching for moments earlier, knocking the Talon over and slamming him into the floor from the sound alone. Moody's nose began to bleed, releasing a murky fluid darker and thicker than blood. And then Dinah flew to Ty's side, barely able to see through her tears, as Larry and Mandy pushed through the crowd to get to them.

The three of them carried a bleeding, barely conscious Ty away from the fighting. Mandy ripped off the sleeve of her shirt, and she and Dinah applied pressure to his wound, begging their closest friend to hold on.

"Please—I'll do anything," Dinah sobbed. *"Please come back."*

Larry listened to Ty's chest, and tears pooled in his eyes. He met Dinah's gaze and shook his head.

He was gone. Protecting Dinah had been Ty's final act.

As Mandy wailed over Ty's body, Larry rushed forward to where Moody lay on the ground, dazed from Dinah's scream, and went in for an attack. Dinah spun around, her entire body on fire with rage, with pain—with power aching to be unleashed.

She ran back into the fighting crowd, passing prisoners fleeing for the doors, and found Oliver in the thick of it, firing arrows at the Talons in the balconies and dodging strikes.

"Can you help me get the rest of the prisoners out of here to safety? I'm about to—to demolish every last Talon in here."

One look at her face was all Oliver needed to see that she was serious. He launched into action, soon joined by Mandy, as the two of them ushered the innocent prisoners through the shattered metal security doors that led outside, toward the front iron gates. It was almost . . . too easy. Where was Mayor Cobblepot, and how was he letting anyone get through those doors?

Dinah glanced back at Ty's body . . . and she had her answer. As Sandra joined Larry in fighting the undead Talon, Mayor Cobblepot slipped toward Ty's body, reaching into his pocket. He pulled out a bottle filled with smoky amber liquid. *The serum.* Dionesium and electrum. And then it occurred to Dinah: there wasn't a single dead body on the floor, even though she'd seen the Talons kill half a dozen prisoners.

Because Cobblepot was reviving them right away . . . turning them into Talons of his own. And now he was going to do the same to Ty, turning Dinah's oldest friend into a monster. Unless Dinah could stop him.

She thought of her mother and Ty, both of their lives cut short by the evil infecting Gotham City. This Canary Cry was for them. And as it came flooding out of her, the bars of Arkham Asylum shattered one by one, spilling shards of metal onto the floor. Dinah fixed her gaze on the fallen debris, aiming her sound wave at the shards—and the force of her scream lifted the pieces, carrying them into the air and aiming them straight into the mayor and the Talons' chests. Like arrows of her own.

The building swayed, the foundation shook. Dozens of Talons dropped to the ground, unmoving. She watched as the undead Talon roared in pain from the force of her scream, clutching his head in agony—until his body hit the ground one last time, shattering to pieces just like the prison bars. Mayor Cobblepot crumpled to his knees as a chunk of balcony from the top floor came crashing down, crushing his skull.

After looking around wildly one more time, to make sure

every last Talon was dead, Dinah grabbed hold of Larry and Sandra. The three of them dodged falling pieces of debris as the ceiling began to cave in. They sprinted through the open security exit just before the roof of Arkham Asylum began to cave in.

Oliver and Mandy rushed toward them as soon as they hit the open air, and pulled them away from the rapidly crumbling building. Dinah turned and aimed one last Cry at the building—her most powerful scream yet. With one last thunderous roar, the walls of Arkham collapsed in on themselves under the weight of the caving roof. The debris exploded into the night, dust spinning high into the air. Arkham Asylum was done. It was over. Together, with the rest of the surviving Resistance prisoners, they stood back, watching as the chaos from within Arkham's walls turned to quiet and the remains of the building settled. There were no screams from within. The Talons, the mayor—they were gone.

Suddenly, Dinah's reverberating cry changed shape.

Her voice lifted into song. A song of relief, triumph, of a battle won. Possibly an entire *war* won in a single night.

Oliver, Larry, Sandra, and Mandy ambushed her with hugs, but Dinah was looking somewhere else. Up above, where a tiny yellow canary fluttered its wings.

"*We* did it," Dinah whispered up to the sky.

CHAPTER TWENTY-THREE

While the rest of Gotham City reeled from the life-altering events of the night before, Dinah wasted no time, returning to Robinson Park as the first rays of morning light filtered through the gray. Even after all she'd just endured and accomplished, she still felt a twinge of nerves as she entered the park. *What if it doesn't work?* What if there was no vault; what if she was putting herself right back into danger, so soon after she'd freed herself from it?

But then Dinah looked down at her black leather costume, the fighting stick bouncing against her palm. She glanced at the two women beside her—the courageous, brilliant mind of the Oracle, and the opera diva who never stopped believing in rediscovering her voice. And she knew this time would be different. Most of all, she wasn't simply Dinah Laurel Lance anymore. She was returning as the Black Canary.

Together with Barbara Gordon and Mariam Noor, Dinah followed the same winding path that began this journey for her weeks ago. They passed the Forum of the Twelve Caesars and stopped to salute the superheroes in the twelve gilded graves. Dinah would soon see what could be done about adding a lucky thirteenth headstone to the group, to honor the original Black Canary.

They waded through the overgrown thicket of grass and trees, passed the rotting reservoir, until at last the white marble palace peeked out through the trees. And as soon as she saw it, Dinah could feel the voices calling out to her, beckoning her forward.

"Go on," Barbara urged softly.

Dinah looked up at the opera house and began to sing. She heard Mariam's astonished gasp at the sound, the first time she'd heard anything like it since their voices were all stolen twenty years ago. But Dinah wasn't thinking about her own voice now. She used it as a tool, a beacon, activating her sonar hearing.

A mix of tones, high and low, light and deep, flitted through her mind like scraps of memory, only these memories didn't belong to her—Dinah was just their observer. All she could do was follow the rising sound. It led her through the double doors of the opera house, which finally swung open. No monsters waited to stop them this time.

Dinah and Mariam walked on either side of Barbara's wheelchair as the three of them entered the time capsule of a frozen opera house—where gold-rimmed glasses still lay in wait on the bar, where a marble grand staircase gleamed with the promise of the lavish productions waiting upstairs. They passed framed posters of the operas from two-plus decades ago, Mariam wiping tears from her eyes as she returned to her old home. And as they moved through the gallery of portraits and posters, the volume in Dinah's ears reached a deafening peak. And that's when she knew: she was looking right at the vault. It was *real*.

Her heart was pounding so fast, she felt like it might fly out of her chest. Dinah moved forward in slow motion, reaching out her hand toward the life-sized black-and-white portrait of an eighteenth-century male opera star hanging on the wall. The three of them worked together to lift it from its perch on the wall—and Mariam let out a cry of shock.

There was another painting beneath the portrait of the man. It was a portrait of *Mariam Noor* herself, in full period costume as Violetta from *La Traviata*. Her buried past, uncovered.

Dinah reached for the side of Mariam's portrait opposite the hinges and swung it outward. And there it was, just as suspected. A tall, vertical vault. She moved her palm across the cool metal door in awe.

No one breathed as Barbara pulled open the metal door. Whatever Dinah might have imagined them finding, *this* certainly wasn't it. Instead of recordings or anything remotely musical, they found a cabinet lined with test tubes, all filled with a swirling, cloudy red substance.

"What is it?" Mariam asked, her face crushed with disappointment.

Barbara lifted one of the vials, and a slight smile lit her face.

"If it's what I think it is—preserved vocal cord tissue from the stolen voices—then I can use it to make an antidote. A vaccine of sorts." She met their eyes, excitement growing in hers. "One that can reverse the Silencing for good."

Four Months Later

As Larry's car pulled up to Gotham City High for the first day back at school, nothing could have prepared Dinah for the sight outside her window. A sight that sent emotion flooding through her body, and that would have seemed like a far-off dream just months ago. But it was real.

Right there in front of her, swarming the school entrance where a GRAND RE-OPENING! banner waved in the wind, were all the female students, returning to the school that had so recently kicked them out. Yet these weren't the same girls who had sat quietly and taken it as Mrs. Pritchard waxed poetic about the Silencing. They weren't the same girls who had passed through these halls in their Court-mandated matching skirts and blouses, weighed down by the consequences of what would happen if they dipped a toe out of line or spoke a word out of turn. Instead, her peers were made almost unrecognizable, flaunting their newly won freedoms. Through the doors of the front entrance, Dinah could see they wore actual blue denim *jeans*—just like the pair Larry had surprised Dinah with, which she was giddy to be wearing now—and bright-colored tops, some emblazoned with slogans, others sleeveless and showing no-longer-hidden skin. They wore sneakers they could run in or dressed up their jeans with heels, and it was these differences that were so striking, so exciting, to Dinah. Instead of one monotonous student body where everyone had to be the same, now she got to see all the different, glorious shades of them.

"Have a great day, sweetie." Larry leaned from the driver's seat to give her a hug, and she squeezed him tight. "I love you. I'm proud of you."

"Thanks, Dad." Dinah smiled at him. "Ditto."

She stepped out of the car into the January chill and a whirl of voices. She could hear fast-paced chatter, peals of laughter, and, woven through it all, snippets of song. Newly unearthed recordings of female pop stars played through some of the students' phones, and Dinah blinked back tears at the sound—especially when her peers started to sing along. As naturally as if they'd been singing all their lives. And her mind rushed back to that incredible, fateful day in the library, when Barbara administered the first antidote to Mariam Noor. Dinah had stood by watching, the hopes of an entire population riding on this moment.

As Barbara injected the serum in the needle, Mariam closed her eyes. And then—

A trilling soprano. Pure and crisp, with a stunning power behind its beauty, as it soared above and around them. More beautiful than she ever could have imagined.

Tears streamed down Mariam's cheeks as the three of them clasped hands in victory.

The lives—their freedoms—were back.

No girl, no woman, would ever have to be silent again.

"Dinah!"

Mandy ran toward her, looking radiant in a peach puffer jacket with a pair of black skinny jeans—skinny jeans being one of their favorite new discoveries. Dinah beamed at the sight of her, and the girls threw their arms around each other.

"Happy New Year! Can you believe this?" Mandy gestured around them. "I never thought I'd live to see the day."

"Same. It's like walking through a dream or something, isn't it?"

Mandy lowered her voice.

"Do you think any of . . . *them* will be here?"

Dinah looked back at the rush of incoming students, feeling her muscles tense up as she scanned the faces, looking for them: the children of the Court. But they were nowhere in sight. She didn't expect to see them again . . . not for a long time, anyway.

The shift had been swift and dramatic after the fall of Arkham and the return of the female voices. It was incredible to see how quickly the Owls lost their power once their weapons were gone. A large group of Talons had perished in Arkham, and without Cobblepot's serum to keep the newest undead additions to the Talon Force alive, the army was a fraction of its size. The Owls must have known they didn't stand a chance against the new and returning superheroes. And if they'd had any hopes of maintaining their positions at the helm of society, those delusions were shattered as soon as women began to sing again. Now that the women had reclaimed what was theirs, there was nothing the Court could hold over them anymore. The Court families were quick to flee the City of Gotham. And without their leadership, the rest of the Talons were soon to follow.

Still, Larry and Barbara had both warned that a time might come, years down the road, when the Owls would attempt to rise again. They had played this game for too long throughout history, a constant power struggle between good and evil, and Dinah couldn't expect that the war was won for good. She had to be at peace with the fact that it was won *now*. And if they did come back . . . then the Black Canary, Green Arrow, the Oracle, and Lady Shiva would all be ready.

"No," Dinah finally answered. "I don't think we'll see them anytime soon."

Mandy nodded, but there was still something clouding her expression. And as Dinah looked up at the school's front steps, she knew who Mandy was picturing there.

"I miss him, too," Dinah whispered.

Mandy blinked back tears. Ty was one of the only things they had a hard time talking about. The loss was too great. But the one fact that sustained Dinah was knowing that those who caused his death were gone. They couldn't hurt anyone again.

Suddenly, Dinah felt a pair of arms wrap around her waist from behind. She broke into a smile and turned to look up into the grinning face of Oliver Queen.

"Hey, Dinah." He bent down, brushing his lips against hers, and Dinah felt a delicious thrill run through her body.

"Hi, Ollie." She wrapped her arms around his neck, smiling as he tenderly kissed her forehead.

"Guys, not to interrupt this charming PDA, but—the

mayor's here!" Mandy's voice rose in excitement, and Dinah and Oliver turned to look, still holding on to each other.

A parade wound down the block with a marching band at the helm, playing an upbeat, joyful tune that made Dinah's smile widen. The procession carried colorful banners that read A NEW DAY FOR GOTHAM CITY! and MAKE YOUR VOICES HEARD! while the crowd of students gathered round, clapping and cheering at the top of their lungs as the parade weaved its way toward the main entrance.

And then the marching band and the other performers stepped aside, revealing Gotham City's first elected mayor in decades. She sat tall and proud in her wheelchair, smiling at the crowd, with a microphone in her hand. *Mayor Barbara Gordon.* Dinah's chest swelled at the sight.

"Happy New Year, all, and welcome, students, to your first day at the new-and-improved Gotham City High!" Her voice was greeted with more cheers, and Dinah and Mandy jumped up and down together, waving at Barbara, who winked in their direction.

"Starting today, you will find an entirely new faculty of teachers, instructors who are both progressive *and* a return to form from the days before our society was shaken. Starting today, all activities and opportunities are open to every single one of you—regardless of your gender, race, orientation, or upbringing." She lifted her face to the sky. "It's a new day for Gotham City, and for all of us."

The new school principal, Mr. Singh—a former faculty member from the pre-Court days who came out of retirement at Barbara's suggestion—beamed beside her. He ceremoniously handed her a pair of scissors, and everyone cheered as she cut the ribbon.

"School is officially in session!"

On cue, the first bell rang. As Mayor Gordon waved goodbye, the students raced up the front stairs, scattering into the different classrooms. Only Dinah, Mandy, and Oliver stayed behind for a moment with Barbara.

"Great first day on the job, Mayor Gordon," Oliver said with a grin, shaking her hand.

"Thank you, Oliver." Barbara smiled back, and then lowered her voice as she turned to Dinah. "I'll see you and Sandra at the library same time tomorrow, okay? Things may be peaceful now, but we can't afford to get lax in our weekly training . . . just in case."

"I'm coming again this time," Mandy chimed in. "I'm basically her workout partner these days, and if you need a fourth Bird—well, I want to be ready."

"Sounds like a plan," Barbara said warmly. "Your loyalty, bravery, and athleticism would make you a strong addition."

Mandy beamed back at Barbara while Dinah leaned over to give her a hug.

"We'll see you tomorrow, Barb—I mean, Mayor Gordon."

They watched her go, the procession moving alongside her. And then Mandy dashed off to her first class, leaving Dinah and Oliver alone as they climbed the steps together. He laced his hand through hers, and Dinah looked up at him with a sparkle in her eyes.

"I meant to tell you . . . I wrote a new song last night."

"Oh, really?" Oliver raised an eyebrow. "Did it have a little something to do with your favorite archer?"

"Maybe," Dinah teased him. "You want to hear it?"

"That depends." He gave her a mock-serious look. "Is it another 'Shattered Fairy Tale'?"

Dinah swatted his arm. She didn't know what had come over her when she decided to share that one with him, but he wasn't going to let her live it down. At least they could both agree: it was one catchy song.

"Come on, sing the new one for me," Oliver coaxed. "Before we go in."

"Okay." Dinah stopped at the top of the stairs, looking out at Gotham City beyond. And then, with Oliver's arm around her shoulder, she began to sing.

ACKNOWLEDGMENTS

Getting to write Black Canary's story has been the "pinch me, I'm dreaming" moment of my career thus far, and I am beyond grateful for all the heroes in my own life who helped me get here. Two literary superheroes in particular, who were most instrumental in this book, are Chelsea Eberly and Sasha Henriques—I bow down to you both! Chelsea, I am forever in awe over the way you instantly saw my vision for this project and believed in it, and me, enough to give me this opportunity of a lifetime. You made an incredible impact on my life in a short time, and I thank my lucky stars that I got to meet and work with you!

Sasha, the lucky stars were out again in full force when we were paired up on this project—you have been an absolute dream of an editor! Your notes and insights were truly brilliant, and you inspired me to step up my writing more and more with each draft. I'm also incredibly grateful for your kindness and understanding while I juggled our schedule with toddler parenting in a pandemic. You've been amazing in every way, and I'm so thankful!

Sara Sargent, thank you for all your support with this book, and for going above and beyond to make sure I had the time I needed to make it shine. You have been wonderful! Enormous gratitude to Michelle Nagler and Caroline Abbey for giving this project the green light—I am thankful and thrilled to be working with your team! To everyone at Random House Children's Books who has had a hand in the making of this book, I thank you with all my heart. Special thanks to Josh Redlich for helping spread the word about this book far and wide; to Jocelyn Lange for taking it around the world; to Barbara Bakowski for the sharp copyediting; and to managing editor Janet Foley for steering our ship on a breakneck schedule (we made it!). Jen Bartel and Regina Flath, there are not enough heart-eye emojis for the gorgeous cover. Thank you for creating the book cover of my dreams!

Ben Harper at Warner Bros., a million thank-yous for your fantastic support of this project and for your invaluable editorial insights! It's such a privilege to get to work with you. Thank you to the entire team at Warner Bros./DC for entrusting me with these iconic characters—it's been the thrill of a lifetime.

To the very first person to suggest I should write a Black Canary story: Sara Miller at DC Comics, thank you *so much* for knowing from the start that Dinah was a character I was meant to write, and for your super-helpful notes on the manuscript. Getting to come full circle at the end of the editorial process, with you reading one of the last drafts, was such kismet!

Michele Wells at DC, our emails and book festival hangs brought me into the DC orbit, and I am so thankful that you saw something special in my work—it meant the world! Sue

Karlin, thank you so much for connecting Michele and me. (And thank you, WonderCon, for being "the room where it happened"!)

To the brilliant creators whose characters and worlds I had the honor and thrill of working with, especially Robert Kanigher and Carmine Infantino for dreaming up Black Canary, Scott Snyder and Greg Capullo for creating the Court of Owls, and Mort Weisinger and George Papp for giving us the Green Arrow. Thank you for your incredible legacy.

To my amazing team, starting with my agent, Joe Veltre, at Gersh: thank you for always taking such great care of me and my career and for moving quickly to connect me with Random House back when I first said I had an idea for a DC Icons book. You are a dream maker! Many thanks also to Tori Eskue and everyone I'm so fortunate to work with at Gersh.

Brooklyn Weaver at Energy Entertainment, thank you for your unwavering belief in me and your enthusiasm for my words—I'm lucky to have you as my manager. Chad Christopher, many thanks for your help on all my contracts and for taking great care of me since I was a newbie writer!

Publicity mavens Crystal Patriarche and Megan Beatie, thank you so much for helping readers discover my books! Special thanks as well to Keely Platte and Paige Herbert at BookSparks for all you do.

Endless thanks and love to Heather Holley, songstress and producer extraordinaire and one of my best friends in the world. Some of the greatest things in my life happened because of you. Here's to many more years of giggling in the recording studio together! ☺

Many thanks to three different people close to my heart who believed in me at pivotal points in my career: Brooke

Kaufman Halsband, Josh Bratman, and Alexandra Cooper. I'm so grateful for each of you!

To my family, starting with my first and forever hero: my dad, Shon Saleh. None of this would have been possible without the incredible, unconditional support you've given me since I was a little girl juggling a notebook, a pen, and a microphone in my hands. The immense love I have for you inspired the father/daughter storyline in this book, and I can't thank you enough for showing me what it means to be a truly great parent—both on the page and in real life.

To my north star and best friend, the one who "Gold Standard" was really written for: my mom, ZaZa. You've been my champion from the start, and everything I am is because of you. There are no words big enough to convey my love and gratitude for you!

All my love to the best big brother, Arian Saleh—thank you for lighting up my imagination since we were kids, and for your invaluable suggestion that I check out *Arkham Asylum*! So grateful to have you, Sai, and Fara Joon!

Thank you to my heroic mother-in-law, Dorothy Robertiello, for stepping in to save the day and helping us take care of Leo during the craziest, busiest time—where would we be without you?! I can't thank you enough for giving me that precious writer's commodity of time and bringing Leo so many smiles and giggles in the process. We love you to the moon and back!

Mia Antonelli, thank you for always being by my side through every book and milestone and life moment—you're more than a best friend, you are family!

Love and thanks to my big, beautiful family on the Saleh and Madjidi sides, as well as my in-laws, the Robertiellos, and my friend-families, the Bratmans and Cohanims. Papa, thank you for lighting up my world and believing in me so strongly from the very beginning—I miss you every day.

A giant round of applause to Mariam Khosravani and the Iranian American Women Foundation for all that you do to support and celebrate our community. There is a reason I chose the name Mariam for one of this book's heroes! ♥

And most of all, my greatest thanks go to the two halves of my heart, who give meaning to everything I do: my husband and my son, Chris and Leo Robertiello.

Chris, you have inspired everything I've created, going all the way back to that first song I wrote about you at age twenty-one. ♥ None of my dreams could ever match the real-life magic of getting to meet and fall in love with you and go on this incredible adventure together, first with our dogs (love you, Honey and Daisy!) and now our miracle boy. Thank you for being so supportive of the unconventional creative life, putting up with all my deadline hours, and being so exceptional at everything you do. Leo and I are the luckiest to have you.

Leo Loulou, the heart of my heart, who waited so patiently for me to finish this book and who, at just two years old, excitedly sang "The Black Canary Sings" right along with me—thank you for filling my every day with joy. I love you more than the whole wide world.

Last but not least, to all the real-life superheroes out there who are standing up for equality, for human rights—your voice is the song we need most. *Thank you.*

ABOUT THE AUTHOR

ALEXANDRA MONIR is the Iranian American author of the internationally bestselling novel *The Final Six* and five other books for young adults. Alexandra spent her teen years as a pop singer before publishing her debut novel, *Timeless*, and continues to write and record music. She lives in Los Angeles with her husband, toddler son, and one fluffy Shih Tzu. To learn more about Alexandra, visit her online.

alexandramonir.com

 twitter.com/TimelessAlex

 @alexandramonir

 @AlexandraMonirAuthor

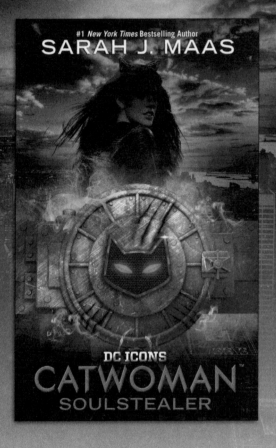

CHAPTER 1

The roaring crowd in the makeshift arena didn't set her blood on fire.

It did not shake her, or rile her, or set her hopping from foot to foot. No, Selina Kyle only rolled her shoulders—once, twice.

And waited.

The wild cheering that barreled down the grimy hallway to the prep room was little more than a distant rumble of thunder. A storm, just like the one that had rolled over the East End on her walk from the apartment complex. She'd been soaked before she reached the covert subway entrance that led into the underground gaming warren owned by Carmine Falcone, the latest of Gotham City's endless parade of mob bosses.

But like any other storm, this fight, too, would be weathered.

Rain still drying in her long, dark hair, Selina checked that it was indeed tucked into its tight bun atop her head. She'd made the mistake once of wearing a ponytail—in her second street fight. The other girl had managed to grab it, and those few seconds when Selina's neck had been exposed had lasted longer than any in her life.

But she'd won—barely. And she'd learned. Had learned at every fight since, whether on the streets above or in the arena carved into the sewers beneath Gotham City.

It didn't matter who her opponent was tonight. The challengers were all usually variations of the same: desperate men who owed more than they could repay to Falcone. Fools willing to risk their lives for a chance to lift their debts by taking on one of his Leopards in the ring. The prize: never having to look over their shoulders for a waiting shadow. The cost of failing: having their asses handed to them—and the debts remained. Usually with the promise of a one-way ticket to the bottom of the Sprang River. The odds of winning: slim to none.

Regardless of whatever sad sack she'd be battling tonight, Selina prayed Falcone would give her the nod faster than last time. That fight . . . He'd made her keep that particularly brutal match going. The crowd had been too excited, too ready to spend money on the cheap alcohol and everything else for sale in the subterranean warren. She'd taken home more bruises than usual, and the man she'd beaten to unconsciousness . . .

Not her problem, she told herself again and again. Even when she saw her adversaries' bloodied faces in her dreams, both asleep and waking. What Falcone did with them after the fight was not her problem. She left her opponents breathing. At least she had that.

And at least she wasn't dumb enough to push back outright, like some of the other Leopards. The ones who were too proud or too stupid or too young to get how the game was played. No, her small rebellions against Carmine Falcone were subtler. He wanted men dead—she left them unconscious, but did it so well that not one person in the crowd objected.

A fine line to walk, especially with her sister's life hanging in the balance. Push back too much, and Falcone might ask questions, start wondering who meant the most to her. Where to strike hardest. She'd never allow it to get to that point. Never risk Maggie's safety like that—even if these fights were all for her. Every one of them.

It had been three years since Selina had joined the Leopards, and nearly two and a half since she'd proved herself against the other girl gangs well enough that Mika, her Alpha, had introduced her to Falcone. Selina hadn't dared miss that meeting.

Order in the girl gangs was simple: The Alpha of each gang ruled and protected, laid down punishment and reward. The Alphas' commands were law. And the enforcers of those commands were their Seconds and Thirds. From there, the pecking order turned murkier. Fighting offered a way to rise in the ranks—or you could fall, depending on how badly a match went. Even an Alpha might be challenged if you were stupid or brave enough to do so.

But the thought of ascending the ranks had been far from Selina's mind when Mika had brought Falcone over to watch her take on the Second of the Wolf Pack and leave the girl leaking blood onto the concrete of the alley. Before that fight, only four leopard spots had been inked onto Selina's left arm, each a trophy of a fight won.

Selina adjusted the hem of her white tank. At seventeen, she now had twenty-seven spots inked across both arms.

Undefeated.

That's what the match emcee was declaring down the hall. Selina could just make out the croon of words: *The undefeated champion, the fiercest of Leopards . . .*

A thump on the metal door was her signal to go. Selina checked her shirt, her black spandex pants, the green sneakers that matched her eyes—though no one had ever commented on it. She flexed her fingers within their wrappings. All good.

Or as good as could be.

The rusty door groaned as she opened it. Mika was tending to the new girl in the hall beyond, the flickering fluorescent lights draining the Alpha's golden-brown skin of its usual glow.

Mika threw Selina an assessing look over her narrow shoulder, her tight braid shifting with the movement. The new girl sniffling in front of her gingerly wiped away the blood streaming from her swollen nose. One of the kitten's eyes was already puffy and red, the other swimming with unshed tears.

No wonder the crowd was riled. If a Leopard had taken that bad a beating, it must have been one hell of a fight. Brutal enough that Mika put a hand on the girl's pale arm to keep her from swaying.

Down the shadowy hall that led into the arena, one of Falcone's bouncers beckoned. Selina shut the door behind her. She'd left no valuables behind. She had nothing worth stealing, anyway.

"Be careful," Mika said as she passed, her voice low and soft. "He's got a worse batch than usual tonight." The kitten hissed, yanking her head away as Mika dabbed her split lip with a disinfectant wipe. Mika snarled a warning at her, and the kitten wisely fell still, trembling a bit as the Alpha cleaned out the cut. Mika added without glancing back, "He saved the best for you. Sorry."

"He always does," Selina said coolly, even as her stomach roiled. "I can handle it."

She didn't have any other choice. Losing would leave Maggie with no one to look after her. And refusing to fight? Not an option, either.

In the three years that Selina had known Mika, the Alpha had never suggested ending their arrangement with Carmine Falcone. Not when having Falcone back the Leopards made the other East End gangs think twice about pushing in on their territory. Even if it meant doing these fights and offering up Leopards for the crowd's enjoyment.

Falcone turned it into a weekly spectacle—a veritable Roman circus to make the underbelly of Gotham City love *and* fear him. It certainly helped that many of the other notorious lowlifes had been imprisoned thanks to a certain do-gooder running around the city in a cape.

Mika eased the kitten to the prep room, giving Selina a jerk of the chin—an order to go.

But Selina paused to scan the hall, the exits. Even down here, in the heart of Falcone's territory, it was a death wish to be defenseless in the open. Especially if you were an Alpha with as many enemies as Mika had.

Three figures slipped in from a door at the opposite end of the hall, and Selina's shoulders loosened a bit. Ani, Mika's Second, with two other Leopards flanking her.

Good. They'd guard the exit while their Alpha tended to their own.

The crowd's cheering rumbled through the concrete floor, rattling the loose ceramic tiles on the walls, echoing along Selina's bones and breath as she neared the dented metal door to the arena. The bouncer gestured for her to hurry the hell up, but she kept her strides even. Stalking.

The Leopards, these fights . . . they were her job. And it paid well. With her mother gone and her sister sick, no legit job could pay as much or as quickly.

The bouncer opened the door, the unfiltered roar of the crowd bursting down the hall like a pack of rabid wolves.

Selina Kyle blew out a long breath as she lifted her chin and stepped into the sound and the light and the wrath.

Let the bloodying begin.

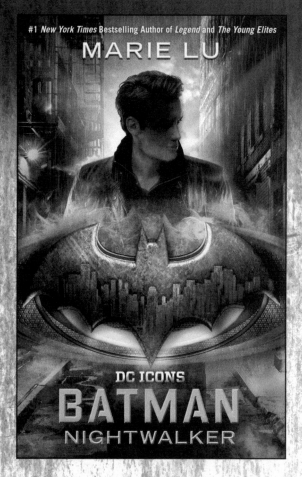

As Bruce rounded another bend, the wails suddenly turned deaf-ening, and a mass of flashing red and blue lights blinked against the buildings near the end of the street. White barricades and yellow police tape completely blocked the intersection. Even from here, Bruce could see fire engines and black SWAT trucks clustered together, the silhouettes of police running back and forth in front of the headlights.

Inside his car, the electronic voice came on again, followed by a transparent map overlaid against his windshield. *"Heavy police activity ahead. Alternate route suggested."*

A sense of dread filled his chest.

Bruce flicked away the map and pulled to an abrupt halt in front of the barricade—right as the unmistakable *pop-pop-pop* of gunfire rang out in the night air.

He remembered the sound all too well. The memory of his parents' deaths sent a wave of dizziness through him. *Another robbery. A murder. That's what all this is.*

Then he shook his head. *No, that can't be right.* There were far too many cops here for a simple robbery.

"Step *out* of your vehicle, and put your hands in the air!" a police officer shouted through a megaphone, her voice echoing along the block. Bruce's head jerked toward her. For an instant, he thought her command was directed at him, but then he saw that her back was turned, her attention fixed on the corner of the building bearing the name BELLINGHAM INDUSTRIES & CO. "We have you surrounded, Nightwalker! This is your final warning!"

Another officer came running over to Bruce's car. He whirled an arm exaggeratedly for Bruce to turn his car around. His voice harsh with panic, he warned, "Turn back *now*. It's not safe!"

Before Bruce could reply, a blinding fireball exploded behind the officer. The street rocked.

Even from inside his car, Bruce felt the heat of the blast. Every window in the building burst simultaneously, a million shards of glass raining down on the pavement below. The police ducked in unison, their arms shielding their heads. Fragments of glass dinged like hail against Bruce's windshield.

From inside the blockade, a white car veered around the corner at top speed. Bruce saw immediately what the car was aiming for—a slim gap between the police barricades where a SWAT team truck had just pulled through.

The car raced right toward the gap.

"I said, *get out of here!*" the officer shouted at Bruce. A thin ribbon of blood trickled down the man's face. "That is an *order!*"

Bruce heard the scream of the getaway car's tires against the asphalt. He'd been in his father's garage a thousand times, helping him tinker with an endless number of engines from the best cars in the world. At WayneTech, Bruce had watched in fascination as tests were conducted on custom engines, conceptual jets, stealth tech, new vehicles of every kind.

And so he knew: whatever was installed under that hood was faster than anything the GCPD could hope to have.

They'll never catch him.

But I can.

His Aston Martin was probably the only vehicle here that

could overtake the criminal's, the only one powerful enough to chase it down. Bruce's eyes followed the path the car would likely take, his gaze settling on a sign at the end of the street that pointed toward the freeway.

I can get him.

The white getaway vehicle shot straight through the gap in the barricade, clipping two police cars as it went.

No, not this time. Bruce slammed his gas pedal.

The Aston Martin's engine let out a deafening roar, and the car sped forward. The officer who'd shouted at him stumbled back. In the rearview mirror, Bruce saw him scramble to his feet and wave the other officers' cars forward, both his arms held high.

"Hold your fire!" Bruce could hear him yelling. "Civilian in proximity—*hold your fire!*"

The getaway car made a sharp turn at the first intersection, and Bruce sped behind it a few seconds later. The street zigzagged, then turned in a wide arc as it led toward the freeway—and the Nightwalker took the on-ramp, leaving a trail of exhaust and two black skid marks on the road.

Bruce raced forward in close pursuit; his car mapped the ground instantly, swerving in a perfect curve to follow the ramp onto the freeway. He tapped twice on the windshield right over where the Nightwalker's white vehicle was.

"Follow him," Bruce commanded.

DAUGHTER OF IMMORTALS.
DAUGHTER OF DEATH.

THEIR FRIENDSHIP
WILL CHANGE THE WORLD.

TURN THE PAGE TO SEE HOW
DIANA'S BATTLE BEGINS
IN THIS DC ICONS STORY!

You do not enter a race to lose.

Diana bounced lightly on her toes at the starting line, her calves taut as bowstrings, her mother's words reverberating in her ears. A noisy crowd had gathered for the wrestling matches and javelin throws that would mark the start of the Nemeseian Games, but the real event was the footrace, and now the stands were buzzing with word that the queen's daughter had entered the competition.

When Hippolyta had seen Diana amid the runners clustered on the arena sands, she'd displayed no surprise. As was tradition, she'd descended from her viewing platform to wish the athletes luck in their endeavors, sharing a joke here, offering a kind word of encouragement there. She had nodded briefly to Diana, showing her no special favor, but she'd whispered, so low that only her daughter could hear, "You do not enter a race to lose."

Amazons lined the path that led out of the arena, already stamping their feet and chanting for the games to begin.

On Diana's right, Rani flashed her a radiant smile. "Good luck today." She was always kind, always gracious, and, of course, always victorious.

To Diana's left, Thyra snorted and shook her head. "She's going to need it."

Diana ignored her. She'd been looking forward to this race for weeks—a trek across the island to retrieve one of the red flags hung beneath the great dome in Bana-Mighdall. In a flat-out sprint, she didn't have a chance. She still hadn't come into the fullness of her Amazon strength. *You will in time*, her mother had promised. But her mother promised a lot of things.

This race was different. It required strategy, and Diana was ready. She'd been training in secret, running sprints with Maeve, and plotting a route that had rougher terrain but was definitely a straighter shot to the western tip of the island. She'd even— well, she hadn't exactly *spied*. . . . She'd gathered intelligence on the other Amazons in the race. She was still the smallest, and of course the youngest, but she'd shot up in the last year, and she was nearly as tall as Thyra now.

I don't need luck, she told herself. *I have a plan.* She glanced down the row of Amazons gathered at the starting line like troops readying for war and amended, *But a little luck wouldn't hurt, either.* She wanted that laurel crown. It was better than any royal circlet or tiara—an honor that couldn't be given, that had to be earned.

She found Maeve's red hair and freckled face in the crowd and grinned, trying to project confidence. Maeve returned the smile and gestured with both hands as if she were tamping down the air. She mouthed the words, "Steady on."

Diana rolled her eyes but nodded and tried to slow her breathing. She had a bad habit of coming out too fast and wasting her speed too early.

Now she cleared her mind and forced herself to concentrate on the course as Tekmessa walked the line, surveying the runners, jewels glinting in her thick corona of curls, silver bands flashing on her brown arms. She was Hippolyta's closest advisor, second in rank only to the queen, and she carried herself as if her belted indigo shift were battle armor.

"Take it easy, Pyxis," Tek murmured to Diana as she passed. "Wouldn't want to see you crack." Diana heard Thyra snort again, but she refused to flinch at the nickname. *You won't be smirking when I'm on the victors' podium,* she promised.

Tek raised her hands for silence and bowed to Hippolyta, who sat between two other members of the Amazon Council in the royal loge—a high platform shaded by a silken overhang dyed in the vibrant red and blue of the queen's colors. Diana knew that was where her mother wanted her right now, seated beside her, waiting for the start of the games instead of competing. None of that would matter when she won.

Hippolyta dipped her chin the barest amount, elegant in her white tunic and riding trousers, a simple circlet resting against her forehead. She looked relaxed, at her ease, as if she might decide to leap down and join the competition at any time, but still every inch the queen.

Tek addressed the athletes gathered on the arena sands. "In whose honor do you compete?"

"For the glory of the Amazons," they replied in unison. "For the glory of our queen." Diana felt her heart beat harder. She'd never said the words before, not as a competitor.

"To whom do we give praise each day?" Tek trumpeted.

"Hera," they chorused. "Athena, Demeter, Hestia, Aphrodite, Artemis." The goddesses who had created Themyscira and gifted it to Hippolyta as a place of refuge.

Tek paused, and along the line, Diana heard the whispers of other names: Oya, Durga, Freyja, Mary, Yael. Names once cried out in death, the last prayers of female warriors fallen in battle, the words that had brought them to this island and given them new life as Amazons. Beside Diana, Rani murmured the names of the demon-fighting Matri, the seven mothers, and pressed the rectangular amulet she always wore to her lips.

Tek raised a blood-red flag identical to those that would be waiting for the runners in Bana-Mighdall.

"May the island guide you to just victory!" she shouted.

She dropped the red silk. The crowd roared. The runners surged toward the eastern arch. Like that, the race had begun.

Diana and Maeve had anticipated a bottleneck, but Diana still felt a pang of frustration as runners clogged the stone throat of the tunnel, a tangle of white tunics and muscled limbs, footsteps echoing off the stone, all of them trying to get clear of the arena at once. Then they were on the road, sprinting across the island, each runner choosing her own course.

You do not enter a race to lose.

Diana set her pace to the rhythm of those words, bare feet slapping the packed earth of the road that would lead her through the tangle of the Cybelian Woods to the island's northern coast.

Ordinarily, a miles-long trek through this forest would be a slow one, hampered by fallen trees and tangles of vines so thick they had to be hacked through with a blade you didn't mind dulling. But Diana had plotted her way well. An hour after she entered the woods, she burst from the trees onto the deserted coast road. The wind lifted her hair, and salt spray lashed her face. She breathed deep, checked the position of the sun. She was going to win—not just place but win.

She'd mapped out the course the week before with Maeve, and they'd run it twice in secret, in the gray-light hours of early morning, when their sisters were first rising from their beds, when the kitchen fires were still being kindled, and the only curious eyes they'd had to worry about belonged to anyone up early to hunt game or cast nets for the day's catch. But hunters kept to the woods and meadows farther south, and no one fished off this part of the coast; there was no good place to launch a boat, just the steep steel-colored cliffs plunging straight down to the sea, and a tiny, unwelcoming cove that could only be reached by a path so narrow you had to shuffle down sideways, back pressed to the rock.

The northern shore was gray, grim, and inhospitable, and Diana knew every inch of its secret landscape, its crags and caves, its tide pools teeming with limpets and anemones. It was a good place to be alone. *The island seeks to please,* her mother had told her. It was why Themyscira was forested by redwoods in some places and rubber trees in others; why you could spend an afternoon roaming the grasslands on a scoop-neck pony and the evening atop a camel, scaling a moonlit dragonback of sand dunes. They were all pieces of the lives the Amazons had led before they came to the island, little landscapes of the heart.

Diana sometimes wondered if Themyscira had called the northern coast into being just for her so that she could challenge herself climbing on the sheer drop of its cliffs, so that she could have a place to herself when the weight of being Hippolyta's daughter got to be too much.

You do not enter a race to lose.

Her mother had not been issuing a general warning. Diana's losses meant something different, and they both knew it—and not only because she was a princess.

Diana could almost feel Tek's knowing gaze on her, hear the mocking in her voice. *Take it easy, Pyxis.* That was the nickname Tek had given her. Pyxis. A little clay pot made to store jewels or a tincture of carmine for pinking the lips. The name was harmless, meant to tease, always said in love—or so Tek claimed. But it stung every time: a reminder that Diana was not like the other Amazons, and never would be. Her sisters were battle-proven warriors, steel forged from suffering and honed to greatness as they passed from life to immortality. All of them had earned their place on Themyscira. All but Diana, born of the island's soil and Hippolyta's longing for a child, fashioned from clay by her mother's hands—hollow and breakable. *Take it easy, Pyxis. Wouldn't want to see you crack.*

Diana steadied her breathing, kept her pace even. *Not today, Tek. This day the laurel belongs to me.*

She spared the briefest glance at the horizon, letting the sea breeze cool the sweat on her brow. Through the mists, she glimpsed the white shape of a ship. It had come close enough to the boundary that Diana could make out its sails. The craft was small—a schooner maybe? She had trouble remembering nautical details. Mainmast, mizzenmast, a thousand names for sails, and knots for rigging. It was one thing to be out on a boat, learning from Teuta, who had sailed with Illyrian pirates, but quite another to be stuck in the library at the Epheseum, staring glazed-eyed at diagrams of a brigantine or a caravel.

Sometimes Diana and Maeve made a game of trying to spot ships or planes, and once they'd even seen the fat blot of a cruise ship on the horizon. But most mortals knew to steer clear of their particular corner of the Aegean, where compasses spun and instruments suddenly refused to obey.

Today it looked like a storm was picking up past the mists of the boundary, and Diana was sorry she couldn't stop to watch it. The rains that came to Themyscira were tediously gentle and predictable, nothing like the threatening rumble of thunder, the shimmer of a far-off lightning strike.

"Do you ever miss storms?" Diana had asked one afternoon as she and Maeve lazed on the palace's sun-soaked rooftop terrace, listening to the distant roar and clatter of a tempest. Maeve had died in the Crossbarry Ambush, the last words on her lips a prayer to Saint Brigid of Kildare. She was new to the island by Amazon standards, and came from Cork, where storms were common.

"No," Maeve had said in her lilting voice. "I miss a good cup of tea, dancing, boys—definitely not rain."

"We dance," Diana protested.

Maeve had just laughed. "You dance differently when you know you won't live forever." Then she'd stretched, freckles like dense clouds of pollen on her white skin. "I think I was a cat in another life, because all I want is to lie around sleeping in the world's biggest sunbeam."

Steady on. Diana resisted the urge to speed forward. It was hard to remember to keep something in reserve with the early-morning sun on her shoulders and the wind at her back. She felt strong. But it was easy to feel strong when she was on her own.

A *boom* sounded over the waves, a hard metallic clap like a door slamming shut. Diana's steps faltered. On the blue horizon, a billowing column of smoke rose, flames licking at its base. The schooner was on fire, its prow blown to splinters and one of its masts smashed, the sail dragging over the rails.

Diana found herself slowing but forced her stride back on pace. There was nothing she could do for the schooner. Planes crashed. Ships were wrecked upon the rocks. That was the nature of the mortal world. It was a place where disaster could happen and often did. Human life was a tide of misery, one that never reached the island's shores. Diana focused her eyes on the path. Far, far ahead she could see sunlight gleaming gold off the great dome at Bana-Mighdall. First the red flag, then the laurel crown. That was the plan.

From somewhere on the wind, she heard a cry.

A gull, she told herself. *A girl*, some other voice within her insisted. *Impossible.* A human shout couldn't carry over such a great distance, could it?

It didn't matter. There was nothing she could do.

And yet her eyes strayed back to the horizon. *I just want to get a better view*, she told herself. *I have plenty of time. I'm ahead.*

There was no good reason to leave the ruts of the old cart track, no logic to veering out over the rocky point, but she did it anyway.

The waters near the shore were calm, clear, vibrant turquoise. The ocean beyond was something else—wild, deep-well blue, a sea gone almost black. The island might seek to please her and her sisters, but the world beyond the boundary didn't concern itself with the happiness or safety of its inhabitants.

Even from a distance, she could tell the schooner was sinking. But she saw no lifeboats, no distress flares, only pieces of the broken craft carried along by rolling waves. It was done. Diana rubbed her hands briskly over her arms, dispelling a sudden chill, and started making her way back to the cart track. That was the way of human life. She and Maeve had dived out by the boundary many times, swum the wrecks of airplanes and clipper ships and sleek motorboats. The salt water changed the wood, hardened it so it did not rot. Mortals were not the same. They were food for deep-sea fishes, for sharks—and for time that ate at them slowly, inevitably, whether they were on water or on land.

Diana checked the sun's position again. She could be at Bana-Mighdall in forty minutes, maybe less. She told her legs to move. She'd only lost a few moments. She could make up the time. Instead, she looked over her shoulder.

There were stories in all the old books about women who made the mistake of looking back. On the way out of burning cities. On the way out of hell. But Diana still turned her eyes to that ship sinking in the great waves, tilting like a bird's broken wing.

She measured the length of the cliff top. There were jagged rocks at the base. If she didn't leap with enough momentum, the impact would be ugly. Still, the fall wouldn't kill her. *That's true of a real Amazon*, she thought. *Is it true for you?* Well, she *hoped* the fall wouldn't kill her. Of course, if the fall didn't, her mother would.

Diana looked once more at the wreck and pushed off, running full out, arms pumping, stride long, picking up speed, closing the distance to the cliff's edge. *Stop stop stop*, her mind clamored. *This is madness.* Even if there were survivors, she could do nothing for them. To try to save them was to court exile, and there would be no exception to the rule—not even for a princess. *Stop.* She wasn't sure why she didn't obey. She wanted to believe it was because a hero's heart beat in her chest and demanded she answer that frightened call. But even as she launched herself off the cliff and into the empty sky, she knew part of what drew her on was the challenge of that great gray sea that did not care if she loved it.

Her body cut a smooth arc through the air, arms pointing like a compass needle, directing her course. She plummeted toward the water and broke the surface in a clean plunge, ears full of sudden silence, muscles tensed for the brutal impact of the rocks. None came. She shot upward, drew in a breath, and swam straight for the boundary, arms slicing through the warm water.

There was always a little thrill when she neared the boundary, when the temperature of the water began to change, the cold touching her fingertips first, then settling over her scalp and shoulders. Diana and Maeve liked to swim out from the southern beaches, daring themselves to go farther, farther. Once they'd glimpsed a ship passing in the mist, sailors standing at the stern. One of the men had lifted an arm, pointing in their direction. They'd plunged to safety, gesturing wildly to each other beneath the waves, laughing so hard that by the time they reached shore, they were both choking on salt water. *We could be sirens*, Maeve had shrieked as they'd flopped onto the warm sand, except neither of them could carry a tune. They'd spent the rest of the afternoon singing violently off-key Irish drinking songs and laughing themselves silly until Tek had found them. Then they'd shut up quick. Breaking the boundary was a minor infraction. Being seen by mortals anywhere near the island was cause for serious disciplinary action. And what Diana was doing now?

Stop. But she couldn't. Not when that high human cry still rang in her ears.

Diana felt the cold water beyond the boundary engulf her fully. The sea had her now, and it was not friendly. The current seized her legs, dragging her down, a massive, rolling force, the barest shrug of a god. *You have to fight it*, she realized, demanding that her muscles correct her course. She'd never had to work against the ocean.

She bobbed for a moment on the surface, trying to get her bearings as the waves crested around her. The water was full of debris, shards of wood, broken fiberglass, orange life jackets that the crew must not have had time to don. It was nearly impossible to see through the falling rain and the mists that shrouded the island.

What am I doing out here? she asked herself. *Ships come and go. Human lives are lost.* She dove again, peered through the rushing gray waters, but saw no one.

Diana surfaced, her own stupidity carving a growing ache in

her gut. She'd sacrificed the race. This was supposed to be the moment her sisters saw her truly, the chance to make her mother proud. Instead, she'd thrown away her lead, and for what? There was nothing here but destruction.

Out of the corner of her eye, she saw a flash of white, a big chunk of what might have been the ship's hull. It rose on a wave, vanished, rose again, and as it did, Diana glimpsed a slender brown arm holding tight to the side, fingers spread, knuckles bent. Then it was gone.

Another wave rose, a great gray mountain. Diana dove beneath it, kicking hard, then surfaced, searching, bits of lumber and fiberglass everywhere, impossible to sort one piece of flotsam from another.

There it was again—an arm, two arms, a body, bowed head and hunched shoulders, lemon-colored shirt, a tangle of dark hair. A girl—she lifted her head, gasped for breath, dark eyes wild with fear. A wave crashed over her in a spray of white water. The chunk of hull surfaced. The girl was gone.

Down again. Diana aimed for the place she'd seen the girl go under. She glimpsed a flash of yellow and lunged for it, seizing the fabric and using it to reel her in. A ghost's face loomed out at her from the cloudy water—golden hair, blue gaze wide and lifeless. She'd never seen a corpse up close before. She'd never seen a boy up close before. She recoiled, hand releasing his shirt, but even as she watched him disappear, she marked the differences—hard jaw, broad brow, just like the pictures in books.

She resurfaced, but she'd lost all sense of direction now—the waves, the wreck, the bare shadow of the island in the mists. If she drifted out much farther, she might not be able to find her way back.

Diana could not stop seeing the image of that slender arm, the ferocity in those fingers, clinging hard to life. *Once more*, she told herself. She dove, the chill of the water fastening tight around her bones now, burrowing deeper.

One moment the world was gray current and cloudy sea, and

the next the girl was there in her lemon-colored shirt, facedown, arms and legs outstretched like a star. Her eyes were closed.

Diana grabbed her around the waist and launched them toward the surface. For a terrifying second, she could not find the shape of the island, and then the mists parted. She kicked forward, wrapping the girl awkwardly against her chest with one arm, fingers questing for a pulse with the other. *There*—beneath the jaw, thready, indistinct, but there. Though the girl wasn't breathing, her heart still beat.

Diana hesitated. She could see the outlines of Filos and Ecthros, the rocks that marked the rough beginnings of the boundary. The rules were clear. You could not stop the mortal tide of life and death, and the island must never be touched by it. There were no exceptions. No human could be brought to Themyscira, even if it meant saving a life. Breaking that rule meant only one thing: exile.

Exile. The word was a stone, unwanted ballast, the weight unbearable. It was one thing to breach the boundary, but what she did next might untether her from the island, her sisters, her mother forever. The world seemed too large, the sea too deep. *Let go.* It was that simple. Let this girl slip from her grasp and it would be as if Diana had never leapt from those cliffs. She would be light again, free of this burden.

Diana thought of the girl's hand, the ferocious grip of her knuckles, the steel-blade determination in her eyes before the wave took her under. She felt the ragged rhythm of the girl's pulse, a distant drum, the sound of an army marching—one that had fought well but could not fight on much longer.

She swam for shore.

As she passed through the boundary with the girl clutched to her, the mists dissolved and the rain abated. Warmth flooded her body. The calm water felt oddly lifeless after the thrashing of the sea, but Diana wasn't about to complain.

When her feet touched the sandy bottom, she shoved up, shifting her grip to carry the girl from the shallows. She was eerily light, almost insubstantial. It was like holding a sparrow's body between her cupped hands. No wonder the sea had made such easy sport of this creature and her crewmates; she felt temporary, an artist's cast of a body rendered in plaster.

Diana laid her gently on the sand and checked her pulse again. No heartbeat now. She knew she needed to get the girl's heart going, get the water out of her lungs, but her memory on just how to do that was a bit hazy. Diana had studied the basics of reviving a drowning victim, but she hadn't ever had to put it into practice outside the classroom. It was also possible she hadn't paid close attention at the time. How likely was it that an Amazon was going to drown, especially in the calm waters off Themyscira? And now her daydreaming might cost this girl her life.

Do something, she told herself, trying to think past her panic. *Why did you drag her out of the water if you're only going to sit staring at her like a frightened rabbit?*

Diana placed two fingers on the girl's sternum, then tracked lower to what she hoped was the right spot. She locked her hands together and pressed. The girl's bones bent beneath her palms. Hurriedly, Diana drew back. What was this girl made of, anyway? Balsa wood? She felt about as solid as the little models of world monuments Diana had been forced to build for class. Gently, she pressed down again, then again. She shut the girl's nose with her fingers, closed her mouth over cooling mortal lips, and breathed.

The gust drove into the girl's chest, and Diana saw it rise, but this time the extra force seemed to be a good thing. Suddenly, the girl was coughing, her body convulsing as she spat up salt water. Diana sat back on her knees and released a short laugh. She'd done it. The girl was alive.

The reality of what she'd just dared struck her. All the hounds of Hades: *She'd done it. The girl was alive.*

And trying to sit up.

"Here," Diana said, bracing the girl's back with her arm. She couldn't simply kneel there, watching her flop around on the sand like a fish, and it wasn't as if she could put her back in the ocean. Could she? No. Mortals were clearly too good at drowning.

The girl clutched her chest, taking huge, sputtering gulps of air. "The others," she gasped. Her eyes were so wide Diana could see white ringing her irises all the way around. She was trembling, but Diana wasn't sure if it was because she was cold or going into shock. "We have to help them—"

Diana shook her head. If there had been any other signs of life in the wreck, she hadn't seen them. Besides, time passed more quickly in the mortal world. Even if she swam back out, the storm would have long since had its way with any bodies or debris.

"They're gone," said Diana, then wished she'd chosen her words more carefully. The girl's mouth opened, closed. Her body was shaking so hard Diana thought it might break apart. That couldn't actually happen, could it?

Diana scanned the cliffs above the beach. Someone might have seen her swim out. She felt confident no other runner had chosen this course, but anyone could have seen the explosion and come to investigate.

"I need to get you off the beach. Can you walk?" The girl nodded, but her teeth were chattering, and she made no move to stand. Diana's eyes scoured the cliffs again. "Seriously, I need you to get up."

"I'm trying."

She didn't look like she was trying. Diana searched her memory for everything she'd been told about mortals, the soft stuff— eating habits, body temperature, cultural norms. Unfortunately, her mother and her tutors were more focused on what Diana referred to as the Dire Warnings: War. Torture. Genocide. Pollution. Bad Grammar.

The girl shivering before her on the sand didn't seem to qualify for inclusion in the Dire Warnings category. She looked about the same age as Diana, brown-skinned, her hair a tangle of long, tiny braids covered in sand. She was clearly too weak to hurt anyone but herself. Even so, she could be plenty dangerous to Diana. Exile dangerous. Banished-forever dangerous. Better not to think about that. Instead, she thought back to her classes with Teuta. *Make a plan. Battles are often lost because people don't know which war they're fighting.* All right. The girl couldn't walk any great distance in her condition. Maybe that was a good thing, given that Diana had nowhere to take her.

She rested what she hoped was a comforting hand on the girl's shoulder. "Listen, I know you're feeling weak, but we should try to get off the beach."

"Why?"

Diana hesitated, then opted for an answer that was technically true if not wholly accurate. "High tide."

It seemed to do the trick, because the girl nodded. Diana stood and offered her a hand.

"I'm fine," the girl said, shoving to her knees and then pushing up to her feet.

"You're stubborn," Diana said with some measure of respect. The girl had almost drowned and seemed to be about as solid as driftwood and down, but she wasn't eager to accept help—and she definitely wasn't going to like what Diana suggested next. "I need you to climb on my back."

A crease appeared between the girl's brows. "Why?"

"Because I don't think you can make it up the cliffs."

"Is there a path?"

"No," said Diana. That was definitely a lie. Instead of arguing, Diana turned her back. A minute later, she felt a pair of arms around her neck. The girl hopped on, and Diana reached back to take hold of her thighs and hitch her into position. "Hold on tight."

The girl's arms clamped around her windpipe. "Not that tight!" Diana choked out.

"Sorry!" She loosened her hold.

Diana took off at a jog.

The girl groaned. "Slow down. I think I'm going to vomit."

"Vomit?" Diana scanned her knowledge of mortal bodily functions and immediately smoothed her gait. "Do *not* do that."

"Just don't drop me."

"You weigh about as much as a heavy pair of boots." Diana

picked her way through the big boulders wedged against the base of the cliff. "I need my arms to climb, so you're going to have to hold on with your legs, too."

"Climb?"

"The cliff."

"You're taking me *up the side of the cliff*? Are you out of your mind?"

"Just hold on and try not to strangle me." Diana dug her fingers into the rock and started putting distance between them and the ground before the girl could think too much more about it.

She moved quickly. This was familiar territory. Diana had scaled these cliffs countless times since she'd started visiting the north shore, and when she was twelve, she'd discovered the cave where they were headed. There were other caves, lower on the cliff face, but they filled when the tide came in. Besides, they were too easy to crawl out of if someone got curious.

The girl groaned again.

"Almost there," Diana said encouragingly.

"I'm not opening my eyes."

"Probably for the best. Just don't . . . you know."

"Puke all over you?"

"Yes," said Diana. "That." Amazons didn't get sick, but vomiting appeared in any number of novels and featured in a particularly vivid description from her anatomy book. Blessedly, there were no illustrations.

At last, Diana hauled them up into the divot in the rock that marked the cave's entrance. The girl rolled off and heaved a long breath. The cave was tall, narrow, and surprisingly deep, as if someone had taken a cleaver to the center of the cliff. Its gleaming black rock sides were perpetually damp with sea spray. When she was younger, Diana had liked to pretend that if she kept walking, the cave would lead straight through the cliff and open onto some other land entirely. It didn't. It was just a cave, and remained a cave no matter how hard she wished.

Diana waited for her eyes to adjust, then shuffled farther

inside. The old horse blanket was still there—wrapped in oilcloth and mostly dry, if a bit musty—as well as her tin box of supplies.

She wrapped the blanket around the girl's shoulders.

"We aren't going to the top?" asked the girl.

"Not yet." Diana had to get back to the arena. The race must be close to over by now, and she didn't want people wondering where she'd gotten to. "Are you hungry?"

The girl shook her head. "We need to call the police, search and rescue."

"That isn't possible."

"I don't know what happened," the girl said, starting to shake again. "Jasmine and Ray were arguing with Dr. Ellis and then—"

"There was an explosion. I saw it from shore."

"It's my fault," the girl said as tears spilled over her cheeks. "They're dead and it's my fault."

"Don't," Diana said gently, feeling a surge of panic. "It was the storm." She laid her hand on the girl's shoulder. "What's your name?"

"Alia," the girl said, burying her head in her arms.

"Alia, I need to go, but—"

"No!" Alia said sharply. "Don't leave me here."

"I have to. I . . . need to get help." What Diana needed was to get back to Ephesus and figure out how to get this girl off the island before anyone found out about her.

Alia grabbed hold of her arm, and again Diana remembered the way she'd clung to that piece of hull. "Please," Alia said. "Hurry. Maybe they can send a helicopter. There could be survivors."

"I'll be back as soon as I can," Diana promised. She slid the tin box toward the girl. "There are dried peaches and pili seeds and a little fresh water inside. Don't drink it all at once."

Alia's eyelids stuttered. "All at once? How long will you be gone?"

"Maybe a few hours. I'll be back as fast as I can. Just stay warm and rest." Diana rose. "And don't leave the cave."

Alia looked up at her. Her eyes were deep brown and heavily

lashed, her gaze fearful but steady. For the first time since Diana had pulled her from the water, Alia seemed to be truly seeing her. "Where are we?" she asked. "What is this place?"

Diana wasn't quite sure how to answer, so all she said was "This is my home."

She hooked her hands back into the rock and ducked out of the cave before Alia could ask anything else.

BEFORE HE CAN SAVE THE WORLD,
CLARK KENT MUST SAVE SMALLVILLE.

TURN THE PAGE TO SEE HOW
THE BESTSELLING DC ICONS SERIES
CONTINUES WITH CLARK KENT!

CHAPTER 1

The storm came with little warning. A flash of lightning lit up Clark's glasses as he huddled beneath the Java Depot awning with three former football teammates, all of them watching the sudden deluge pound the streets of downtown Smallville. The whipping rain had forced them elbow to elbow, and if Clark exercised a little amnesia, it almost felt like old times, back when he and the football squad were thick as thieves.

He doubted they would ever be close like that again.

Not after he had quit on them.

Clark had always marveled at the power of thunderstorms, which put even his own mysterious strength into perspective. For others, the storm was nothing more than a nuisance. An older businessman, holding a briefcase over his head, sprinted toward a silver SUV, where he beeped open his door and dove inside. A drenched calico slunk beneath an industrial trash bin, looking for a dry place to wait out the downpour.

"We can't just stand here all day," Paul shouted over the roar of the rain. "Come on, let's make a run for the library."

Kyle shot him a dirty look. "Dude, this shit is, like, biblical. I'm not going *any*where."

"I guess we could just do this here." Tommy glanced back at the closed door of the coffee shop before turning to Clark. "Cool with you, big guy?"

Clark shrugged, still wondering what "this" was.

And why no one else could be within earshot.

He had been more than a little surprised when Tommy Jones, a lumbering offensive lineman, approached him at school wanting to "hang out." He'd been equally surprised when Tommy then showed up at the coffee shop with star running back Paul Molina and full-back Kyle Turner. After all, they'd wanted nothing to do with Clark for the better part of two years—since the day he abruptly left the freshman team midseason.

Now here they all were, kicking it on Main Street again.

Like nothing had ever happened.

But Clark knew there had to be a catch.

Tommy raised the brim of his baseball cap and cleared his throat. "I'm guessing you know our record this past season," he began. "We sort of . . . underachieved."

"That's one way of putting it," Kyle said, and Paul shook his head in disgust.

Clark should have known. This meetup was about football. Because when it came to Tommy, Kyle, and Paul, *everything* was about football.

"Anyway, us three have been talking." Tommy slapped a big, meaty hand onto Clark's shoulder. "We'll all be seniors next year. And we wanna go out with a bang."

A massive clap of thunder echoed overhead, causing the three football players to flinch. Clark had never understood that reaction. How even the bravest people he knew could get so spooked by a little thunder. It was yet another example of how different he was from his peers. The guys tried to play off their jumpiness by checking their phones and studying their drinks.

That's when Clark noticed something odd.

About thirty yards to his right, a wire-thin man in his early twenties was standing in the middle of the road, holding out his arms and staring up into the pouring rain. He had a tight buzz cut, and he was dressed head to toe in brown. Brown long-sleeved shirt. Brown pants. Brown combat boots. Clark had an uneasy feeling about the guy.

"Look at *this* freak," Paul said, noticing him, too.

"Who?" Tommy asked.

"Over there." Paul pointed, but a slow big rig rumbled by, blocking their view. When it had passed, the man was gone.

Paul frowned, scratching the back of his shaved head and scanning the empty street. "He was standing out there a second ago. I swear."

Clark searched for the man, too. Random strangers dressed in all brown didn't just appear on the streets of Smallville, only to disappear seconds later. Who *was* he? Clark glanced back through the Java Depot window, where a dozen or so people he recognized were sitting at little round tables, drinking coffee and talking. Doing homework. Taking refuge from the storm.

He wondered if any of them had seen the guy.

As swiftly as the storm had begun, it now slowed to a quiet sprinkle. Steam rose off a drenched Main Street. Heavy drops fell from the trees. They streaked down the windshields of parked cars and zigzagged down street signs. The road was a sea of puddles.

"Let's walk," Tommy said, and they set off toward the public square, Clark still looking for the man dressed in brown.

The four of them had to veer around a series of orange cones blocking off yet another construction zone. A surging local economy had led to a serious transformation of downtown Smallville over the past several years. Gone were all the boarded-up storefronts and dilapidated buildings of Clark's youth. In their place were trendy restaurants, real estate offices, a luxury condo development, and two shiny new bank branches. Multiple construction projects seemed to always be under way now, including the future headquarters for the powerful Mankins Corporation. But there was no work being done this afternoon. The storm had turned Main Street into a ghost town.

"Look, Clark," Tommy said, attempting to pick up where he'd left off, "we all know how much better we would be with you in the backfield. I mean, there's a reason we were undefeated in the games you played freshman year."

"Yeah, before he bailed on us," Paul scoffed.

Tommy shot Paul a dirty look. "What'd we talk about earlier, man? This is about moving forward. It's about second chances."

Clark shrank into himself.

Two years later and he still couldn't stomach the idea that he'd let the team down. And then lied to them. He hadn't quit football to concentrate on school, like he told everyone at the time. He quit because he could have scored on just about every play from scrimmage. And the urge to dominate—wrong as it seemed—grew stronger with each passing game. Until one day he ran over Miles Loften during a tackling drill, sending him to the hospital with fractured ribs. And Clark had only been going about fifty percent. After practice, he'd climbed the bleachers and sat alone, long into the night, contemplating what was no longer possible for him to overlook—just how drastically different he was. And how bad it would be if anyone found out.

Before leaving that night, he'd decided to hang up his cleats.

He hadn't played an organized sport since.

When Tommy stopped walking, everyone else did, too. "I'm just gonna come right out and say it." He glanced at Kyle and Paul before turning back to Clark. "We *need* you."

Kyle nodded. "Come back soon and you'll be able to reestablish yourself before summer workouts. Shit, Coach would probably even make you a captain."

"What do you say, Clark?" Tommy play-punched him in the arm. "Can we count on you?"

Clark wanted so badly to come through for these guys. To put on the pads and get back to work. To feel like he was a part of something again, something bigger than himself. But it was impossible. Injuring teammates and scoring seven touchdowns a game was bad enough when he was a freshman. Imagine if things like that happened on *varsity*. With everyone watching. He just couldn't risk it. His parents had warned him how dangerous it could be if the world were to discover the depths of his mysterious abilities. And the last thing he wanted to do was bring trouble to the family. Kids at school already teased him about being too good. Too perfect. It was the reason he'd started wearing glasses he didn't actually need. And mixing in a couple of Bs on his report card.

Clark adjusted his glasses, looking at the sidewalk. "I really wish I could," he told Tommy in a lifeless voice. "But I can't. I'm sorry."

"See?" Paul said. "Told you he didn't give a shit about us."

"Unbelievable," Kyle added, shaking his head.

Tommy turned away from Clark. "Easy, fellas. We can't *force* the guy to be loyal—"

The man in brown turned a corner and cut right through the four of them. He forcefully bumped shoulders with Tommy, causing him to fumble his iced coffee to the ground.

Clark and his ex-teammates were struck silent for several seconds, until Kyle kicked the plastic cup across the sidewalk and called after the guy, "Hey, asshole! You need to watch where the hell you're going!"

The man spun around and shouted something back at Kyle in Spanish. Then he spit on the sidewalk and held up a small blade, as if daring them to say anything else.

"Yo, he's got a knife!" Paul shouted.

When Clark stepped in front of his friends, he saw how jittery the man's bloodshot eyes were. And he was mumbling under his breath.

"What's he saying?" Kyle asked Paul, who was Mexican and spoke Spanish at home.

Paul shook his head. "I don't know. Something about getting back to Metropolis."

Clark wondered if the guy might be on drugs. What else could explain his bloodshot eyes and the way he'd been standing in the pouring rain? And he wasn't just staring at Clark now. He was staring *through* Clark. "Let's leave him alone," Clark said, focusing on the knife in the man's left hand. "There's something off about the way he's acting."

"Screw that," Kyle said, elbowing past Clark. He pointed at the man, shouting, "Nobody slams into my teammate like that without apologizing. You think I'm scared of that little bullshit switch-blade?"

The man lunged, swinging the knife violently, the blade grazing Kyle's forearm, before quickly retreating.

Kyle looked at the blood trickling down his arm. He looked at the man.

Then all hell broke loose.

Clark bounded forward to kick the knife out of the guy's hand, sending it skittering under a parked car. Tommy and Paul threw their backpacks into the street and charged. They tackled the man onto the hard, wet pavement, but he managed to scurry out of their grasp, leap to his feet, and retreat.

Kyle made a move to join the fray, but Clark pulled him back. "Hang on!"

"Oh, hell no! He just cut my ass!" Kyle took a wider angle this time and joined Tommy and Paul as the three of them stalked the guy, backing him into a row of parked cars.

Clark knew how lopsided the fight would be. The man was wild-eyed and showed no fear, but he was clearly no match for three hulking football players.

Clark's instinct was to rush in and break everything up before anyone got seriously hurt. But things had gone horribly wrong the last time he'd used his powers in public. It had been winter. He'd been walking to the library when he spotted a big rig careening across a large ice patch on Highway 22. Without thinking, he'd sprinted over and used his strength to grab hold of the massive truck before it could flatten the Alvarez Fruits and Vegetables stand at the side of the road. Only he'd somehow overcorrected the big rig's momentum, toppling the heavy trailer, spilling dozens of oil drums out onto the two-lane highway. Oil had gushed everywhere.

Clark would never forget helping the driver from the wreckage. The man's face had been as white as a sheet, his leg twisted grotesquely. Would he have even been hurt if Clark hadn't stuck his nose in things? The question haunted Clark, and he'd promised himself to stop and think before physically intervening like that again.

But he could use his voice.

"Let him go, guys!" he shouted at his ex-teammates. "It's not worth it!"

The man in brown backed right into an old truck before slipping between parked cars and scurrying away.

Tommy turned to Kyle, grabbing his bloody arm and studying the cut. Paul huffed into the middle of the street to retrieve his backpack.

Clark cautiously followed the man in brown down the next block. He had to make sure he was really leaving, so no one got hurt. He stopped in his tracks when the guy began pounding his bare fists against the side of a beat-up white pickup truck while the driver cowered at the wheel. Clark stood there watching, absolutely baffled. What was wrong with this guy? And why was he beating on this one particular truck? It had just been innocently idling there at the side of the road. And the man was attacking it with a shocking ferocity, bloodying his fists in the process.

He turned suddenly and stalked back the other way, in the direction of Clark and the football players. Clark made a move to cut him off, but the man lunged toward the silver SUV instead, the one where the gray-haired businessman was waiting out the storm. The man in brown flung open the driver's side door, threw the businessman onto the street, and climbed in to start the engine.

Clark's eyes widened with panic when the SUV lurched out of its parking spot and then sped forward, seemingly headed directly toward Paul, who was still kneeling in the street, zipping up his backpack.

"Look out!" Clark shouted.

Paul looked up when he heard the screaming engine.

But he was still just kneeling there, a sitting duck.

Then came the familiar weightlessness of Clark reaching warp speed.

His skin tingling and raw.

His throat closing as he bolted soundlessly into the street, eyes fixed on the SUV barreling down on Paul.

Clark instinctively calculated his angle, the speed of the SUV, and the potential for destruction, and then he dove at the last possible second. And as he tore through the air, he peered up into the crazed eyes of the man gripping the steering wheel, and he saw how lost the man was, how bewildered. In that instant, Clark understood this was an act that ran far deeper than he or anyone else could know.

Then came the bone-crushing impact.